THE NIGHTMARE EXPLODES . . .

There it was, that shiny, three-inch edge glistening high in the air above the man with the outraged, determined look, high above the wide-eyed little girl with her head pressed back against his body, the pounding pulse of her pure white throat seemingly visible to Devlin.

"Don't!" pleaded Devlin. He ventured another step closer, stopped when the razor trembled in the sun. The policeman kept his gun-heavy hand behind his back. He held his left palm forward in supplication.

Devlin saw the man's lips quiver. The razor-tipped arm began to fall . . .

RAZOR GAME

RAZOR GAME

James Grady

BANTAM BOOKS

TORONTO · NEW YORK · LONDON · SYDNEY · AUCKLAND

RAZOR GAME
A Bantam Book / March 1985

ISBN 0-553-24826-X

Published simultaneously in the United States and Canada

Bantam Books are published by Bantam Books, Inc. Its trademark,
consisting of the words "Bantam Books" and the portrayal of a
rooster, is Registered in U.S. Patent and Trademark Office and in
other countries. Marca Registrada. Bantam Books, Inc., 666 Fifth
Avenue, New York, New York 10103.

PRINTED IN THE UNITED STATES OF AMERICA

O   0 9 8 7 6 5 4 3 2 1

Razor Game is a work of fiction. Any similarity between the story and reality (other than historical points of reference) is coincidental illusion. The author has taken poetic license with the organization and history of the Baltimore Police Department, and for that as well as for their generous assistance, he owes his appreciation and gratitude. The author is also grateful to a number of journalists on the Baltimore *Sun* and the New York *Daily News* for their assistance, to the Drug Enforcement Administration for technical help, and to a number of friends who prefer never to be named anywhere.

RAZOR
GAME

one

Detective Sergeant Devlin Rourke couldn't understand why they hadn't killed him yet.

He also didn't know who "they" were, where he was or why he was there.

He'd been wondering what there was to eat in his refrigerator, fumbling in his pants pocket for his apartment key as he walked through Baltimore's hot summer sunset toward the intersection of 28th and St. Paul. There'd been a stinging pain in his left leg. Then oblivion. When that dark fog lifted, he found himself sitting in some rich man's lawbook-lined library. Two greasy, sullen hoodlums in tacky polyester suits stood across from him. When they were sure, one yelled, "He's awake." Moments later a third man entered the room. He was about 50, with a happy bounce in his step and a carefree smile. His expensive suit seemed a size too large for his bony frame.

"Tranquilizer gun," said the smiler. "A simple *pop!* and three steps later you're out like a precious baby. We've relieved you of your gun, handcuffs, badge, watch, wallet, anything that might tempt you into trouble. Don't worry: you'll be just fine."

The smiler left Rourke alone with the two silent watchdogs.

They didn't stay a trio long. The two watchdogs suddenly jerked to attention as another pair of their kind marched through mahogany doors, glanced around the room, then

1

parted to let the man they escorted enter. He was a beer-keg person, 240 pounds of muscle and meanness stamped into a 5'6" frame. He had the face and bristly hair of a gorilla, with long arms and paws to match. His name was Anthony Cardozo, and Rourke now knew who "they" were.

Smart people respectfully called him Mr. Cardozo or Tough Tony. He was 59 years old and could crush any college athlete with his bare hands. He'd been active in the old-line organized crime circles dominated by the Italian and Sicilian Mafia families since his teens. His only conviction sent him to prison for three years in 1948 for extortion and assault. He'd been suspected of five separate murders plus a legion of lesser crimes. After his release from prison, Cardozo held a phoney job for a shipping company while he settled union problems on New York's docks. Part of his legend claimed he once used stevedore hooks to carry a corpse he made the length of a New York wharf in broad daylight. He dropped the body into the ocean while a hundred of the dead man's terrified co-workers watched.

Five years earlier Rourke had drawn temporary duty with a joint city, state and federal task force to probe the organized crime rumors which abound in Baltimore. The task force easily found prostitution, gambling, narcotics, loan sharking and various other illegal economic enterprises. But the entrepreneurs in these endeavors were individuals with small gangs. The task force could never prove any of the businessmen mixed their activities—say, dabbling in loan sharking, prostitution *and* gambling—had any working links with other groups in other cities, or were part of anyone's umbrella operation.

"Everybody here is too macho to organize," an informant told Rourke's partner on the task force.

The task force disbanded. Their official report noted that "no organized crime of any significance exists within Baltimore."

Six months later Tough Tony Cardozo moved to Baltimore. Rourke's former partner on the task force took an assignment on the skeleton-staffed police unit with a low-priority duty to guard against organized crime. Nobody but he paid much attention to new and persistent Mob rumors.

One night this cop showed up drunk at Devlin's apartment, took him for a giddy ride to the suburbs. They parked outside an overrated steak and seafood restaurant. Two hours later, the beer-keg gorilla emerged, accompanied by two sharply dressed, wary-eyed cretins who kept their hands close to their flapping coats.

"See that guy?" slurred his friend. "Look at him really good. He doesn't exist. We don't have an official file on him. Tough Tony Cardozo. Got a fortress home in the burbs, just bought three tailor-and-laundry shops, one big one down by the docks, but he doesn't exist. Brought in a bunch of new tailors to help him run things. Half a dozen from New York, one or two from the West Coast, three out of Detroit, two out of Chicago, a Philly man who drives back and forth at least three times a week.

"Somebody's decided it's time to organize Bal'more. Hell, the All-American City is making an economic comeback, right? Lots of nickels and dimes. We got the hookers and the porn shops on the Block, the dirty-flick places. They buy their goods from O.C. wholesalers. Somebody's got to watch the tail end of that trade, right? And maybe fuck around with all those vending machines—a quarter here, a quarter there, a ton of dirty money laundered a few cents at a time through dirty movie machines. Then there's the hookers. Somebody could arrange insurance policies for them. No pimps, no houses to manage, no flashy new dudes on the street. Just quiet insurance policies, low-key salesmen backed up by acid and baseball bats. Same deal for the local loan sharks who bleed some poor steelworker who starts a few bucks short and ends a lot of bucks beyond forever. Then there's the gamblers who don't want their games knocked over or their numbers banks held up. Plus the docks, $12 billion a year shipped into Baltimore docks, $1 million a year stolen that we know of. God knows how much cargo really vanishes, how much shit is smuggled in. And don't forget government Social Security scams running out of the national center at the edge of town.

"Who're the local creeps going to complain to? Us? 'Please help me, Mr. Policeman. I'm a crook who doesn't want to be eaten by bigger crooks!' If they try to complain, they'll end up as Homicide business. 'Course, crackerjack Detec' Rourke won't see those stiffs. Somehow I'll betcha some real conscientious Department *badge* gets those cases. Cases that'll stay open just as long as those guys stay dead.

"So take a good look at that guy. The word out of New York is that he's finally gotten his reward for years of hard service. They've given him Baltimore to shape up and bring into line.

He's the big shark somebody put here to eat all the little sharks, the monster who doesn't exist. He's a sadist, an absolute O.C. man. The worst thing about him is he's smart."

Now that gorilla Devlin had first seen that night stalked across the room to where the detective sat. Devlin saw the open paw curve up in a low, slow swing as Cardozo cuffed him just hard enough to snap his face to one side.

"That's so you's pay attention," snarled Cardozo. "You know who I am?"

"I've heard the stories. I recognize the smell."

Cardozo's backhand smacked Devlin three times as hard as the first slap. White fire roared through his mind, then vanished. The salty taste of blood filled his mouth.

"You say you heard the stories. You heard the one about the guy what got dumped over the edge of the dock in front of all his buddies?" Cardozo paused long enough for Devlin to nod. "True. Only you probably don't know that the guy was alive when I sunk the hooks into him. I carried that creep a hundred feet. He quit screaming before I dumped him in the water. I'd like nothing better than to rip your fucking ribs open with my bare hands or sink a hook into your skull and drag you around the front lawn for a while. Your badge don't mean *shit*. I can pull it easier than you can spit. I want you dead, I pick you off the street in ten seconds. No place you can go, nothing you can do I can't hook into you. You fuck up, I get you for Christmas—anytime of the year. So don't fuck up or piss me off.

"There's a man in there," he said, jerking his huge head towards a set of sliding doors. "He wants you should do some things for him. He tells you to jump, you ask how high. He tells you to go downtown and fucking shit on the Police Commissioner's desk, you fucking do it or dead is the best you're going to get. Anything he fucking wants, you get it for him. You understand me, *cop*?"

"I heard what you said."

"Stand up."

Rourke complied. The gorilla reached out and with surprising gentleness rearranged the detective's blazer, straightened his knit tie, tucked in his blue shirt. Like grooming a child. Devlin's flesh crawled at the man's touch. "I learned about clothes in the joint," Cardozo said. "These are nice threads. You got good taste. Your tailor ain't terrific, but you got good taste.

"Hey!" he hollererd over his shoulder to the four goons who waited his commands. "The fuckin' cop's got good taste. You's guys should maybe learn a little from him." The goons smiled, nervously wondering if they should laugh or chorus their assent. Devlin's gaze flicked towards them. A new light flashed in Cardozo's eyes. Devlin sensed the change too late. The gorilla's huge fist slammed into Devlin's stomach and drove all the air from his lungs. While Devlin gasped and retched, the monster once again gently adjusted his clothing.

"When you's can talk and walk normal, *with respect,* you go in here and you be a 100-percent good boy. You understand?"

Rourke could barely nod.

"That's smart," Cardozo said. He released Devlin's shoulder and stalked out the way he'd entered, leaving the detective to stagger and wheeze his way upright under the nervous watch of his original two guardians.

two

"Enter."

The private office beyond those double doors cost a fortune to create. Floor-to-ceiling curtains prohibited Devlin from seeing out French windows. Indirect lighting cast warm shadows over rich mahogany paneling. Thick carpet absorbed his ginger steps.

"Hey buddy, glad you came out of the tranquilizer so well."

The smiler beamed his concern, led Devlin to a fragile antique wooden chair. The small cushion didn't pad the wood beneath his bottom. Smiler settled into one of two comfortable-looking stuffed armchairs posted across the room. The second armchair already overflowed with another man's bulk. When that man stood, Devlin guessed he would top 6'5". Beneath his three-piece, fawn-colored summer suit was the finely sculptured body of a weight lifter. The man's chest was five feet or more around. His upper arms were thicker than

Rourke's thighs. This slab of muscle had blond hair and blue eyes that regarded Devlin with quiet contempt.

Rourke's uncomfortable chair sat ten feet in front of a massive desk covered with tidy stacks of paper. The man who'd commanded him to enter sat in a swivel chair behind those papers.

Never had Devlin seen green eyes with such fire and depth. Their emerald glow burned all the more brightly because of the shocking contrast with his thick, white hair which was fashionably cut and styled into a wavy crown of snow. The long-fingered, carefully manicured hand resting on the desk was strong, supple. His lean face was lightly tanned, barely wrinkled.

"Good evening." His voice was even, rich, carefully polished and accent free. "My name is Salvatore Matella. That means nothing to you. The two men seated to your right are my immediate assistants. You have already met Joseph Kibler." The smiler waved. "Seated next to him is Randy." The strongman inclined his head the merest fraction of an inch. Rourke glanced toards them, but made no response.

"You've also met my associate Mr. Cardozo," continued the white haired old man. "Mr. Cardozo is a regional commander for a large consortium of which I am nontitular head. My name and the simple fact of my existence are known to no more than 100 people. I have gone to great lengths to preserve as much anonymity as possible. I am sure you understand your responsibilities in that regard.

"You are Detective Sergeant Devlin Rourke, 30 years of age, single, currently assigned to the Baltimore Police Department's Homicide Squad. Your personnel file shows high intelligence, strong motivation traits, a brilliant track record and a rebellious streak. You are the right man in the right place at the right time. Therefore, you will complete a necessary task for me."

"No thanks," said Devlin. His throat was dry, words hard to form. "I wouldn't enjoy playing on your team."

"What makes you think you have any choice? But I understand your reluctance. You will not sign your name on our pad. You may, if you wish, but I assume you will never want to, and any efforts to persuade you to do so would be wasted. You're too honest—not to the system: you know you ultimately serve yourself, and you know man must be true to some allegiance. You will not betray the police force, because you will not violate your quaint concept of justice.

"I don't need or want you to be a crooked cop. We have an adequate number of those for our needs.

"I want you to catch a murderer."

three

"Who's been killed?"

"In Baltimore? Probably no one. Yet."

"My badge has a limited jurisdiction."

"I'm as aware of your limitations as I am of your abilities!" hissed the old man. His tutorial tone returned.

"Last year I learned of the existence of what is loosely called a homicidal maniac. He refers to himself as the Reaper, sometimes as The Reaping Angel. This person, almost certainly a man, selects children as his primary victims. He has killed victims in 8 different American cities. I've established his body count as at least 16 people."

"Nobody kills 16 people. Not without notice. I've never heard of this Reaper."

"As with myself, few people realize the Reaper exists. Juan Corona killed 24 people in California before he was caught. Peter Kurten, a mass murderer in Düsseldorf, Germany, just prior to World War II, killed 8 people in 10 months, attacked a score more. Most of his crimes were committed long before his existence was realized. Unlike these two killers, our man does not limit himself to an easily defined killing zone. He strikes in one city, then moves on. There is no organized effort to connect random murders on a national level. All the cases are seen as individual, unsolved crimes within the cities where they occur.

"Halloween night, 1978, my 10-year-old grandson became the Reaper's seventh child victim. The boy's name was Peter Jenkins. He went trick-or-treating with his friends, under the supervision of one of their parents, in a middle-class suburb of San Francisco. His family has no contact with my activities. My son long ago had disowned me and changed his name. Little Peter ran down one hill alone to be the first to solicit a block while his friends dawdled at other doors. Pete was costumed as a ghost—a white bedsheet with eye-holes. Some five minutes later, his friends ran after him. They began stopping at homes, and soon realized that Pete had not been there before them. They became alarmed, but after all, it was Halloween. Then one of them saw Peter's sheet flapping with the breeze in the darkness behind some bushes. They sneaked up to scare him—and discovered his body, his throat cut from ear to ear, the blood still pumping all over the white sheet."

"Jesus."

"Yes, it must have been quite a sight. I saw my first corpse at about that same age.

"I learned of the murder later that night. I immediately probed all the possibilities in my world: No one killed that boy because of my work. The next suspects are, of course, his immediate family. The police easily established their innocence. The boy had not been sexually molested, nor had any such attempt been made. None of his school friends, his teachers or the adults he routinely came into contact with proved to be viable suspects.

"I then assumed that the killer was a local madman. But after two months, the police had no new leads and no similar offenses. The police did an excellent job. I made sure of that. Eventually, however, they were forced to move on, leaving the case open but unsolved.

"Such an ending was not satisfactory to me. I deduced that perhaps there might be more to my grandson's killing than a solitary event. My people were able to uncover a similar murder which happened in March 1978, in Kansas City. A 10-year-old boy had his throat slit—case open, unsolved.

"I arranged for a private detective firm to take over the investigation along lines I suggested. They uncovered a total of 8 children, each in a different city, whose throats had been cut by an unknown assailant, with the first murder taking place in November 1975. They finished their investigation the same week the last child was murdered—in Boston, this February."

"You're supposed to be Professor Moriarty, not Sherlock Holmes."

"What an ironic analogy. And accurate. Holmes is your job."

"Why me?"

"You're the best homicide detective in Baltimore, one of the best in the country. The pattern I discovered in the killer's routine leads me to believe he will soon strike in Baltimore, where you will apprehend him.

"I mentioned that there were a total of 16 victims. Before each child murder, a prostitute in the same city is killed in the same manner, throat cut by an unkown assailant. My common sense—backed up by expert psychiatric analysis—dictates that the two crimes are linked, that the Reaper first kills a prostitute, then a child.

"The private detectives stumbled on another common factor in all the crimes. Our killer runs newspaper ads in each city prior to each crime. It is from these ads I have taken the name *Reaper.*"

"What does he advertise? Two slashings for the price of one?"

The green eyes showed no anger at Rourke's insolence. The cop needed to spar with his captors, to retain some semblance of courage and control. Besides, the old man obviously expected it of him.

"Our man is a religious hysteric. He buys two small display ads in the local newspaper, jumbles of twisted scriptural language and Bible quotes. One runs shortly before he kills his prostitute, the other runs shortly before he kills the child.

"Three seemingly coincidental events: A series of harmless, nonsensical newspaper ads depicting religious fervor. A murdered prostitute. A murdered child. All in one city. Then another. And another. And another. The pattern is too tight to be coincidence. The cause is *a* killer.

"You don't need to chase the Reaper around the country, Sergeant. He's come to Baltimore. The Reaper's first ad ran in this morning's *Star.*

"Once I knew the pattern, I needed only to alert my network. All over the nation, in every city of any consequence, someone from my organization has been carefully reading more than the sports page of the daily newspaper. It was only a matter of time. The Reaper is in Baltimore, Sergeant. He will soon kill. And you will catch him, so that we may both see justice done."

"What makes you think I'll be your manhunter?"

"I've arranged for you to be officially assigned to the case. Then there's the sport. You're an egotist. You went into police work as the ultimate challenge, handicapping yourself with a creaky, blundering bureaucracy to pursue your quest for justice and revel in the chase. You've been in Homicide, the ultimate game, for three years. You've been promoted to sergeant. Ninety percent of the time such a promotion means a transfer back to uniform and an administrative or supervisory post. But you fought that. You don't want to be hamstrung with the details of command or lose the thrills of hunting in the street. For once the Department realized its own best interest, and has basically freed you to play your game. Now comes the Reaper. He will be the hardest and thus your most rewarding opponent ever.

"Besides, you have no choice about this hunt: I needn't threaten you with my power. Your own folly has given yourself over to my game, and I'll use the laws represented by your own badge to control your play. Besides ego and a talent for detection, you and Sherlock Holmes share one other common trait: a fondness for cocaine."

four

"Maybe that was just a phase I've finished," argued Devlin. Denial seemed useless. "A one-or-two-time thing."

"Don't be absurd. My eyes are everywhere. Since cocaine is not physiologically addictive, we can't use the term addict to describe you. And so far, you seem to have avoided letting it psychologically take over your life. But you use it as frequently as you can—which is one aspect of your life that puzzles me. Surely you know there is a fair chance of long-term physical and mental-health problems, to say nothing of the risk you expose yourself to—risk which has now trapped you. Besides, why play with your already fine mind, your keen perceptions? If it's merely a phase, it's an absurdly dangerous one."

"Maybe I get no kick from champagne."

"I have never needed such kicks. At most, I take wine with a meal or as a social ritual. My virtue has been amply rewarded. Just as in your case, your indiscretion has become your damnation."

"You're extremely sure of yourself."

"Completely. I devote enormous energies to being sure. This is but a side show, yet I treat it with all my talents. Believe me, we have you. Enough evidence to present to any grand jury, and from there to a prosecutor who would win a conviction even without our help—which would be there, should the judge or jury seem reluctant to do their duty. The police department would sacrifice you to the jackals of civic decency without hesitation. You have no resources or ammunition to defeat such attacks.

"Yet, perhaps rather than deal with us you will sacrifice yourself. Luckily, you have another weak spot. Your supplier is an old friend, a civilian lab technician within the Police Department. Dennis Garn, a nice man, with a wife, a new son, and a clever system for stealing impounded drugs. We will let the truth and your system ruin him completely if you're foolish. You are far too loyal and conscientious a friend to inflict such pain on him.

"But look at the bright side. You have a chance to capture a monster who destroys innocent children. Blood need not stain Baltimore's streets. Think of the challenge! This man is cleverer than Kurten, more complex than that slobbering Son of Sam, more precise than Corona, more resourceful than Jack the Ripper.

"Not only will the Department be behind you, we'll be behind you. All the resources, all the power you could possibly want or need. All you have to do is use it."

The white-haired man leaned back in his chair. His fire-green eyes roamed over the detective.

"What happens if this doesn't play out quite like you want?" asked Rourke. "What if I don't measure up to your expectations?"

"Ah: Randy."

That giant, living Apollo moved behind Rourke's chair with frighteningly quick grace. He gripped the back two legs of Rourke's chair in his hands, smoothly lifted the antique higher until Rourke's ashen face was but inches from the ceiling.

Devlin clung to the chair as Randy held him there for a moment . . .

Then released his grip. The chair crashed to the floor, Rourke atop it. The fragile antique *cathumped* into the thick carpet, splintering into dozens of valueless bits as Rourke's body slammed through the old wood.

From where he lay Rourke could see only Randy's expensively shoed, huge feet, the front of the desk and the splinters of wood all around him on the carpet. His legs ached, his head ached, his ribs ached, his back ached, his stomach ached, and he'd twisted his wrists when he hit the floor. But he clearly heard the old man hiss: "If you fail, deliberately or not, or if you decide to play some other game, I'll crush you like a cockroach on a concrete floor."

five

"Randy and Joseph will see that you get home," announced Matella as Rourke painfully picked himself up from the floor.

"Won't you be worried without your babysitter and bully boy by your side?" asked Devlin: *Keep scrapping.* He saw Randy's fingers flex ever so slightly. Devlin braced himself. This time he would strike back.

"Sergeant, like you I take great pains to insure that I am always capable of acting on my own. The value of assistants lasts only as long as they are dispensible. I need no one. I can—and often do—go my own way. Alone. Joseph will give you a phone number. Memorize it. When you need anything, call that number and ask for him."

"Nice to be working with you," said Kibler, smiling. "Call me Joe."

Devlin said nothing.

The two assistants to the emerald-eyed man led him back to the library. The goons who'd guarded him earlier were still there. Call-me-Joe Kibler, with a wry, apologetic grin, handed him a black hood without eye holes. "It's either this or the tranquilizer gun."

Darkness. Thick, impenetrable cloth darkness. There was even a drawstring to cinch the hood tight around his neck, cutting off all light and any glimpse of the world passing beneath his feet. Randy's iron grip on his right arm steered him through several rooms and out on to a wide porch. Five steps down, across a crushed rock drive to where the sounds of opening motor vehicle doors waited. Devlin strained to sense the muffled world. The clean, wet smell of greenery, of trees and shrubs and lawn, filtered through wet cloth. He heard chirping crickets and the electric buzzing song of an insect whose name he could never remember. Somewhere not far away a deep-throated church bell rang. The thick heat of the August night trapped beneath his hood baked streams of sweat from his face. Randy guided him into the rear of a van-type vehicle. He sat with his back against the wall. Randy sat between him and the door. He was sure Kibler sat across from them. *Someone else must be driving*, he thought, *maybe one of the goons*. The van lurched forward, slowly curved onto the road, then onto a highway. Devlin felt the speed, heard the hum of tires, the blare of a semi's air horn as it passed them.

For over half an hour they drove him around—freeways, city streets, in and out of alleys. No one spoke. The van lurched to a stop. Randy opened the rear door and guided Rourke out. He untied the drawstring, removed the hood. Rourke blinked: the dimly-lit alley seemed familiar. A few lights shone through shade-covered rear windows. No one was watching. He didn't bother trying to see the license plate on the van: it would be phoney.

Kibler handed him his gun, handcuffs, badge, watch, notebook, pens, change, nail clipper, bullets (six more than the spares he carried, so he assumed his gun was empty), keys and a card with a phone number printed on it.

"Here you go, buddy. Call any time, for anything you need. You'd be amazed at the things one little phone call will help you accomplish.

"And don't worry. Working for Mr. Matella won't be bad. Hell of a thing, ain't it? Some religious nut chopping up little kids. Love thy neighbor, butcher his child. But we'll get him, yessir, we'll get him. I got a lot of faith in you.

"Oh, by the way. I almost forgot something." Kibler reached

into his suitcoat pocket. He brought out a gently clenched fist.
Rourke tensed, then relaxed. This wasn't another terror time.
Besides, Kibler didn't look capable of any violence, and the
loosely clenched fist was finger-side up—peculiar preparation
for a punch from anyone but a seasoned karate expert. Kibler's
fist opened. Two clear plastic bundles, each smaller than a
thimble, lay in his palm. The corners of household plastic food
bags had been cut out to form a pouch for white crystalline
powder. Two paper-covered wire twists held the bundles shut.

"Two grams of terrific cocaine, or so they tell me. I don't use
the stuff myself. I know it won't make me see God and run
naked in the streets, but hell, I'm too timid to try. Go on, take
them."

Rourke hesitated. Randy leaned against the back of the van.
Devlin didn't think the generosity was avoidable. He cupped
his hand, and let Kibler dump the two almost weightless
bundles on his palm.

"Maybe it's Mr. Matella's way of apologizing for your
inconvenience," said Kibler. "Stay in touch."

Kibler climbed in the van. Randy coolly appraised the
detective one last time, then he too climbed in the rear of the
vehicle, shutting the door behind him. The goon driving let in
the clutch, and the machine rolled away.

Rourke carefully looked round the alley, waiting, watching.
He gingerly dumped the two plastic bundles in his suit pocket,
then reloaded his snub-nosed .38 Smith and Wesson. He
holstered it, but did not snap the gun in tight. The walk to the
end of the alley took forever. He emerged on 31st Street, with
Calvert to his left and St. Paul to his right: three blocks from
home. He walked towards St. Paul. The streets were deserted.
His watch said it was 1 A.M. He'd been snatched around 8. For
five hours he'd been out of control. Water gurgled through a
storm drain at the corner. It must have rained while he was
unconscious. He glanced around. Still no one in sight. He
reached into his pocket and carefully cupped the two small
cocaine packets. He avoided touching them in such a way as to
leave even the hint of a print, although they could have set
that up while he was unconscious. He squatted, glanced into
the open, two-foot slash in the concrete curb where the
overflow from summer storms and winter meltings ran from
the streets to the Chesapeake Bay. A flick of his wrist sent the
two packets deep into the swirling void. He peered after them,
but saw only roaring, rushing blackness.

six

"Hey Devlin . . . Captain wants to see you in the big conference room upstairs."

Devlin nodded to the uniformed sergeant standing behind the horseshoe reception desk in the main hall of Baltimore's coolly modern marble Central Police Headquarters. He couldn't suppress a yawn from the sleepless night before. No ambushers had been waiting for him in the streets or his third-story walk-up apartment. After being sure his closets held only clothes and his chain bolt was snug, he'd gone straight to his drug stash. A cigar-box-size Chinese tea chest held yet another container, this one a small elliptical pewter jewel box given him by his last lost love. The tea chest also held what was left of an ounce of marijuana he'd purchased a year before. Devlin wasn't addicted to tobacco, and seldom smoked grass anymore. He set the plastic baggie of grass on the table, then opened the pewter box. A plastic bundle similar to the two he'd thrown down the storm drain lay inside the metal container on a bed of instant rice. The rice absorbed spoiling moisture. Devlin had paid $45 for the gram which he'd barely touched. Half the street price, if he could find stuff that good in the street. He flushed the cocaine and grass down the toilet. Then he searched his apartment as thoroughly as he'd searched any crime scene, even checking the stitching along the edge of his mattress to be sure it hadn't been disturbed. He found pencils and pens in the bowels of the couch, ticket stubs to a movie he couldn't remember in the pockets of a pair of jeans, and two dead bugs amid the dustballs—but no planted contraband. He showered, lay down on his bed, and thought until well past dawn. Then he went to work to await whatever happened.

Which didn't take long, he thought as he stepped into an elevator with three uniformed cops he vaguely knew. Normal-

ly he went straight to the Homicide room on the sixth floor.
Today he punched the top button marked 9.

"Go right in, Sergeant," said the receptionist outside the
conference room's double doors, "they're expecting you."

Baltimore's newly-renovated harbor and downtown skyscrapers sprawled out beyond the windows of this command
level conference room. The people shuffling over the summer
streets below seemed as far away as the clouds floating across
the blue sky. The room was spotlessly clean, cooly air-
conditioned. A bronze abstract star sculpture hung on one
wall. Devlin didn't know if the artist intended his creation to
represent something about police work or an ethereal object of
the heavens. Devlin didn't care. A large video-tape machine
stood in the corner, its television set mounted so all of the
seven people sitting at the conference table were beneath the
gaze of its dead green eye.

That city's police department is headed by a commissioner.
Next down the command ladder come deputy commissioners
and division directors, then chiefs, who command various
sections, as do some captains. Devlin was assigned to the
Homicide Squad in the Crimes Against Persons Section in the
Criminal Investigations Division of the Operations Bureau.
The Deputy Commissioner for the Operations Bureau (DC/
OB) presided from the head of the table. The rest of the table
was balanced, with three police officers (two captains and one
lieutenant) to his left, three civilians to his right.

The first captain was Ted Goldstein. He'd been battered by
seventeen years of police work, but he hadn't lost his edge on
life. Not yet. Goldstein commanded the Homicide Squad, and
kept himself and his troops as free of the bureaucratic traps
and political pitfalls as anyone could expect.

The second captain headed the Crimes Against Persons
Section. He should have held a higher rank, but for bureaucratic reasons favorable to him, he had not yet accepted
promotion.

The Lieutenant was the Commissioner's chief aide, his
hatchet man when necessary. He was only 32, lean and sharp
in his formal blues. The Lieutenant's bureaucratic savvy pulled
him through the ranks over the bleeding backs and broken
careers of anyone who got in his way. Rumor claimed that the
Commissioner kept the Lieutenant close to him because he
needed someone to do the dirty work and because the

Commissioner knew his right-hand man only too well: better to direct the Lieutenant's schemes than to suffer them.

The three civilians sitting across the table from the policemen were a mixed lot in age, sex and appearance.

The man to the DC's immediate left could have come from any county courthouse where backdoor deals decide what's what. He was 60, with a rumpled, factory-cut suit two days overdue for pressing. His lined and sagging face looked as tired as Captain Goldstein's, but this man had a fiesty twinkle in his blue eyes. He was the DC's top civilian aide, a man who'd been part of Baltimore's old-time political machine and who'd survived its demise through one public job after another. He was a fixer when the urban juggernaut jammed, a counselor for those who kept it running. He stayed in the background, and he stayed around. Few people ever knew precisely what he did or how he did it, but no one who'd been around the right circles in Baltimore doubted that he did it better than anybody else.

Biz Grey was the only woman at the table. She was a divorcee who'd put the pieces of her shattered suburban dream in the garbage can, walked away from a past fantasy that hadn't worked, to a dream she'd denied because when she was younger society convinced her such dreams weren't for her. Society had been wrong, but finding sufficient faith in herself had been a hard battle, one she still fought despite her achievements of having worked her way through law school and proving her skills as a tough Baltimore prosecutor. Devlin's respect for her brains, for her guts, for her skills was enough to make him feel a gap separated them—with her far above his street-cop-with-an-unfinished-bachelor's-degree league.

But Biz had more than brains, guts and accomplishments going for her. She was one of those women who quietly grows more beautiful each year, so that the high school cheerleaders who eclipsed her at 17 were wilted flowers next to her radiance by the time they all reached their mid-20s. Now, at 29, with the force of her personality finally free and shining from within, Devlin found her breathtaking. Her long slim legs, taut and neatly tucked bottom, trim waist, firm high breasts, her classic lean face marred only by what purists would call a too generous and wide mouth, her widely set deep-blue eyes and tawny bronze hair that was just barely flecked with silver strands she refused to color made Devlin feel the gap between them even more.

The third civilian was a stranger, a lean, high-strung, chrome-domed man in a pinstripe three-piece suit. The stranger repeatedly thrust his chin forward, stretching his neck as if his shirt collar were too tight. Then he'd push his finger against the nosepiece of his glasses to be sure they hadn't slipped too far down his prominent hooked beak.

"Come in, Sergeant," said the DC. He gestured to a chair at the end of the long table.

"Sergeant, I think you know everyone here but Greg Sonfeld." The DC nodded towards the pinstripe suit. The nervous man stretched his neck, pushed his glasses, then jerked a nod towards Rourke. "Mr. Sonfeld is with the Mayor's office.

"The Commissioner and the Mayor have been made aware of what could be a most serious situation, one which it's been decided that you are the best-equipped officer to handle."

And then the DC described the exact homicidal maniac scenario Matella told Rourke the night before.

"We realize that this type of investigation is unusual. That's why we've given it to you. You'll receive everything the Department can give you. The Mayor wants me to assure you that the rest of the city's agencies will also cooperate. As will the prosecutor's office, which is why Ms. Grey is here. The state police can be brought in, any other agency you need or want. We don't want this Reaper creep in Baltimore. If he comes, if he kills, we want you to nail him. Do you have any questions?"

What Devlin wanted to ask was how the Commissioner and the Mayor had "been made aware" of "the situation." But Devlin assumed any answer he'd get from the DC on that topic would be worthless.

"I have no questions, Sir."

"Then go get him."

"Yes, Sir."

"Ah, if you don't mind, Sergeant," said the Lieutenant, interrupting Devlin's exit. "There are one or two points I'd like to make."

"Of course, *Sir*." Everyone heard the slight lilt Devlin gave the last word. No one acknowledged it.

"You have a reputation, Sergeant."

"If you're complimenting me for having the best closure and conviction rate on the squad, thank you Sir."

"That wasn't what I had in mind."

"I'm sure you know what you mean, Sir."

A tiny hint of a smile turned Biz's lips upward. Devlin wasn't the only one who noticed it, for the old fixer arched his eyebrows her way.

"I want *you* to know what I mean, Sergeant. Precisely what I mean. I don't care that you're a cowboy, I don't care that you think you can always get away with doing precisely what you want. I care about getting this job done."

"So do I, Sir."

"Really? Be sure of that. This is big time, Devlin. The Department is out on a limb, and you're the one we've tapped to play. If you cowboy around and blow it, you're going to take the fall."

"Is that your analysis, Sir?"

"That's the *Department's* position, Sergeant! And not just ours. The Mayor's office agrees. Isn't that right, Greg?"

So that's your game, thought Devlin. He wondered how much of this political theatrics the two young and ambitious aides had rehearsed.

"The position of the Mayor's office is, of course, pro public safety." The bald man's voice was nervous, shaky and high pitched. "Closely allied with that is public confidence. The Baltimore Better Government Committee is being particularly aggressive in second guessing civic affairs these days, and we have reason to believe they're keenly interested in police procedures. I'm sure Sgt. Rourke has perfectly valid explanations for his record and the press it's received. . . ."

"What record?" asked Devlin. "My valor awards or the court testimony I've given that put away guys who killed somebody?"

"The details are unimportant," continued the aide with a wave of his hand. "The point is this must be handled with extreme delicacy and discretion, so that the public perceives this as a positive police action that reflects well on everyone concerned."

"Even the killer?" said Devlin, his patience wearing thin.

"The point is . . ."

"Whose point?" snapped Devlin. He glared at the Mayor's

man, who in turn shrank back in his chair and looked to the Lieutenant for support.

"I'm a bit confused," interrupted the old fixer in a steady voice that overpowered all other emotions in the room. "Are we all on the same side of the fence here? Seems to me you two guys are trying to jerk a cop around instead of helping him catch a killer. Unless you can explain to an old civil servant like me why we ought to do that, maybe we should turn Sgt. Rourke loose. Are there any objections?"

There were none.

As the meeting broke up, Captain Goldstein drew Devlin aside.

"Parcel out your case load. Finish what you must, but this Reaper thing is your only priority." The Captain's wise eyes looked around them, looked back to his best man. "There's a big piece of shit in this somewhere, isn't there?"

"There usually is, Captain."

"Oh balls. You know what I mean; you smell it too. Maybe you even know something about it. I figure you're smart enough to tell me if I can help above and beyond all our official duty crap. Just be smart enough to make sure that you don't give the Lieutenant and that punk from the Mayor's office an excuse to hang you from City Hall."

Devlin and Biz somehow were the last to leave the conference room. He yawned as the two of them waited for the elevator.

"Looks like you're stuck working with me again," he said.

"I can think of worse fates," she replied.

Devlin yawned again.

"You should try getting to bed more often," she said.

"You know how it is," he said: "A man's work is never done."

"If you can ever get him started," she said.

Before Devlin could reply, the elevator doors slid open, disgorging a too-tall scarecrow of a man in a threadbare suit. A moth-eaten briefcase weighed down the man's thin frame, dragging his right hand and long wrist even further than usual beyond the ends of his too-short jacket sleeve. Black hair twisted from his head in a curly electric Semitic Afro, accentuating his pale skin, long nose and small mouth. The man was so deep in thought he almost stumbled over Devlin and Biz.

"Excuse . . . Hello Biz," he said, his voice changing from gruff to glad.

"How are you, Jeff?" she replied.

"Fine, and seeing you makes me feel even better, although I suddenly seem to smell . . . What is it? Something foul in this whitewashed building. Oh, *Sgt. Rourke!* I didn't see you slouching down there. I should have known."

"One can't be omniscient all the time, Counselor."

"Big words for a little man. I know a great deal more than you think, Sergeant. For example, I know you've been handed some cushy new assignment through somebody in City Hall. Who's your rabbi there, Rourke? What dirty deed are you going to do for law and order now? Gun down some other poor soul for the political hacks downtown?"

Rourke's eyes narrowed, but he said nothing.

The gangly attorney shifted the weight of his briefcase, then thrust his bony finger towards the policeman.

"I haven't forgotten you, Rourke. I'll never forget you. You step out of line, you fuck up, you play too cute and too cozy just *once*, and I'll nail your ass to the wall with your shabby little badge!"

The lawyer stomped away. Three steps into his exit he turned and said, "Biz, I thought you had better taste than to hang out with crap like that."

Biz glanced at Rourke as the lawyer's wake receded. She pushed the button to bring back the impatient elevator that had not waited until after the tirade. As the doors slid open, she said, "How did you get to be such good friends with Baltimore's White Knight?"

"Counselor Stern and I go way back, before your time. You joined the prosecutor's office two years ago, right?" he asked as they stepped into the empty elevator.

"Three days after law school graduation." She punched the button for the first floor and the elevator sped down the shaft with an effortless hum.

"That was my first year on Homicide. One of my first cases was the Ortega girl."

"Why do I know that name?"

"It was a big case that got lots of press play. She was 19, an illegal Latin working in a seafood bar and grill place out at the Point, a dollar an hour paid off the books with half her tips kicked back to the owner. No green card, hiding from

Immigration. One night the cook, a 50-year-old mean puke, got together with two of his buddies who hung around after closing time. They beat her up because she was a no-good foreigner sneaking in and taking jobs from decent Americans, then took turns raping her for a couple hours, finally threw her out into the street. She crawled back to the basement she was living in with her mother and sick father, spent two days healing up. She kept her 'shame' secret, told them she'd been mugged. They were illegal: who could they complain to? Besides, in her country the police were as bad as the outlaws.

"She got hold of a .45 automatic and a couple ammunition clips that one of her father's friends carried on a security job at the docks. The third day she staked out the restaurant, and when the cook put out the garbage cans, she stepped out of the shadows in the alley and from six feet away blew five holes through him."

"Now I remem . . ."

"I got the case. Took about eight hours to learn about the 'sport' night from the cook's cronies, which gave me a motive and at least one good suspect. What I didn't know was in that eight hours, the girl broke down and told her mother the whole story. Her mother went to some priest, who convinced the girl to talk to Jeffrey B. Stern, Attorney-at-Law, friend of the helpless downtrodden. This was before he took over the Baltimore Better Government Committee. Back then he ran a storefront legal aid place—some government bucks, a few measly private contributions and his own blood, sweat and tears. After listening to the girl's story, he linked up with one of your predecessors, started dickering on an easy way into the system for her.

"But nobody thought to call the cops. I was pretty good back then. I found out where the girl was hiding, showed up with two uniformed bulls, one of whom supposedly spoke Spanish. I should have come alone. She saw an army coming to drag her away, figured everybody had betrayed her, panicked, ran down an alley. We chased. She started blasting with that .45, winged one of the uniformed guys pretty good. Then she ran out of bullets. She slapped another clip into that gun as we ran toward her. I saw her work the slide, figured there was no talking her out of shooting me. I popped two quick rounds her way. One shot broke her collar bone, the other slammed into her chest and put her down hard."

"She was lucky you didn't kill her!"

"It wasn't for lack of trying. In the street you shoot for what you can hit and hope to hit as much as possible as hard as possible.

"She stood trial. The Department pushes police shootings as far as they can. She got that charge on top of a murder one count. And the wounds. And all the trauma from the rapes, the beating. She's in prison for most of the good years she's got left. When she gets out, she'll be deported. Counselor Stern thinks she got the rawest of raw deals, and he holds me responsible."

The doors slid open and they stepped out. A distraught mother and father mumbled their way past them into the elevator.

"I can understand his feelings," said Biz. "That poor girl! But she murdered a man, she shot a cop, she might have killed you if you hadn't shot her. He shouldn't blame you, you were just doing your job."

Devlin shrugged his shoulders. "I think she got the rawest of raw deals, too."

seven

The boys from the blue Ford were nowhere to be seen, so Devlin jogged across the open-air concrete court with its fountain spraying into the summer humidity and raced up the steps of the Federal Building. He dropped fifteen cents in the lobby pay phone and dialed the number listed in the phone directory.

"Good morning, Federal Bureau of Investigation."

"Agent Cowan, please."

"I'll see if he's in. Please hold."

The boys in the blue Ford had been waiting for him that morning when he pulled his dented 1967 Chevy Camaro away from the curb outside his apartment. They turned when he turned, they parked not far from the municipal lot where he had an assigned space. He'd glanced at them briefly as he entered the police station. Three indistinct male figures sitting in a parked car on what was bound to be a hot summer day.

They were still sitting in the Ford when he came out of Police Headquarters with Biz. He used some half-assed excuse to walk her to her office, an excuse which she surprisingly didn't question. Two of the men climbed out of the car and fell in step about a block behind them. Devlin studied their reflections in a store window as they walked up Fayette Street, avoiding the seamy Block section on East Baltimore Street. Except for a slight insolence in their step, they were just average guys. He led them to Biz's building. They stayed outside. When he finally left her building, he did so as a passenger in the car of another prosecutor who kindly agreed to give him a ride. As they pulled out of the basement garage entrance Devlin doubled over to the floor. He spent an entire block "tying his shoe." While the prosecutor thought Devlin weird and uncoordinated to take so long, he never noticed that the soft leather, thick rubber-soled shoes Devlin always wore to work did not need to be tied.

Devlin had the obliging prosecutor drop him three blocks from the plaza where the black-glass main federal government office building is dominated by even taller glass-and-steel insurance company lairs.

The on-hold buzz ended: "Good morning, this is Special Agent Cowan."

"Danny, how are you?"

"Well, if it isn't my favorite flatfoot! How are you?"

"In need of sustenance. Buy me a cup of coffee."

"Listen, us Feds are important people! We can't just take off in the middle of the day like you city boys. Do you realize what could happen to our nation's security if I'm not sitting around with my eyes open and my pile of forms stacked at attention?"

"Danny, I really, *really* need a cup of coffee."

The two men had worked together on the Joint Organized Crime Task Force. Cowan thought a moment, then said, "That thirsty, huh?"

"That thirsty."

"When and where?"

"Fifteen minutes. Where we had breakfast that time you slid the scrambled eggs all over your suit."

"Jesus, don't remind me. They bounced when they hit the

floor. I still don't know how I survived that meal. I'll see you there."

Special Agent Daniel Cowan, Federal Bureau of Investigation, wore a $400 pinstripe suit, $75 shoes, a $25 tie, and a $50 shirt, but his wife was a whiz of a stock market analyst and his father had been generous with the family millions, so opulence on a mere civil servant didn't worry the city detective in the wooden booth of the hole-in-the-wall downtown diner. The FBI agent looked out of place in this seedy, musty atmosphere, but no one there cared enough to notice.

"What's all this secret rendezvous and tapped telephone crap?" Cowan asked his friend after the waitress slammed down their two tan mugs with spoons jutting out steaming black liquid.

"These are harsh and tricky times."

"And I suppose you want me to help you get through them."

"I could use a friendly face on my side."

"What can I do and what are we doing?"

"First off, you can't ask me any questions. . . ."

"I hate blind man's bluff."

"It's the safest way for you to play this one."

"Second, I want you to ask about a name for me with the Bureau's best O.C. guys, and do it so the question doesn't even come from the Baltimore field office. I don't care where you lay it off, but no links back here."

"Touchy, but I know a guy in Philly who supposedly knows *the* guy in O.C. these days. My guy owes me. What name?"

"Salvatore Matella. Probably mid-to-late sixties, refined Don type. White hair, hellfire green eyes. Maybe out of New York or Vegas, Miami or Chicago. No accent, no scars. Probably an old-line family man somewhere back in time, but I don't know for sure how he's hooked up now. The guy could be a retired college professor."

"Never heard of him."

"Me either."

"Until . . ."

"Until I asked you."

Cowan sighed. "Okay, that's the way we'll play."

"We'll use pay phones, random and different ones, third-party cut-outs to set us up. No visible contact."

"You're really in the shit, aren't you lad?"

"I've been there before."

eight

Five heavy document boxes covered Devlin's office desk. The manila envelope taped to the top box contained an inventory of the files, plus the name of the private detective who'd supervised the case. Devlin glanced at the letterhead: InterDec, Inc. He vaguely knew their reputation as an ultra-sophisticated, posh corporation of ex-FBI, CIA and big city police types with offices in most major American cities as well as overseas branches. Eminently respectable, allegedly super efficient. Now he knew them as consultants to organized crime.

Devlin dialed the number on the letterhead, asked for the man in charge.

"Look," Devlin asked him after they exchanged amenities, "before I read it all, can you tell me what's important in this stuff?"

"I can tell you what we dug out of it. Eight cities, sixteen victims. The weapon is probably always the same, a sharp steel instrument like a butcher's filet knife, a scalpel or a barber's straight razor. The wounds were long cuts, strokes and slashes. No deep stabbing penetrations, so we don't think the thing has much of a point.

"The children are all 12 or under. One of the biggest puzzles is how he gets to them so easily. Almost like they know him and trust him, or he appears to be so harmless they ignore all the advice their folks taught them. While the victims *may* be random, I think he picks and stalks the kids. He's too clever with them for random improvisation.

"There seems to be no pattern among the whores, except he didn't go after girls working in a house or with a pimp close by.

"We're assuming the killer is male, and we're assuming we're dealing with one individual. We've pretty much ruled out a Manson-like cult or a double-nut team. The male angle

26

comes from the whores. It doesn't make sense that any woman would get close to them. Of course, given their profession, any sexual examination of the corpses to determine bloodtype of their assailant was worthless. Besides, maybe the only way this guy got his rocks off with them was spilling their blood."

"What you're saying is we've got nothing."

"But *we* don't have it anymore. *You* do. And I'm glad of that. We busted ass for months on this. We've handled lots of homicides, had lots of successes. But this one . . . We've no clues, no precedents to learn from, no patterns to follow. Just corpses all over the country."

"Now Baltimore."

"Listen, at least you know what you're up against. None of the other cops did. They still don't. They know we've got some hypothesis, but nothing as complete as what you've got has been put before them. You have a jump on this guy. Maybe your fresh eyes will see something we didn't, maybe you can even collar him before he knocks off the whore."

"You taking bets?"

"Not on your side. By the way, the memo lists the phone number of a shrink we used to help us with the psychiatric profile. He couldn't tell us much, but he didn't try to bullshit us either. Dr. Herman Weis, works in Manhattan. I'd keep in touch with him. Who knows, huh? We'll do whatever we can, probably for free. We hate this guy."

"Thanks."

"Listen, I got a question for you. You don't have to answer, even if you can."

"Shoot."

"Okay. Our client was Frank Stoner, father of Andrew Stoner, the sixth kid killed, a manager of a Kansas City hi-fi store. He told us some story about a foundation offering to fund the investigation, and damned if there wasn't one: The National Foundation for the Advancement of Justice, Law and Order. They do a few good deeds, give a few cops awards. A funny group, but we didn't have the *knockus* to crack it without an angle, so we let it lay. But hey: it's fishy. Even Stoner knows so, though he won't admit it. What I want to know is who set up this whole big buck bankrolled deal, the hunt and what started it where and why? Who's our client's angel?"

"Beats me," answered Devlin.

nine

Even after four readings, the bizarre ad in the previous day's Baltimore *Star* made little sense to Devlin. He raised his head from the black blur before his tired eyes, glanced at the gap between the boxes on his desk, yawned. He shifted his body, propped his feet up on his desk, leaned back in the swivel chair and tried again.

> *"And He that sat on the clouds thrust in His sickle on the earth and the earth was reaped."*— *Revelations 14:16, sayeth the Lord, so beware Baltimore, for the day of Judgement and Salvation is at Hand and we must prepare the way for the Lord's return. Let all preparations be made and let the sinners beware, even The Mother of Harlots, who is drunk with the blood of saints, for this is what is and must be done, and We are who will Be the Way and do the deeds the Reaper must do as is and always shall."*

He closed his eyes, rubbed the bridge of his nose. Maybe tonight he could sleep. At least he had a better idea of the game he was playing. He opened his eyes, stared at the newspaper ad, but again it blurred. He'd skimmed through the major files in the carton for three hours. He focused his burning eyes on the far wall to counter the strain of close work. After a moment, he pulled his vision away from the soothing green plaster, through the squad room, back through the canyon between the cardboard boxes on his desk, back to his crossed feet. He noticed a dab of glue on the side of his right heel where the shoe repairman had been sloppy affixing the inset heel to the bottom sole.

But he'd never had his shoes repaired.

That took a moment to sink in. He bent his leg to examine

the heel. In addition to the small glob of freshly dried glue, he saw other tendrils emerging from the seam. He glanced around. Three other detectives worked at their desks. Uniformed patrolmen strolled in and out of the office. The Captain wasn't in his glass-walled office, but should he return, he could see Devlin's desk without any problem.

The toilets in the bathroom didn't have flat lids, but the stalls afforded Devlin unquestioned privacy. He sat on the horseshoe flap as he worked his unfolded buck knife across the seam. Within seconds, he pried apart two rubber sections, the still-fresh glue crackling in the process.

A small black metal capsule lay in the scooped out center of the heel. Devlin shook it free of the glue.

"I'll be damned," he said. They'd done more than guard him while he was drugged. The black capsule was an electronic transmitting device. The boys in the blue Ford had been camouflage, a blind. Somewhere close by, probably moving parallel with him all the time, was another, more sophisticated set of watchers with electronic eyes.

Devlin spread his legs wide and held the capsule above the water. Somehow the prospect of the bug merely clogging up the Department's plumbing didn't seem sufficient. He slipped the capsule into his pocket, pressed his shoe back together, and left the stall.

A walking mountain in a police uniform almost ran Devlin down as he turned the corner near the elevators. The mountain bounced back from their collision, unsure of itself and barely able to keep its balance.

"Hey Sgt. Rourke!" The mountain's name was Liam McKinnon. He had the red hair and florid face though not the brogue of his Irish ancestry. KcKinnon was 35, a big man made even bigger by his love of hot-fudge sundaes and gallons of beer. The creaky black Sam Browne utility belt still shoved much of his expansive gut up and outward, but the brass buckle would soon be covered by a drooping stomach. McKinnon's uniform was immaculate, his black shoes spit-shined to a luster rivaling the mirror sunglasses he habitually wore. His mother crisply ironed his blue shirt and trousers every morning. His sergeant's stripes pointed at exactly the proper angle. McKinnon loved being a policeman, wearing the uniform, riding around in the white squad cars with their red-and-blue stripes and the single blue light on top. He loved the way civilians

stared at him: nervous awe tinged with proper doses of fear
and respect. He went to every police movie, watched every
police TV show. He knew all the cinema slang, although it
sometimes confused even him when he parroted it back to
others. He thought he looked like a movie-star cop, kind of a
red-headed Clint Eastwood. He cultivated that self-image,
even cajoling the Department into letting him carry a highly
unorthodox and forbidden .44 Magnum revolver—just like
Eastwood's most famous cop character.

McKinnon reminded his fellow officers of a movie star too—
though not Clint Eastwood. They'd called him by a star's name
so long many of them had forgotten he had another identity.
The entire force knew this man as the Duck, after that famous
cinema star, Daffy Duck, and he was the dumbest man on the
Baltimore police force.

It is not unusual for a fool to rise to such an exalted rank as
police sergeant, but the Duck's elevation was no mere accident
of bureaucratic osmosis. His uncle had been a policeman, as
had his father. The Duck's well-earned reputation for dumb-
ness was matched by his father's equally justified reputation for
cunning. Under a previous Departmental organization and the
old Baltimore political machine, the Duck's dad climbed from
the ranks of patrolman to commander of the vice-riddled
downtown police district *and* the district which covered most
of the posh Baltimore neighborhoods where the monied and
powerful citizens lived. He became a power within the city,
living well and prominently in the rich neighborhood he
guarded. The Duck's father died of a heart attack shortly before
a massive federal probe of Baltimore police corruption. He
received one of the largest funerals in the city's history. His
powerful friends, out of loyalty, nostalgia and the fear that the
father's ghost would haunt them through secrets entrusted to
the Duck's mother, made sure that the son never lost the police
job his family had arranged.

The Duck had no duties. The Department long before had
discovered the dangers of assigning the Duck to even routine
police functions. He could be trusted to foul up all but the
most basic tasks. No one liked to work with him. Nominally he
was assigned to the Patrol Division. The Duck drove his
cruiser in city parades, though never as the lead cruiser
because of official fear that he might take a wrong turn. On
days when Baltimore hosted no parades, the Department

shuffled the Duck around the city. He spent most of his time aimlessly driving his cruiser. He was under strict orders not to respond to any radio calls. No dispatcher would ever assign the Duck to a run, but the Commissioner wanted to be sure the Duck didn't answer a general alarm.

The only police assignment the Duck drew besides parade detail was his role as bagman for a small but dedicated core of cops on the take. They reasoned that (1) Duck was too stupid to understand what he was doing, (2) he was therefore unlikely to rip them off, and (3) he was so well connected he would not be bothered by Internal Affairs or outside reformers who had been increasingly vigilant since the Great Vice Squad Purge of 1974, when most of the cops in charge of policing immorality were found to be wallowing in their work. If the Duck were caught, reasoned this contemporary crop of crooked cops, he would take the full fall. The logic was impeccable. Once a week, Duck received a phone call from a captain he'd never met, a voice on the end of the phone. The captain's name didn't exist on the police roster, but Duck never thought to question orders from a superior officer. This mysterious voice dispatched the Duck all over town. He'd shuttle from bar to bakery to street corner, picking up packages and paper sacks from toilet stalls, bus lockers, and occasional seedy strangers, delivering them to a broom closet or some other location in one of the district station houses. That he was entrusted with such special duty filled the Duck with pride, even if he didn't understand his top-secret mission.

But sometimes the Duck grew weary of the nebulous nature of his career. After all, his father always told him that a policeman should be more than someone in a blue uniform who drives around in a squad car.

"Boy am I glad I found you, Sgt. Rourke!" said the Duck.

"Hello . . ." Devlin couldn't remember the seldom used real name of the grinning man, ". . . Sergeant."

Duck glanced to both sides in his best cinema tough guy fashion. He inclined his head towards the far wall, motioning Devlin to follow him.

"I heard you got some special assignment," whispered the Duck. "I don't mean to pry. I just heard about it in the hall downstairs. I was dropping something off in a broom closet when . . . I can't talk about that! Anyway, the lieutenant from the Commissioner's office and some bald guy were talking in the hall about how if they were lucky Detective Rourke's new special assignment would become his final bow. I don't understand what they meant, and I didn't hear what the assignment was—you don't need to tell me! I know how these things are."

The Duck winked.

"Look," he continued, "I've pretty much got my duties down. I like 'em and all, but . . . between you and me, I think some people might think the only reason I got my stripes and other stuff is because . . . well, because my father was big in the Department."

"No!"

"I know: you're going to tell me I'm wrong, just like all the brass I talk to does. You're going to tell me what a swell job I'm doing and how important I am to the Department and the safety of the citizens of Baltimore."

"Not in quite those words."

"I just can't help feeling there's more to being a cop than doing a good job like that. I can handle a whole lot more than I've got now, but nobody will give me a break. They think I'm too busy or too important to ask for help on something routine that they're doing like a murder or a robbery or a rape.

"So I've decided it's gotta be up to me. If I'm ever going to be something more than just another good cop on the beat, doing his duty, drawing his pay, putting his life on the line, I've gotta take the initiative. That's why I've come to you. Us meeting in the hall like this just shows you how it must be fate."

"What fate?"

"Well . . . You know," insisted the Duck.

"No, I don't know."

"This special assignment you got. Let me help. Just a little. That's all I want. I'll be *so* good I'll show you and the whole Department! Why . . ."

"Sergeant, I don't think . . ."

"I'll do anything! Anything, if you just give *me* the chance! I'll work all hours! I'll go undercover! I'll . . . I'll walk a beat if you want me to! Just let me do something. I don't care what! *Please?!*"

A strange but beautiful vision rose through Devlin's mind.

"You know, Sergeant," said Devlin with a smile, "I think I've got a job for you." He reached inside his shirt pocket. "You see this?"

"A black capsule."

"An extremely *important* black capsule. We'll put it here," said Devlin, reaching out, sliding it into the properly buttoned shirt pocket of his fellow officer. "And that's where it must stay. On you at all times. I want you to guard this black capsule for me."

"With my life!"

"And one other thing."

"Name it!"

"I want you to stay as far away from me as possible."

"Sir?" said the Duck, forgetting he was speaking sergeant-to-sergeant.

"Just stay far away. They can't get both of us if we're not together. Go where I'm not, where you figure you'll never find me."

"Yes, Sir!" cried the elated policeman.

"And Sergeant . . ."

"Sir?"

"This is a secret mission."

"You can count on me, Sir!"

"I'm sure I can," said Devlin as he walked to the elevator. His loose sole slapped on the floor. He felt the eyes of his new assistant on his back. For once the elevator opened immediately after he touched the button. He turned when he entered the elevator and saw the Duck proudly smiling at him. Suddenly the Duck frowned, held up his hand. Devlin instinctively punched the "Door Open" button and stopped the machine from whisking him away.

"Excuse me, Sir," said the Duck, showing off his powers of observation, "but one of your shoes is broken."

"Don't worry, Sergeant," said Devlin, lifting his finger off the hold button. The doors started to slide shut. "I've fixed it."

ten

The phone booth in the lobby reeked of tobacco smoke and the dried sweat of desperation, but Devlin felt more secure using this line than the phone on his desk.

"Marberry Realty." The lilting feminine voice sang the words with just the right touch of snobbery.

"Lisa Lemick, please."

"One moment. I shall see if she's in."

"This is Lisa Lemick. May I help you?"

"Hello Lisa."

"Devlin! Oh Devlin! How are you?"

"Pretty good."

"Just pretty good? Can't you tell me you're doing great?"

"Hey, I'm fine, Lisa. Really I am."

"I hope so Dev. I still worry about you. But you promised me you'd do okay, and you're a man of your word. Remember how I insisted you promise to do terrific things? You gave me your best smile of the afternoon and said that right then okay *was* pretty terrific, all things considered. How 'bout now, Dev? Wasn't I right? Aren't there just whole lots of terrifics for you?"

"You couldn't guess how many if you tried, Lisa."

Her laugh still sounded like golden bells.

"Oh Devlin! How are you, really? How have you been and what can I do for you?"

"Good, better, and I'm looking for a house."

"A house? From our firm? Devlin, I assume you're still a sergeant. I'm afraid my company is out of your league."

"It always was."

"Now don't start that foolishness again, Dev. I simply mean our property is too rich for your wallet."

"Me too."

She sighed. "Let's be serious, Dev. If you are looking for a house, this isn't the firm for you. I've got some great contacts who will be able to help you and I'll double-check everything they tell you, help you with inspections and settlements and . . ."

"I'm not looking to buy, Lisa. I'm looking for *a* house."

"Oh. You mean I finally get to be part of police business."

"In a way."

"Will you tell me about it?"

"About the house, yes. About anything else, no. About how you should be extremely circumspect and cautious in your inquiries, never—repeat, never—mentioning me or the Department. . . . Yes, I'll tell you about that."

"Devlin, I never did understand your life."

"I sympathize with you there."

"Okay. I'll help. Obviously this house is expensive or you wouldn't be coming to me."

"I always said you were the best realtor for the rich in the state. Would you want me to settle for second best?"

She laughed again. "Never you, Devlin. Now, what can you tell me about this house."

"It's big. It has a dark wood-paneled library with a private office off that. Floor-length windows in the office that might overlook a garden or lawn. A large entryway with double doors. The entryway is white, the stairs leading up to the second floor out of the entryway are maroon carpeted. It has a porch with five steps down to a gravelled, probably circular driveway that's about . . . fifty, sixty feet or so from the entrance to the house. It's off an oiled road, maybe in the suburbs or along one of those private lanes you were always driving us around on Sundays. It's quiet. You can't hear any traffic over the crickets and the electric bugs."

"Electric bugs?"

"You know, those bugs: Zzzzzzzzz! I even have them in the trees by my place."

"Cicadas. You mean cicadas."

"If they're the electric bugs, I mean them. One more thing: Sometimes a big church close by sounds its bells."

"Church bells?"

"I think so. But then, you know how sometimes I think I hear church bells and I'm wrong."

She laughed a third time. "Oh Devlin!" Her voice dropped and he heard her concern. "This is serious, isn't it?"

"Would I bother you with anything less?"

"No, not now. Maybe once, but not now. I'll see what I can come up with, though you've given me absolutely nothing to go on. Is this place for sale?"

"I doubt it, but I don't know. It might be vacant, rented, hell, maybe it's supposed to be vacant and really isn't."

"Who's supposed to live there?"

"That's what I want to know. Probably somebody with a lot of money to afford such a house."

"You'd be surprised, Dev. People borrow the kinds of lives they want to lead, and play them out as long as they can. Should I call you at home or your office?"

"Neither. I'll call you."

"You and Hollywood. I gave up waiting for their call a long time ago. I used to wait for your calls, though, Devlin. I really did. With a smile."

"Keep smiling. I'll call you again soon."

"But not that way, Dev. You know not that way, don't you?"

"Yeah, I know."

He hung up. He sighed, and the odor he sucked in with his deep breath sickened him.

"Aw shit," he said.

eleven

The first victim had been beautiful. Stephanie Phillips, age 24, a chestnut-brown brunette with big blue eyes, a fine profile, full lips, heavy breasts and a walk that drove men wild. She'd switched from being a stewardess to a high-class call girl at age 22. At age 24, when her lush ripeness would normally just be gaining class and maturity, she had her throat cut in a Chicago hotel room. The crime lab photos of her naked body sprawled out on the dark-stained hotel carpet showed none of the sensual talent that she'd turned into a hollow economic lie. Devlin glanced down from the wide glassy eyes and half-open mouth to the gaping wounds on the piece of meat that had been her throat. Two long slashes: a left to right, somewhat shallow cut, and a right to left, deeper, more jagged slash. From the condition and position of the wounds on Stephanie and the other victims, forensic pathologists agreed the odds were 70 percent that the killer was right-handed.

After looking at her pictures, the shots of her in life acquired from friends and former employers, and the shots from the Chicago police morgue, Devlin didn't feel tired anymore.

Four days after a maid found Stephanie Phillip's butchered body, Elizabeth Jackson, age 9, a Caucasian girl average in all respects, right down to the report card she carried home to her father, a linotype operator, and her mother, who occasionally sewed for the neighbors while mothering three children, disappeared. Shortly after noon on an average November Chicago school day, someone snatched little Elizabeth off the playground. Someone enticed her into a car. How, no one knew, since her parents insisted she knew the dangers of strangers with candy. Two days later, Cook County sheriff's deputies responded to a hysterical mother of a 13-year-old quarterback in a northwestern Chicago neighborhood. Someone had gently placed little Elizabeth's throat-cut body in the middle of the boy's sandlot playing field. Elizabeth had not been sexually molested or otherwise mistreated. Merely murdered.

Devlin closed his eyes—to think, not to rest. He was the only detective in the squad room. The other detectives had current corpses to account for, clues to track down, cases to close. He had to plan for disaster. And avert it. And destroy it. And survive it. He opened the large bottom desk drawer. A rank odor rose from behind the file folders. A mixed collection of his dirty clothes waited there—some socks, two old shirts, even a pair of underpants, clothes soiled in the course of his work. Clothes he'd replaced from a nearby store because he hadn't had time to go home and change during the middle of a case. He pawed beneath the soft material, turning his nose as far away from his task as possible, until he found the small recipe box full of index cards. As soon as he had the box on his desk, he slammed the drawer shut.

The regular files were fine for detailed information, but on a case like this they were too cumbersome for quick reference. Soon much of the data would soak into his memory. The cards would help that process and give him a quick reference system until it was complete. With a red felt tip pen, he wrote in the upper left corner of a card:

Victim/Whore #1

On the card below he printed Stephanie Phillips. For easy alphabetical filing of the card, he underlined her last name. On the card he recorded her age, hair color, city of death, place of death/body discovery, and race, as well as the name of the chief investigating officer and next-of-kin and their phone numbers.

He used a black felt-tip pen on a second index card:

Victim/Child #1

On that card he wrote Elizabeth Jackson, undelined her last name, noted her age, from where she'd been snatched, where she'd been discovered, her race, pertinent dates and the same type of phone numbers.

The other cards took him a half-hour, a mechanical chore which he performed automatically while his mind percolated. When he was finished, he picked up his telephone.

His first call was to Vice Squad. He ordered all assaults on prostitutes to be reported to him immediately, and told the Vice Commander to have his detectives warn all suspected and known hookers to be wary and report unusual customers.

He called Communications Division and arranged for a 24-hour line with an officer to answer it to be assigned solely to him, then arranged for it to be hooked into his desk phone as well as the main switching center.

He encountered no difficulties until his third call, this one to the Department's Planning and Research Division. He worked his way up the chain of command with his request, finally ending up with the Director, who expressed sympathy but could promise only that the help Devlin wanted might take three weeks to arrange. When Devlin informed him that the killer usually struck down his first victim within two to six days after the appearance of the ad, the Director repeated his litany of technical, bureaucratic and budgetary problems. Devlin hung up swearing. Then he remembered a suggestion he'd gotten from one of the lower-level officers in the Planning and Research Division, who'd tossed out an idea as a "too bad you can't" bit of information.

Why not? he thought a moment later. *Why not play that card and see what it's worth?*

The phone on the other end of the number Kibler gave him rang twice. A strange male voice answered: "Yes?"

"Tell Kibler he's got a caller."

The man grunted. All sound died on the other end, as if Rourke had been placed on hold. Then Devlin heard a series of clicks, as if he were being electronically transferred time and time again. Finally Kibler came on the line.

"Is that you, Buddy? How you doing?"

"I want a meeting. Now."

"Well, I'm a ways away from you. Let's say . . . Hey! It's almost lunch time. I'll buy you a sandwich at the Lexington Market. You know the Polish sausage place? Meet me there in 30 minutes. Okay with you, Buddy?"

"Just fine with me."

twelve

The boys in the blue Ford were waiting for him when he pulled his Camaro out of the parking lot. The walkie-talkie all Baltimore detectives carried squawked a run for a numbered cruiser as it lay on the seat beside him. He briefly considered having the blue Ford stopped and its occupants rousted, but that would be a juvenile response. He drove a mile up East Baltimore street in a careful and prudent fashion. The blue Ford had no trouble staying on his tail.

There are actually two Lexington Markets in Baltimore, one right next to the other. Lexington Market East is a block-big warehouse with fruit stands, flower stands, vegetable stands, butcher shops, bakeries, candy stands, tobacco stands and even an old magazine collectors' stand clustered on a sloping concrete floor beneath an open girdered, corrugated roof.

"Hey Buddy!" Kibler waved a hot-dog-filled hand at him

from the stand that billed itself as the home of the original Polish sausage sandwich. "What'll you have? My treat."

A chubby teenage girl in a T-shirt looked expectantly at Rourke from behind the makeshift counter.

"A Polish and a cup of coffee," he told her. "Black."

"You want onions on the Polish, Mister?"

"Sure, I don't need to worry about offending anybody."

Rourke waited until he had the styrofoam cup in one hand and the greasy sausage dog in the other. A half dozen onion cubes fell onto his shirt, flecking it with grease stains. Arms outstretched, he gingerly made his way towards an empty wall. Kibler followed. He wondered if Kibler noticed his flapping shoe, or if he'd been informed by the electronic watchers that the man now with him wasn't the man with the bug. He settled his back against the wall, took two bites of his spicy sandwich, washed them down with a long drink of coffee, and said, "I need a computer."

"No problem," said Kibler.

"A *particular* computer. There's a man named Jackson Brickler who runs a computer program of some kind at Johns Hopkins. He came to the Department with a proposal a few months back, but nobody had the bucks to talk to him. His project may have folded out there, but you can find him. I need him, his computer, whatever he needs to use it. Fast."

"No problem. Anything else?"

"Yeah. Tell Cardozo to put the word out on the street, warn the hookers, the girls in the bars, the hotels, the call girls. He'll know the circuit to hit. They're to watch their ass, do nothing with nobody they have any questions about, stick close to their safest patterns, and call the Vice Squad or a 24-hour number I'll give you if they have any suspicions, any problems, any rough or peculiar customers."

Kibler carefully wiped a dab of mustard from one finger, then vigorously rubbed the paper napkin across his mouth. He wadded the napkin into a ball, and threw it into a nearby garbage can.

"I'm sorry friend. I really am. But I can't do that. Mr. Matella has already vetoed that idea."

"What the hell are you talking about?"

"I know what you're thinking. If we can stall the Reaper finding a whore to kill, maybe you'll have more time to catch him. Maybe a cautious whore will help you catch him with nobody getting hurt. Maybe if a girl goes down, you will have made the scene so tense the Reaper will overplay his hand and you'll get him that way.

"But maybe if he can't get a whore, he'll skip Baltimore. Maybe that will throw him off his pattern, which could shut him down or change him round. We'd never get him then. Mr. M. won't allow that. So we keep his hunting ground open for him. You nail him that way.

"Don't worry. They're just whores. Replaceable. The special ones we've already warned to lay off until we say it's okay. The rest take their chances, just like always. They sell themselves for money in a rough business."

"Just like you, Kibler? Is that what you do? Aren't you as replaceable and respectable as the whores?"

"Aw, buddy: the old wedge technique. You are gutsy, I'll give you that. Mr. M. said you'd try to drive a wedge between us, work something to your advantage. He's a smart man, that Mr. M. Smartest I've ever seen and I've seen a lot.

"Life's grand, ain't it buddy? I really mean that. *Grand*. But it's like I heard on the radio driving here, some song by somebody. I couldn't understand most of the words, one of those hoarse-throated rock guys singing through his nose. But the chorus came through loud and clear, said you gotta serve somebody. They got that right. Everybody's got to serve. Priests get their three squares and niche in life serving the Church. The guys out at Sparrows Point serve the steel companies, the guys in the car factories serve Detroit. The shopkeepers on the corner, they serve the public, and the people who put them on the corner, the bankers probably. Everybody pays some kind of service somewhere down the line. Lots of times it comes down to that dollar that lets them live. Cops, they serve the Commissioner, the Mayor, the City Council, the do-gooders, all the rank and file, plus the citizens too. Plus maybe us, if they're smart. You serve who or what can jerk your chain. Everybody's chain can be jerked, somehow.

"There's guys like you and the Boss. You try to beat that game, make it so's you can say *fuck off* and take whatever jerk hits your chain, take it and win or die not caring because you gave it your best shot. You think you're good at that. Hell, Mr. M. makes you look like a clown. But you guys serve too, even if you only serve something that's in your head.

"Not many of us can be as out there upright and alone as you. We need this or want that, or are afraid of this, or can't do that or tire easily or just don't want to fight the crowd more than we must. We're the folks who really serve. The only question is who. Me, I figure if you got to serve, why not serve folks who know that game backwards and forwards, folks who give pretty good for what they get."

"They take all you have," said Devlin. "They use you to hurt others worse than they could hurt them without you. They make you whore your soul. They never give back a fair return for any of that."

"So who out there in the marketplace gives any better? Listen friend, the only folks who come close to not serving are nuts like this Reaper. He's like you and Mr. Matella, only he really gets the job done. Still, he's trying to serve something in his head. I think he got too tangled up in his own chains and he's jerking himself around, chopping up little kids while he does it. That makes him a loony killer, because they ain't Commie gooks in some pissant country. But he's put himself above questions like that. He might be loony, but he's freer than you and me.

"Look around, Buddy. Listen. Hear that hustle and bustle? That's life, common, ordinary life. The guys over there eating oysters on the half shell work construction someplace. They're real people. They go home at night to one of those flat houses with a marble stoop. That's all most people see of Baltimore. They drive by it, come through on the train, look out their windows and what do they see? Row after row, block after block, of houses flat from one end of the street to the other, all the same, with a little marble three-step stoop to the sidewalk. No grass. No trees. Stone canyons, block after block after block. They see that, and they go *Yech!*

"Me, I think it's beautiful! I love this city. I ain't from here, but I love it. It's real, not all phoney glass and tackboard like other places . . . California, for instance. This city's got old neighborhoods with real people. In lots of those neighborhoods folks go out and scrub those stoops with a brush and bucket every day. Some of those folks live in houses that their parents owned before them. The people on those blocks have been there for years. A kid gets married, moves down the block to the same kind of house, buys it from somebody when they're ready to die. The kid goes to work in the steel plant with his old man. Makes another kid to do it all again. Real people, Buddy, and I love it."

"So you come here to bleed them."

Kibler smiled, shrugged his shoulders. "They gotta serve too, friend. They gotta serve."

"You know that's why Matella is in this Reaper thing, don't you?" said the detective. "He's serving too. He doesn't give a rat's ass about catching a madman. He doesn't care about the women or the kids. He's not even out for revenge because of his grandson. He wants to nail the Reaper because the Reaper insulted him. The Reaper had the balls to kill Salvatore Matella's grandson. He's serving his own monster ego. More than that, I'm betting he wants the Reaper nailed because it's expected of him. He stays in power because of the image two-bit hoods and fat-cat Dons have of him. If he lets the killer of his grandson walk, well, maybe somebody will think old Salvatore ain't quite tough enough, ain't quite as good as he used to be. That's why he's gunning for the Reaper."

Kibler shrugged; neither the gesture nor Devlin's words bent his smile. "I don't worry about 'why's.' I leave that to guys like you and Mr. M. Now is there anything else I can do for you?"

"Yeah. Jerk my tail. Those guys in the blue Ford you've got dogging me all over town cramp my style. They'll make me fuck up. I don't want that. Neither does Matella."

"We'll jerk the tail, but we'll keep our eyes on you. After all, you're our latest investment."

"So trust me to pay off or cash me in, but don't play my hand for me."

Kibler leaned away from the wall as if to go, then turned back to Rourke. "Did you enjoy the little bonus we gave you?"

Devlin said nothing.

"You threw them away, didn't you? No, we didn't see you do it. Mr. M., he predicted it."

"What if I hadn't? How would you have known?"

"You gotta understand Mr. M.'s way of thinking. He's a brilliant, brilliant fellow. Don't ever forget that, Buddy. Please, don't ever forget that.

"You having the coke hobby gave us the hook into you, but it also bothered Mr. M. Made him wonder about your smarts. He decided to be sure you were the right guy, that you were running the coke and not the coke running you.

"He figured if you *were* the right guy, the thing you'd be worried about first was whether we'd set you up for something you didn't see for a reason we didn't tell you. We didn't—I think you know that now. That meeting this morning should have convinced you we were serious and straight. But we had to be sure of you, so we gave you those two grams. Mr. M. said if you were dumb enough to keep them around after how, why and when you got them, then you were too dumb to be the right man for the job. We might have planted the stuff on you deliberately for a bust by your own people. He also figured if you were dumb enough to keep the stuff around, you were weak enough and dumb enough to try it by now. If you were that lame, we had to know right away. Then maybe the Reaper would win a free shot at Baltimore, 'cause Mr. M. says you're the best on the Baltimore force and if you weren't good enough, why waste our time and effort? We'd've waited until the guy hit here, then followed him to his next city.

"We had to know. So we gave you two grams of primo quality cocaine. But it wasn't a clean cut. We mixed it 70-30 with pure heroin. Not enough to smell over the coke, nothing that a kitchen test would show. But plenty strong enough. High-quality horse. If you'd been dumb, if you'd've been the wrong man for the job, you'd have kept that stuff and tried it by now. One hit of that mix, the heroin goes into you, maybe two minutes before you're dizzy as well as high. Half an hour later you're in a coma. An hour later you're dead. Checked out and dropped down, d-e-a-d, dead. The newspapers get a story 'bout a crooked cop who did one too many drugs. The Department would dump all over your corpse. How could they explain an overdose any other way, especially when somebody would dig up witnesses to say you snorted coke, blew grass? And even if the brass and your buddies didn't believe it all, who could unravel it? All the trails would start and end up your nose.

"But you are the right man for the job, so that didn't happen. So far you pass, friend. I want you to know I'm real glad about that, because I like you, I really do.

"Oh . . . Mr. M. said that since you've passed, you can have some high quality coke. He said you probably had some and dumped it along with the other. Consider the offer a reward for doing well so far, and a replacement for the trouble we caused you. Absolutely clean, safe as any shit can be. If you want it. But only now, after you've passed, when you've shown you don't got your nose up your ass. You pass friend. So far, you pass."

thirteen

Devlin rubbed the sleep from his eyes. His watch read 9:02. Soft morning sunlight waited outside his open bedroom door and beyond the thick blackout shade over his bedroom window. He was still tired. After his lunch with Kibler, he'd returned to Police Headquarters and ordered the Ballistics Department to examine his service revolver. The gun was in perfect working order, though a bit dirty, and demonstrably hadn't been fired for at least three weeks. They chided him about keeping better care of his pistol. The bullet matched the markings of his file bullet. It was his gun, it hadn't been used by anyone but him. They gave him a full written report so stating. He refused to answer their curiosity. Another base covered.

He spent the rest of the day reading the Reaper files. When he finished each file, he called the chief investigating officer and the person identified as closest to the victim to introduce himself and probe them with random questions. Had they thought of anything new? Was there anything they remembered differently? He made sure that he always reached the investigating officer before the next of kin, because he knew that most of the citizens would immediately check with their local police department. He didn't want to step on any toes or ruffle any feathers.

The calls wore on his professional stance. Maybe if he'd not been so tired he could have handled them better.

Maybe he wouldn't have found himself almost crying with Mary North's mother when she talked about how her little 8-year-old ran up to the concessions stand at the drive-in theater all by herself that June night in Houston. The Norths had been so proud of their little girl. So bright. So cheerful. So friendly. And so fiercely independent, anxious to please. She'd be safe on that short of a solo mission. One hour later, ushers searching the grounds with flashlights found her bloody little body behind a toolshed 100 yards from the concessions stands. A blood-splattered box of Pom-Poms lay not far away. Five days earlier, police had found the almost decapitated body of Sally Florence, 19, a mousy brown-haired skinny wretch of a girl in an alley not far from the Houston massage parlor where she turned tricks. Sally had been dead a week; in the time she'd been missing, nobody cared enough to search for her.

Maybe if Devlin hadn't been so tired he'd have had the answers for the father of little Matty Lopez, age 9. Matty was found under a car in a Los Angeles parking lot when the owner of the vehicle stepped in the sticky river of Matty's blood. August, 1979. "I'd done everything right," Matty's father told Devlin. "So had Matty. We emigrated, no wetbacks, no illegal aliens. We're citizens, we don't even need green cards. Matty was born in this country. He was so fine a child, so bright, so happy, so alive. He loved baseball and movies and flying and the little girls who chased him. I worked so hard to do everything right. Then for no reason, Matty is taken from us. Why, Sergeant? After his mother and I did all the right things, why did this terrible thing happen to innocent little Matty?"

Devlin had no answers. Maybe he could have at least come up with some platitudes if he hadn't been so tired.

Maybe if he hadn't been so tired he wouldn't have felt so badly for Marilyn Mason either, the dyed-blond 28-year-old whore who'd spent 10 years on Sunset Strip selling her body in the street because nobody ever liked it enough to put it on the screen. The devils in the city of angels called L.A. all drive cars too: Matty's body had been found in a parking lot where cars rested; Marilyn's body was found dumped along a road in the south L.A. suburb of Marina del Rey, the blood from her gaping wound flowing toward the not-too-distant thunder of the Pacific Ocean.

And maybe if Devlin hadn't been so tired, so disgusted with the gore he found in those manila files, gore he forced already wounded, innocent people to relive with a stranger over the phone, he wouldn't have asked Mr. Stoner of Kansas City how

and why he happened to hook up with the National Foundation for the Advancement of Justice, Law and Order.

After long moments of silence over the telephone wires, Mr.
Stoner answered:

"One evening you're sitting at home with your wife and your
only living son and the doorbell rings. It's a hot-shot local
attorney who says he's got a client who wants to remain
anonymous. A guy who's fixed it so this rich foundation will
give you what you don't have, the money to go after the guy
who somehow cut your little 10-year-old Andy's throat, cut it
right there in the living room of your own home and then left
him, bleeding like a fountain, left him for your other boy, little
6-year-old Ricky, to come home and find all by himself when
the school bus dropped him off, left him there for Ricky to
freak out over and stay with alone, crying and staring and
puking for an hour and a half before a neighbor notices the
door ain't shut and peeks in. This foundation is willing to help
you get that creep who's taken your oldest boy, left your
youngest boy a nervous wreck before he's even a teenager, left
your wife a gutted woman because she went to tend to her sick
mother instead of staying home with her son who had a cold,
thinking he was a big boy and would be all right anyway. So
now she's living with guilt you can't even imagine. And then
there's me. I got a fire in my guts that won't quit. I feel like
crying every time I come home because there doesn't seem to
be anything I can do to make it better. So this lawyer has a
client and a foundation that's willing to foot the bill for what it
takes to run this creep sicko down, a creep who's done this to
other parents too. All you got to do is sign some papers. Now
maybe you think that this client and the foundation are fishy.
But would you say no to the first chance you've had since
March 3, 1978, to do something besides bleed like little
Andy?"

Devlin couldn't answer that, just as he couldn't answer the
still-stunned parents of Lieu Thee, a 24-year-old Vietnamese
who'd fled the chaos and disaster of war for the promised land
and ended up as a slaughtered whore riding an automatic
elevator in a Kansas City hotel. Devlin couldn't tell them how
or why their daughter got there. Maybe that was just because
he was too tired.

So after he'd gone to the display ad department of the
Baltimore *Star* and discovered no one there remembered the

person who'd paid cash for two ads, one in hand, one to be
delivered by mail. After Devlin arranged with the paper to be
called as soon as the letter bearing the next ad arrived, he went
home. By then it was 7 P.M. He stopped at a deli not far from
his house and ate a meal he quickly forgot. He was in bed by
8:30. Despite the exhaustion of the hard day's life on a
sleepless previous night, he lay between his sheets, the
window air conditioner humming, his eyes wide open and full
of bloody manila files. His gun, handcuffs and his silver-and-
blue detective's badge in its leather case rested on his bureau.
Baltimore police badges are rotated: when an officer leaves the
force, his badge number goes back into the pool until a new
recruit picks it up. Devlin's badge was number 47. He had no
idea who carried that badge before him, or who would carry it
after. All he knew was that he had it now, and it lay waiting on
his bureau while somewhere out in the summer blackness of
Baltimore waited another shiny steel object. A sharp steel
object.

No one in his city had been killed with that unknown sharp
steel object.

Yet.

The first thing he did when he woke the next day was call his
24-hour number. No news to report. But the general police
switchboard had a message for him to call Mr. Smallwood.

Like the Duck's Captain, Mr. Smallwood didn't exist. He
was the code name FBI Agent Cowan used to signal his friend
Police Sergeant Rourke to call him.

It made no sense to trust his home phone any more than his
office extension. Devlin showered, shaved and dressed, gulp-
ing down a cup of coffee while putting on his clothes. He
looked at the jumble on the floor of his closet. He couldn't
wear his regular shoes, the flapping sole drove him nuts. He
owned three other pairs: a hiking type boot he wore in the
winter to keep from freezing to death on cold investigations,
his regulation blacks which had always hurt his feet and were
three years overdue for a shine, and a pair of electric blue-and-
white racing-striped running shoes.

"The Lieutenant will love this," he said as he picked up the
running shoes.

The nearest pay phone was at the deli two blocks away. He
walked beyond that to a deserted Esso station. He saw none of

the boys from the blue Ford, but that didn't mean he was as clean as Kibler had promised.

"Federal Bureau of Investigation. Good morning."

"Agent Cowan, please."

"Agent Cowan, can I help you?"

"This is Mr. Smallwood," said Rourke, pen poised above his notebook.

"487-1213. Ten minutes."

Ten minutes later Cowan was talking to him from a pay phone by a book store not far from the Federal building.

"Matella's name rang bells at the top. The number one O.C. man in the Bureau got back to me direct when I passed the question around."

"Did he know anything?"

"This guy didn't *answer* questions, my man, he *asked* them. Hard. I used my famous professional and personal discretion, and decided to give your name to him. His is spelled funny, pronounced simple: B-e-q-u-a-i, Beck-way. Gus Bequai. Special Agent in Charge, though what he is SAC of I don't know. I only know he is hot to talk to you."

"Got his phone number?"

"Man, he's in Baltimore! Made the trip up special from D.C., just to meet little old you. Only he's not *in* Baltimore, know what I mean? My SAC doesn't even know he's here. He's not your standard Bureau boy."

"Is he straight?"

"Like a fucking arrow."

"How do we know?"

"Oh we know. I'm surprised his name didn't ring a bell with you, but then it happened in Connecticut when Bequai was assigned to the New York field office. 1977. He'd just transferred from Chicago, before that, Miami. Worked with a couple of strike forces other places too. A rising star. Well, he pissed off somebody in the Mob. One day he and his wife and two-year-old son go out to get in his car. Usually he drove to work alone, leaving his wife the proverbial station wagon. But she thought she'd take him into the city, see some kin of her adopted old man. She was an orphan raised by an uncle who just happens to be a U.S. senator on the judiciary committee which oversees the FBI, all of which doesn't hurt the husband who's so brilliant he doesn't need such connections. They get settled in the car, wife turns on the engine, little boy remembers he forgot his teddy bear. Since the missus is driving, Gus volunteers to go get it. He leaves her there, car idling, while he goes to the door, fumbles with the keys, runs through the house, finally finds the teddy bear, brings it out, locks the front door, turns to go to the car, and BLAMMO!

"They'd rigged a time-delay fuse on the bomb so he'd be on the highway when it went. That model of car had gas tank problems, maybe it could have passed as an accident. But they didn't figure on the wife, the kid, the teddy bear and the long idle. Gus got blown back off his feet. He rolled over and saw his old car in a twisted heap burning like it had been napalmed. He knew what was inside.

"That was the first outright Mob hit on an FBI agent. Let me tell you, the shit flew. We spread out 150 agents. God knows where we pulled them from. No trouble getting volunteers. We jerked around every Mob guy we could find. New York, Chicago, Miami, Los Angeles, Vegas, Philly, Cleveland, Nashville, Dallas, Detroit. We made U.S. attorneys prosecute Mob guys for spitting on the sidewalk. We were none too gentle in interrogations. Something like 50 soldiers and half-a-dozen lieutenants bought hard time. We found three guys we knew were bombers and the Cappo who probably oversaw the contract garroted beside a New Jersey highway two days after the funerals, but we didn't let up for months.

"Bequai was into intense investigation, and they must have thought the heat was worth it to stop him. Not only did they catch more heat, their team blew it. You know where Bequai lives now? FBI Headquarters in D.C. Somewhere in there they made him a little apartment. He's got round-the-clock guards. They wanted him to do the I.D. dip, set him up somewhere else, but he said no, and the wife's grieving senator uncle helped him pull it off. Now he spends full time on O.C. stuff. Most of the time in the Hoover building, sometimes doing the Phantom bit, popping up with his army here or there to come down on somebody. He's got more clout than a baseball bat. And there's no question of his being straight. You couldn't buy him with anything but blood."

fourteen

On Rourke's two previous visits to the Ebbit Hotel there'd been no elevator operator. This time he found a tense young man in a three-piece suit feigning nonchalance as he asked for floors. The elevator operator's suit coat was unbuttoned. From the awkward way he used his left hand to press the buttons, Devlin knew he was right-handed. That primary skill hand hung by his side—empty, waiting. Devlin stared at the elevator doors, his own hands carefully folded in front of him.

Two other tense young men in three-piece suits waited on each side of the elevator when the doors slid open to the sixth floor. They flashed a badge, asked for his I.D., and frisked him. Devlin started to protest when they took his gun from his holster, but thought better of it. One of the young men pointed him down the hall. Two more of their type stood in front of a door, and another two stood guard in front of the stairwell at the far end of the corridor.

As soon as Devlin reached the two men guarding the door, one of them called out, "He's here." Yet another of their kind threw open a door two rooms *behind* Devlin.

"Oh that's real cute," said the Baltimore policeman in sneakers, crumpled navy blazer and knit cloth tie to the three-piece suit crowd. Devlin blinked. All these hard young men from Washington blurred into one anonymous face, as if they were cloned from a single model and given different color hair and suits only for cosmetic purposes.

"In here, Rourke," commanded a voice from the open room. *The rest of the corridor must be empty*, thought Devlin. That wasn't strange for the Ebbit, which was a far cry from Baltimore's best. But maybe the Bureau rented the whole floor. A floor of rooms with the sole function of being empty and therefore safe. An interesting use of tax dollars.

Devlin knew the man sitting inside the dimly lit, curtain-

drawn room was the clone maker. Two more of his creations
waited with him, their nervousness keener than their corridor
comrades who worked further away from the master's eye.

"What the hell are you doing poking around with Matella?"
The man who barked at Devlin from the chair was almost an
older version of his guardian clones. Almost. He hadn't been
allowed to mature naturally. His short grey hair was combed
flat along the sides of his head. His left cheek was a hairless
sheen of abnormal flesh. A plastic surgeon repaired something
there, probably a burn. The man's classic chiseled features
were a bit off too. The surgeon needed to remold a man who'd
been too close to an explosion to walk away unscathed. The
surgeon had been able to fix the damage to the face and body,
but no medicine had been found to ease the angry ache in the
man's brown eyes.

"I said what the hell are you doing messing with Matella?"
"Who wants to know?"
"FBI."
"Bullshit. You're not the Bureau. You might be part of them,
but that's all. You and your clone army aren't here officially and
I didn't ask officially. You got less legal clout in this place than I
do. I don't like your whiz kids patting me down. I don't like
you barking orders as if I were one of your trained seals."

The angry brown eyes blinked, then slowly roamed over
Devlin. They stopped when they reached his blue running
shoes. "What the hell is it with the sneakers, some kind of
joke?"

"Who's laughing?"
"Leave us!" barked the man, and the two bodyguards who'd
been itching to slap down Devlin's arrogance stalked from the
room disappointed but with military precision.

"Sit down," the voice said. The tone was softer, almost
polite. Devlin lowered himself to the edge of the bed. The
man sighed, and put his hand on top of the blank TV screen.
When he laid aside his iron-guard commander role, he seemed
older and more exhausted than his 45 years.

"You're right about my guys. They are trained by me or
because of me. Our Academy plus Secret Service plus some
other schools you don't need to know about. There are just
barely enough such men. To some degree they are clones. I
bred them from and for a mold, even going so far as to recruit
some of them in college. I'm going back to high schools now for

the next generation. That's the only way I can be sure who they really are, who I'm trusting with my life and my work. You I don't know from shit. Cowan is supposed to be clean. He says you are. He's a smartass too, but you're both supposed to be good cops.

"That's what I used to be once. I had it all: career, mission, ideas and ability, wherewithal to make something of what I had. Plus the dream home life. The dream. I was so good I began to find out things the Boys don't want known. I found out a name. When that name found out I knew his secret, everything I had went on the line.

"The craziest part of all was it wasn't supposed to work out this way. He said to neutralize me. He meant I should suddenly find my funds for investigations dried up, or that I should get transferred to an Indian reservation in the middle of nowhere. The old Butte Montana syndrome, banished to bureaucratic Siberia. Or maybe even promoted up to a high level of ineffectiveness. But his underling was a bit overzealous and . . . traditional. So he blew my life away. It cost him his own, plus those of the guys who'd botched the contract. Those four deaths were supposed to help level things out, end the exchange, them plus all the busts and trouble we gave them while they were rebuilding me at Walter Reed.

"But all that doesn't even come close to evening the score. The man who raised his hand: when he's down, then maybe it's enough of a loss for me to let go. Of course, the opposition fails to agree. So I'm back as a target. And the Bureau is locked into the game whether they like it or not. Because of that man."

"Salvatore Matella."

"Salvatore Matella. Now where and how and why did you cross that name?"

"I can't tell you. Not yet."

"You're crazy!"

"Listen, I know he's terrible. And I'm locked into something involving him. But I can't tell you. There are a hundred ways he can find out. If he does, I lose and you lose. You've got to trust me on that."

"Why?"

"Because it makes sense and because there's no other option."

The men stared at each other, then the scarred FBI Agent

sighed again. "All right. I'll do that. For now. And God help
you if you're not straight. What do you want?"

"Everything in the world you know about him."

"That won't take long. Salvatore Matella. He's 74 years old.
Up front, he's a barber who still putters around his Brooklyn
barbershop. Owns a couple small townhouses he rents out, an
office building. But he's been Mob ever since the old days,
since he was little more than a boy. He used to do his killing
personally. A score or more, for all we know. I think he liked it.
Then he moved into management, and, brother, was he
brilliant.

"The only other mobster who's still around, active and older
than Matella is Saul Leibowitz, the money man for the boys
since the thirties. If you think he's retired down there in
Miami, then you're either a fool or ignorant, which Cowan
claims you're not. Our boy Matella latched on to Saul in the
forties. Matella merged himself with the national and international scope of the Mob rather than tying himself to any one of
the 27 major families in the cities. Smart move. Our boy
missed a lot of internecine warfare that way.

"Maybe he figured on replacing Saul someday, maybe not.
Matella always hid in the shadows. Deep, deep in the
shadows. He was kind of a cross between a protégé, a partner
and a right hand for Saul. But a successor . . . Well, there's
two other guys angling for that. Have been for 20 years, but
Saul won't die. Neither of them are anywhere as brilliant as
Matella, but they're younger.

"Maybe Matella realized all this or maybe he knew something else. For whatever reason, he got to do something very
few of the Boys are allowed to do. In 1970, partially as reward
for his lifetime of loyal and outstanding service, they let
Matella retire.

"But then in 1977, The Boss, Guisseppe Ganaldo, also did a
rare thing: he died of natural causes. He was succeeded by a
guy we joke about as 'G-2': Marcello Giordano, a real brutal
Don. And flashy. Big cars, loud scenes in restaurants, the
whole deal. He attracted a lot of attention from the press, and
from us.

"Giordano's heavy act annoyed the Council. They couldn't
pretend they didn't exist when he was driving around in block-
long limos, thumbing his nose at everybody. They also worried
that as brash, crude, arrogant and maybe crazy as he was, he

might take a fall. In his position, if he went down, everybody might topple.

"But they couldn't just replace Giordano with another Boss of Bosses drawn from the ranks of Dons. Their egos were involved, their power, their rivalries. There'd have been a bloodbath beyond belief, in part because Giordano didn't step aside for anybody.

"But the Council persuaded him to accept an alternative. The fact that he finally got jail time for some weak federal charges helped. They came up with a man they could all trust, someone without ambition to set up a personal empire. Someone too old to change into a strong shark who'd try to eat all the other sharks. Someone who was a proven, experienced, brilliant, safe bet."

"Salvatore Matella," said Devlin.

"That's one name," replied Bequai. "His consorts sometimes call him by an Italian nickname based on his green eyes: Two Emeralds. *Due Smeraldi.*" The FBI agent's Italian was limited to classic O.C. terms and phrases. He pronounced the nickname with reverent care: *Dō-a Smarellde.* "Sometimes he's referred to as the *consigliere tu consiglieri*, the councilor of councilors, the adviser above all advisers. But those titles are incomplete. He does far more than advise the Council, the Families; he directs them, coordinates them, leads them, juggling all the rivalries and all the power they give him into the smoothest-working machine they've ever had.

"When he accepted the offer to come out of retirement, Matella insisted on one condition: absolute anonymity—which suited the Council fine, for the public nature of Giordano was one of the problems to begin with. Few mobsters beneath the ruling clique of each family know that Matella even exists, let alone know his name. They might believe that someone like him does and sense an unseen hand guiding their Don. But they know no name. Those who do don't speak it lightly. Due Smeraldi has the death sentence on any who do.

"For a while, the transition from the brash and bullying Giordano to the caretaker with green eyes went well. There were some 'adjustments', some bodies ending up in car trunks. But Matella kept everyone in line. With the support from the Council, with his ties to his old mentor in Florida and Caesar Boniventre, an old 'retired' Don who still pulls strings in New

York from Phoenix and who could have been Big Boss if he wanted to, Matella was safe. Everybody was happy.

"Everybody except Giordano, who was marking time in a federal prison in Atlanta. Marking time, living the life of a prison God, and knowing his empire was crumbling over the horizon.

"One day Giordano announced at handball that from then on, anybody playing against him had to hit the ball high on the wall so he could hit it back easily. Only he, the grand and powerful Giordano, was allowed the low shots. 'I win all games,' he said.

"Somebody questioned this, and got slapped around by Giordano. 'I rule everything,' claimed Giordano. 'When I get out of prison, I'll show everyone who's Boss. Due Smeraldi will deal with me. He'll kiss my hands or he'll kiss my ass.'

"Giordano became the prison handball champion. He won the trophy set up by the rehabilitation boys. And Matella got detailed reports of his every move, including his little speech in the yard.

"In May, Giordano got out of prison. He dropped out of sight until June, then surfaced and began making the rounds of all his favorite spots in New York. The Council had let him resume control of his old Family, but told him moving back up to Boss was out for the time being.

"Giordano made no secret of his displeasure, but he did nothing overt. We think he was trying to gather support, find dissident members of the Council to back him in a coup. He may have made some progress, but not enough.

"One day he pulled up to a small family restaurant in Little Italy not far from where Joey Gallo got hit a few years back. He was going to have lunch with one of his friends. Giordano had been playing it smart: always changing his schedule, always riding with a couple bodyguards.

"But he wasn't smart enough. He'd just started his pasta when three guys came out of the kitchen blasting away with shotguns and an M-16. The two bodyguards and Giordano's luncheon guest, an old sycophantic civilian friend, died. So did a busboy. So did Giordano. And after he was dead, his chest blown out by a shotgun, one of the gunmen pulled a pistol, stood over the corpse and shot out the eyes. It could have been meaningless mutilation. Or it could have been a signature from the man with emerald eyes, Due Smeraldi, who was in his barbershop that noon with a dozen witnesses.

"That's all I know. I've been living with that man at the center of my life for two years. I almost died for knowing ten percent of that when I started on the idea of a grand consigliere in 1977.

"My world has shrunk to a few institutional blue-and-green walls in the largest civilian office building in the world. My fortress and my prison. Where else could I go? What else could I do?"

Rourke shrugged his shoulders. He couldn't involve himself with such questions from this man. Not then. "I need some other things maybe you can help me with."

"Go."

"First, can you set up a hotline to you? One independent of the rest of the Bureau? One you can check for taps at least once a day? I might have stuff for you and I might need cavalry from some other army besides my own."

"The line within six hours. And I'll have five agents waiting your orders in Baltimore. The guys in the hall, you've seen them, they've seen you."

"Second, arrange so I can acquire and possess narcotics and other controlled substances carte blanche in the process of an ongoing, unspecified investigation. And get me that cover absolutely secretly."

"Done. Go."

"I need a wire, a body bug I can carry that will escape a good frisk."

"My technical man can pull one out of the CIA, have it ready to hook up to you in . . . say five hours."

"I won't need it quite that soon, but that's good. What I do need is for you to keep all this buried so deep no one knows it's there."

"It's with me. That means it's dead."

"If it isn't, I am."

"Which brings up an interesting point: I'm trusting you on this. I'm backing you all the way. But you gotta know something down to the bottom of your soul. If you play footsie with Matella, or fuck up a chance to nail him, or fuck me over, I'll draw a circle around you, stick your ass up at the headquarters range, and personally shoot the first volley with the troops."

*   *   *

A pigeon warily pecked at the scraps of someone's discarded junk food hamburger bun next to Devlin's parked car. Devlin looked at the pigeon, then at the tops of the high buildings and the blue sky. The Department of the Interior was conducting a pigeon control and wildlife regeneration experiment in Baltimore. Two peregrine falcons had been resettled atop one of the skyscrapers, set free to live in the city and feed on pigeons. The pigeon's nervous pecks came between upward glances as if he knew that at any second death could dive out of the sky to smash him at 180 miles per hour, faster than he could hear, faster than he could see, faster than he could certainly dodge.

"I know how you feel pal," said Devlin who normally hated pigeons. "If I'm a little careless or unlucky, Matella will crush me like a cockroach, the Lieutenant will hang me from City Hall, Stern will skewer my ass with my badge and Bequai will take me to the wall for the federal firing squad. Hell, the Reaper might even cut me down if I get too close. It's great to be popular."

fifteen

"Hey Sergeant, I love those shoes!" called the uniformed officer at Central Headquarters' reception desk. This cop was also a sergeant, a thick-skinned old bull who'd tenaciously clung to his badge through all the shake-ups and bureaucratic wars, through all his own deeds and misdeeds, and who now sat secure in his pension-building job as meeter and greeter, always a kind word and a smile for the right persons, the unerring ability to pass the buck when need be, and just enough civility to deal with stray members of the public who wandered in with curiosity about their police department. The old sergeant had a scar running diagonally from his left eyebrow to his receding hairline. The implication was that the officer had been wounded in performance of his duty. Actually, his wife had connected with a surprise right hook when they'd been drunk one night. Her fist contained a beer bottle which broke across the sergeant's broad forehead, leaving him with a colorful scar. He had another scar, this one hidden from the public by his uniform, a long thick welt branded into his back by a red-hot water-pipe. He acquired this second scar when he charged into a burning tenement in the black ghetto and pulled three unconscious children from the incinerator that minuted before the furnace explosion had been their substandard home.

Rourke waited for the elevator with no reply.

"You detectives will do anything to catch a crook!" yelled the uniformed bull as the elevator doors shut behind Devlin.

"There's a call for you on 3-2!" yelled one of Rourke's fellow detectives as he entered the Homicide room.

"Thanks Paul. How's it going?"

"Ahh, quiet night. We got a line on that arsonist who burned down the warehouse with the wino inside."

"Terrific!"

"Me and Perry hope to make the collar at the guy's job today. We're cutting the papers for the warrant right now."

"Get him good," said Devlin as he settled in his chair. He punched the blinking light on phone line 32. "Detective Rourke."

"Detective, this is Jackson Bricker at Johns Hopkins computer center and you've made my year! I don't know how you did it, but yesterday afternoon the project I thought was on the junk heap is funded with all the bucks it needs from some foundation out of Chicago! Supposedly you had something to do with it because you're trying to catch a killer, but hell, what do I care! We're going to make it work! I haven't been this excited since I programmed the machine to handicap last year's pennant race at the start of the season and came up with the Yankees!"

"Glad you're glad. I've got a ton of material I want you to start on. You may need some people. . . ."

"Got 'em. Programmers I trained myself. Guys who understand data instead of just processing it."

"I'll be right over."

Devlin hung up, then called the motor pool and arranged for an unmarked car. He glanced through the room. The only other detective present was Paul McKee, and he was busy

preparing paper work for the arson murder bust. The Captain
sat in his cubicle, wearily explaining something to someone on
the telephone. The five heavy boxes sat on Devlin's desk. The
quickest answer would be found at the front desk.

"Look," Devlin asked the old bull sergeant who answered
his call, "you got any uniforms around? I need two or three of
them to help tote some boxes, one of them with his own
cruiser so I won't need to ferry them back."

"I got two cadets here who think they're off duty and
stopped by to shoot the shit. They just volunteered. They can't
take a cruiser. . . . Wait a minute, I see another animal I can
send up."

"Thanks Sergeant."

"Hey, Fleetfoot: for you, anything."

Three minutes later the sound of footsteps entering the
squadroom keyed Devlin. He turned and saw two nervous
cadets.

And behind the tall one, sheepishly waiting, stood the
Duck.

"The desk sergeant said you wanted me!" explained the
Duck to what even he recognized as an angry look.

Time was too important to waste waiting for someone else.

"Is your cruiser in the lot?"

The Duck nodded.

"Grab one of those boxes. Stick it in your car, and then I'll
follow . . . No, you'll follow me to Johns Hopkins."

The two cadets lugged their burden through the doorway
first. Duck looked over the box between his arms as his new
commander shifted the last heavy cardboard container off the
desk. The Duck wished he could carry two at once like the big
cadet so his new commander wouldn't need to sweat.

"I've been doing real good," he said, hoping to make Sgt.
Rourke feel better.

"Glad to hear it," said Devlin, wishing he'd picked a lighter
box. Two dozen more steps to the elevator. He could hold the
box that long, rest it on the railing inside.

"I mean, except for today, you haven't seen me, have you?"

"Can't say I have," agreed Devlin.

"Sergeant?"

"Yes?" replied Devlin, straining to control both his impa-
tience and the weight of the box.

"Should I wear sneakers too?"

Devlin looked at the eager, questioning eyes of the uniformed man before him. He heard the elevator stop. As the doors slid open, he said, "You can wear whatever you want."

sixteen

"I want it all in there," Devlin told the bearded little man in wire-rim glasses. "Names, dates, places, numbers, nothing is too trivial. Program it the best way you can. You know we're dealing with a psycho, but there's bound to be a pattern somewhere, somehow. Find me coincidences, conjunctions, similarities I don't already know. Some little scrap of data, some quirk we can turn into a handle. If there isn't a motive beyond the killing itself, at least find me a pattern."

"I feel awful for the people who got killed," Jackson Bricker told him. "But I'm so excited! This is such a challenge. I only hope we can do it. The machine can help you look, but it can't find what isn't there. Maybe there is no pattern."

"Then we're in worse shape than I think."

"Is there a deadline we're working against?"

"We've passed it."

seventeen

For the first time, Devlin felt good about the case. He was moving, he was doing, he was exercising his intelligence in the street. His odds were going up. The computer might help him find the Reaper. The alliance with Bequai might prove enough to help him weasel away from Matella without a bullet or a stevedore's hook in his back. If he could win those two, then skating by Jeff Stern's vindictive traps and the Lieutenant's caginess should be easy. Force and counterforce. Analyze, understand, act.

He glanced in the rear-view mirror. No one had followed his two car parade to the University. He'd seen no one follow the Duck when he ordered that man to leave and continue his "avoidance" mission. Devlin saw no one behind him now. Matella might actually have pulled the tails. Might. By now they knew their electronic eyes were locked on the Duck's confusion, not Devlin. They wouldn't admit to it, just as Devlin would not flaunt his play to them. This was a quiet exchange which both sides would accept, waiting for the other side to err by making something of it.

The computer arrangements had taken longer than he planned. Up the road on the right he saw a bank of pay phones. Why not see how efficient Bequai really was?

Extremely efficient. The pay phone linked him to one of the three-piece suit clones.

"We're in place for back-up and ready with the wire," said the clone. "The tech man will be waiting for you when you want, where you want."

"Why doesn't he meet me. . . . Have him go to the Attorney General's Violent Crimes Liaison Unit first thing tomorrow morning. Have him ask for Biz Grey. She'll tell him where to go, I'll meet him there. It's safe for us both to show up at that office. He should use the name Sherman, Walter Sherman."

"Got it."

Another 15 cents connected Devlin to Lisa. *As if it were that easy,* he thought grimly.

"You know Dev," she said, "you didn't give me a whole lot to work with. I can't even narrow it down to neighborhoods. Do you know how many thousands of churches Baltimore has?"

"I don't . . . Wait a minute! I think a lawyer or a judge, somebody involved with the law owns the place. The library was full of law books."

"Do you know how many pages of lawyers there are in the phone book?"

"But there's only one realtor who can put it all together."

"Flattery gets you shit, Devlin. With a smile, but still shit."

"How about if I appeal to your sense of pity, civic duty, and old times?"

"You bastard," she said without anger. "You refuse to give me a reason that matters, so I assume there *is* a reason that *really* matters and that makes it even harder to do anything but practically kill myself helping you."

"You're a good person, Lisa."

"You used to say 'a good woman.' Give me a few more days, Detective Rourke, and I'll see what I can come up with."

"I don't know how much time I have, Lisa."

"Then give me what you can. And call when you must."

While technicians across the city poured similar data into an emotionless machine, Devlin used his card index system to finish out the day calling the rest of the policemen and next-of-kin of the Reaper's crop.

He talked to the parents of Thad Gardner, age 6, who'd wandered away from his Manhattan school group touring the Museum of Natural History. Thad ended up dead in a seldom-used subway tunnel. The parents of Charlotte Bumby, a 21-year-old scrawny natural blond junkie from Minneapolis who'd been slashed to death by the Reaper in a Times Square flophouse that same March in 1977, acknowledged Devlin's call, but they wanted no more of their daughter's history or policemen.

The mother of little Jimmy Austin, who at age 7 had been snatched from a car she insisted she'd locked and left safe in a

Denver parking lot, needed more than the questions Devlin asked. Her son had been found two days later, executed in a graveyard. Since that July, 1977, her life had first frozen, then shattered into little pieces she carried with her. Her marriage disintegrated. Devlin heard behind her nonchalant explanation of events an aching she controlled but couldn't relieve. He gave her no help. Just as he found no help from the Denver policeman who'd tried in vain to track down 28-year-old Myrna Shull's next-of-kin or any friends beyond the maid who saw her "entertainer" employer once a month. Myrna's maid found her decaying corpse one Friday in July when she came to clean the black call girl's apartment. The Reaper was the last customer she entertained.

Devlin exercised his greatest tact when he called the parents of the Reaper's seventh victim, Peter Jenkins, the 10-year-old boy who had a green-eyed monster for a grandfather. Devlin asked all the usual questions, got all the usual answers. He was about to end the conversation when John Jenkins né Matella softly asked, "Is my father involved in this?"

"Not . . . not on the Reaper's side."

"His side is always the Reaper's side," insisted the son.

Another son in San Francisco held a peculiar opinion of his parent. "I know what she did," said the son of Andrea Compton, who had been a successful prostitute at age 42 when most women in her profession are usually dead, burned out or broken husks. "I think she was an angel. She was with the angels here on earth in her own way, and she's with them in heaven now. Whoever left her like that in the alley behind that hotel just changed her physical dimensions. Her inner spirit will always be pure and free."

The last and latest Reaper victims had been in Boston. The Reaper's first victim there was Lois Palmer, 27, an enterprising businesswoman who filled in for a subordinate in the outcall massage service Lois managed. Her initiative earned her a scarlet ribbon all the way around her pale neck. And lastly came little Maggie O'Donovan, age 5, a flower-girl at her big cousin's High Mass wedding in Irish Southie. She and the ring-bearer had been playing hide-and-seek at the back of the church, a frightening but thrilling adventure for youngsters who were just beginning to understand the terror of sacrilege. The boy heard whispers, then the rear door opened and Maggie giggled as she slid out into the cold February air. He'd run after her, jumping out into the alley with a triumphant yell. But she was nowhere to be found. He hunted until his fingers were cramped with the cold, until his little body wouldn't stop shaking inside the small suit his aunt had sewn for him. When he ran back to the vestry and the merry wedding reception, he desperately believed he would find Maggie there. But he was wrong. The men from the wedding, after carefully reassuring everyone of what they tried to believe themselves, fanned out through the neighborhood crying Maggie's name. The last place they thought to look was back inside the church. She'd probably never left there. The opening door had probably been a ruse to send the young boy away. Maggie's butchered body, her tiny white dress drenched in crimson, lay stretched out on the altar.

eighteen

"Devlin! How did you get my home number? I'm not listed!"

"Your secretary is and she was happy to give it to me when I called her last night," he said into the pay phone not far from his apartment. The morning was already turning hot. "She thought it was a great idea to tell me. Said you wouldn't mind."

"Well, I . . . I don't, but why didn't you call last night? It's . . . 7:15. It's a good thing I'm an early riser."

"Look Biz, can I drop by your office this morning? I know you're working on that arson case even though it's Saturday. I figured your office would be open. Crime doesn't care about weekends."

"Devlin . . . Sure."

"Another guy will come too."

"Another guy . . . You mean it isn't just you wanting to drop by my office. This is a group affair."

"Sort of."

"Sort of."

"His name is Walter Sherman and he'll ask for you at the reception desk."

"Walter Sherman. What am I supposed to do with Walter Sherman?"

"Put him in your office and stick out the 'Do Not Disturb' sign."

"I had another use in mind for the office and that sign."

"Look, this is really important."

She sighed. "Okay. I'll move in another chair so we can all be comfortable."

"Ah . . . Biz?"

"Yes?"

"That's the other thing. I need to see Mr. Sherman alone."

"You mean you don't want to drop by my office this morning to see me; you want to drop by the building this morning and use my office. You and Mr. Sherman no doubt need some place private and quiet where you can be alone and not disturbed. Some place discreet."

"That's it."

"You son of a bitch."

"Biz! This is important!"

"It normally is. Normal doesn't seem to apply to you, though, Detective Rourke. All right. I'll let you and your Mr. Sherman do whatever it is you are so eager to perform in my office, and I'll meekly slide off into the sunset."

"It'll be this morning, Biz, not this afternoon."

"You don't even leave a woman a metaphor, do you?"

"Biz, you don't need anything you haven't already got," he joked.

"I better not," she replied without a trace of humor, "because it doesn't look like I'm going to get it."

'Walter Sherman' turned out to be 50, pudgy, and so short Devlin (who stood just under 6') could look down to the top of his bald head. Sherman must have bought his two-piece suit off the rack at K-Mart, then picked up his shirt and tie at a table not far away. He smelled of the heat of the day and giggled at his own jokes. Besides his badge and the ends to which he lent his skills, he had nothing in common with Bequai's Fed clones. Devlin liked him immediately.

"This is a great set," insisted the electronics wizard as he unpacked his beat-up case. He dropped a pair of needlenose pliers on the varnish of Biz's desk. Devlin winced: the scratch wouldn't improve her disposition. "An absolute beauty of a set! The CIA is trying to sell the State Department on using them. That way it will be easier for the diplomats to remember what it is they agreed to.

"We're way beyond wires these days. The pen is the transmitter," he said, handing Devlin an innocent appearing ball point pen. "You activate it by twisting this clip once around clockwise. The clip holds the pen in your pocket. The pen actually writes—not much, but enough to pass a test. The receiver and a tape recorder are built into—" He rummaged in his bag of tricks and pulled out a pair of brown wingtip shoes. "—Ta da! These! Bequai said you needed a new pair anyway." The wizard glanced at Devlin's blue running shoes. "They're cute, but hard to hook up."

"I know what you mean."

"All the stuff is in the left shoe. They're both built up a little, so you'll be maybe a quarter inch taller than in a normal pair of this model. Slouch if you're worried it'll be noticed. You turn the heel like this. . . . And voila! It swings open to a special tape recorder with cassette already in place and ready to pop out . . . thusly . . . into your hands. The antenna wires and other stuff are woven through the sole so most of the heel room is for the recorder. You can tape 90 minutes on one side. Shuts off automatically. The shoe is waterproof, but don't go wading. You can't trust guarantees these days. The unit will take the shock of your normal walking, some running."

Devlin slipped out of his sneakers and into the wingtips. They fit, but were stiff.

"Good thing we got your size. Somebody at the Bureau pulled your personnel file out of the task force papers."

"That file is popular reading these days."

"Oh yeah? Listen, I'd rather read the file on the chick who gave me this here office. I mean, let me tell you!"

"Why don't you tell me how to turn on the tape recorder?"

"The recorder is signal-activated. That means when you turn your mike on, it transmits a sound which turns on the recorder.

"That's an extremely sensitive pen. Wear it in the lapel pocket of your suitcoat, if you can get away with it. If not there, an inside suitcoat pocket. Third choice is your shirt pocket, but that gives you more operator interference than the other options."

"Operator interference?"

"Your heartbeat. Boy is that errie, listening to a tape of guys talking with this *babumpa babumpa babumpa* in the background. Spooky. Cuts down on the clarity too."

"I'll try to remember."

"Here are some spare cassettes." The man picked up his tools and toys, packed them in his trick bag. As he did, he knocked over a framed picture of Biz's godchildren. The glass cracked. He either didn't notice, or, like Devlin, was too embarrassed to make a point of the accident. He handed Devlin his running shoes. Devlin took them; they'd go in the desk drawer with his dirty laundry.

"One more thing, if you've got a minute," asked the detective.

"Hey, I got all day. Nobody needs the Wizard until tomorrow."

"Here's a pad and pencil." Rourke hoped Biz didn't need those supplies. "Note the time, the date, where you are and who you're with, then take notes." Devlin glanced into the Wizard's bag: Why not do it in style? "May I?" he asked, pulling out a small tape recorder. A suction cup dangled from the same wire as the microphone.

The Wizard nodded. Rourke inserted a fresh cartridge, plugged the machine in and turned it on. "Testing, testing." Satisfied with the level shown by the needle dials, he sat down, spoke into the microphone.

"This is Detective Sergeant Devlin Rourke, Baltimore Police Department, Badge Number 47. It is Saturday, August 4, 1979, 9:30 A.M. I'm in Room"—Devlin read the reversed number on the back of the fogged glass door they'd closed behind them— "814d of the Municipal Building in Baltimore. I'm about to place a call to . . ." He stopped. The Wizard would tell Bequai whatever he learned. "I'm about to place a call to number Alpha in the course of an ongoing investigation. There is one other person in this room. Would you identify yourself please?"

The Wizard leaned forward, as eager as any child with a new toy. It dawned on Devlin that for all the time and energy this man spent taping others, he was himself probably seldom recorded.

"This is Fred L. Fogworth, Special Technical Agent for the Federal Bureau of Investigation, I.D. number 17302," he announced solemnly. Wizard Fogworth leaned back, his face eagerly searching for Rourke's approval.

"Mr. Fogworth, is everything I've said correct?"

"Yes it is."

"I'm about to make the phone call, using the office phone number 546-8519." Devlin attached the suction cup to the mouthpiece of the telephone. "Testing, testing, into the telephone receiver." The needle jumped as Devlin spoke. He dialed the number.

"Yeah?"

"Get me Kibler."

The same whirring and clicking ensued. Devlin wished the Wizard could hear it, but the knowledge he gained might be more than Devlin wanted to give.

"Hey Buddy! How are you?"

"I'm fine, Joe. How are you?"

"Good. Got any news? Got any needs?"

"I've decided to take Mr. Matella up on his offer. I want some high-quality stuff, in quantity, if he really means it. Chalk it up to psychic assistance."

Devlin held his breath. He had Kibler identified. He needed two more things in the conversation: Matella's name, which he'd supplied. He now had to hope that Kibler would suppy an essential element for a strong case. He had to hope Kibler mentioned the word cocaine.

"I think I know what you mean," replied Kibler. Devlin silently mouthed 'Damn!' "Call me again in an hour or so. You can give us a progress report then too." The phone clicked dead.

The Wizard was furiously scribbling notes when Devlin hung up.

"It's not much," said the Wizard. "Obscure and inconclusive. It's probably admissable in court, for whatever you're building, but it's prima facie harmless. A couple names. He didn't admit to a relationship with Matella, or agree to do anything."

"It's what we've got now. Of course, feel free to tell Bequai all about this."

"I will," said the Wizard. "And take him the tape?"

"Not yet. But your notes are acceptable as evidence too. And he'll probably be amused by them."

"He'll have more than my notes to play with," said the Wizard smiling and patting his suit pocket. "You see, I carry a pen too."

nineteen

Lazeretto Point thrusts out into the Chesapeake Bay from the middle of Baltimore's extensive docks area. The water lapped at riprap 15 feet from where Devlin stood beside his car. He'd worked his way through ramshackle industrial areas, over potholed roads, down canyons with walls of boarded-up buildings to this wide, wet patch of sooty ground. On an island half a mile out to sea sat Fort McHenry, where Francis Scott Key composed his greatest hit. A huge 15-star flag flew from the Fort. Devlin had rented apartments smaller than that expanse of red, white and blue cloth. A bridge named after the songster was hidden by the old warehouse to Devlin's left. A sightseeing tug with a few curious tourists chugged slowly between Devlin and the Fort, then was gone. He breathed deeply the tangy air of the sea, the stench of industrial development and dead things floating in the bay. The sun beat down on the green water, making him squint. His shirt was soaked with the humidity and tension. He'd thrust the walkie-talkie in his back pocket, the volume turned high enough so he could understand the calls. The pen mike should pick that up, he thought, another identifying piece of data. And just like in Dallas and John Kennedy's assassination, the radio traffic tapes could be matched. And maybe Devlin would live long enough to call for help or pull his gun from its unsnapped holster, should things go wrong. A gull cried as it circled overhead, then flew away to more hospitable zones. Off in the distance he heard the rumble of tractors and unloading machines driven by hard, sullen men who'd stared at his car as it bounced past them to this quiet zone. This empire of sweat, toil and tears served Tough Tony Cardozo. Never had Devlin felt so alone, vulnerable and desperate.

"It's 1:42 by my watch," he said, trying not to move his lips, staring out to sea so no one could observe him talking. "I'm still waiting at Lazaretto Point as designated by Joe Kibler, assistant to Salvatore Matella, as a rendezvous where he will give me, on instructions from Matella, a quantity of cocaine in turn for services rendered contrary to my official capacity as a police officer."

Devlin paused for breath. With his bad luck, the pen recorder didn't work. Gravel crunched behind him.

"Red 1978 Chevy Impala, Maryland plate 503-391. Joe Kibler, muscleman named Randy, unknown driver, all getting out. Kibler and Randy approaching."

"Hey Buddy!" called Kibler. "How you doing?"

"Fine Joe, just fine. Why did you bring Randy and the driver with you?"

"The streets aren't safe for anybody these days," answered Randy. He looked at Devlin as if the detective were a piece of meat sizzling on the grill. "Muggers, junkies. Lazy cops sitting on their ass, scared shitless."

"Maybe we can find a midget to hold your hand," said Devlin.

"Hey now guys, come on!" insisted Kibler. "None of that. It's too nice a day."

"Is this what you wanted?" Kibler asked. He handed Devlin a plastic baggie containing a mound of white crystals large enough to fill his fist.

"Jesus!" swore Devlin in spite of himself.

"Clean, if you know what I mean. Just like you requested."

Devlin looked at the man smiling in front of him. Kibler could be playing the conversation safe, he could not be playing at all.

"How we doing, Buddy?"

"Could be better," replied Devlin, "could be worse. We're closer to catching the Reaper than before."

"How much closer?" demanded Randy, his voice booming over the water to where the fishes waited.

"Three days."

"So far you've only marked time?!"

"Look," snapped Devlin, genuine anger pouring onto the

tape, "you tell Matella that he's put me out on the line, but I go
down it my own way. He gets progress reports from me when
I've got them, not before. If he wants to bug me with a leash, if
he wants to jerk it just for fun, if he doesn't want to help, fine,
but then he can't blame me for not doing the job!"

And with all the cool he could command, the cop turned his
back on the two crooks, stomped to his car, and roared away.

twenty

"This stuff is incredible, Devlin!" hissed Dennis Garn after
the computer analysed identified the few grains of white
powder from two gram-sized plastic packets Devlin had cut
from the package now hidden in his apartment. The two
friends leaned on a counter not far from the large police
laboratory's glass wall. The hallway ran along the other side of
the glass. A college criminology class in town for a weekend
field trip watched the two men from the other side of the
soundproof pane. The other lab technicians were working out
of earshot. Just after Dennis's barely concealed outburst, the
class wandered down the hall under the protective care of an
officer from the Community Relations Department.

"I mean this stuff is dynamite!" continued Dennis. "It's
absolutely as pure as it can be after refinement to a usable
level. I've only seen this quality stuff twice. The Drug
Enforcement Agency training seminar had some, another time
was off a bust they made of a diplomat at BWI airport with our
boys. And two grams! I can step on this three, four times, still
keep it top quality!

"Look, you didn't get this stuff off a bust or a corpse, did
you? I should have heard if you did."

"I didn't."

"Jesus, man! Where did you get it?"

"That's not a question you ask, Dennis."

"Hey, I know that! If you've got a new guy who can get you

this quality, buy it no matter what it costs. Have you tried it yet?"

"No, I wanted to be sure of it."

"What's to be sure of? Listen: all I'm asking is a return of a favor. Buy all you can, bring me what you don't want. I'll pay your cost, maybe a little more. I'll step on it then, and get it to some friends."

"That's not the way to play this, Dennis."

"Why not? What do you mean?"

"Have you been . . . careful?"

"What the hell are you saying, have I been careful?!" The bottom suddenly fell out of the lab man's life. "Of course I have! You think I'm crazy?! What the hell is going on here? What the hell have you heard?!"

"Nothing. But lay low for a while."

"Come on, man! You're scaring me! My ass is on the line here! Is somebody zeroing me for a bust or what?"

"Nothing like that, Dennis. I just got a bit of attention on me right now. We're friends—known, *innocent* friends, so some attention might come to you. Don't worry, don't look like that! The paranoia can beat you faster than the system. I've fixed it, and nobody even knows what's been fixed. But lay low, huh?"

"Are you shitting me? What is this lay low crap?!"

"I'm not shitting you."

"Are you sure you're not shitting me?"

"I'm sure."

"Don't scare me like that, friend!"

"I won't."

"Don't fuck me like that! I mean . . . Just don't scare me like that!"

"I know."

"I've put together a foolproof system for skimming stuff out of here for me and my buddies and you do me like that! . . . You know how many nightmares I've had? Don't scare me like that. Not ever!"

"I'm sorry, I won't."

"Not *ever*!"

Devlin met the wild man's stare.

"So," Dennis said as soon as he quit shaking, "What do you want me to do? Forget I ever saw this great stuff?"

"No. Take these two grams, but . . ." Devlin paused as a risky idea came to him. Risky, but . . . "Step on them once, good. Make quality stuff, but step on them. You get the skim. Log the two mixed, cut grams minus the test amount. Log them to me, open case number. Send one to Property, standard procedures. Keep one gram here, all properly tagged and guarded in the lab safe. I may have another officer come pick it up. He may even be a Fed, FBI. Whoever he is, he'll have true I.D. in his name, but will call himself . . . Agent Bozo. And he'll ask for you by name."

"I don't like getting that close."

"It makes the cover work, my man. You slide under my umbrella this way. You gotta be close to get under."

"That means if you get folded, so do I."

"Never happen. And if it does . . . maybe you'd get folded anyway. Besides, you got the system licked, right?"

"Right," repeated Dennis. "Right." But with none of his old confidence.

Devlin found a message slip on his desk: Call Biz. He frowned, wondered if he should use his office phone, decided not to, and took the elevator back to the entrance and the stinking pay phone. He'd used that phone twice now, and he knew he'd soon need to avoid it too.

"Look," said Biz when he finally got her on the line, "I think we're pretty good friends. We've always been that, I thought. Even . . . comrades in arms. But I'm getting tired. I mean, I didn't like the office bit, turn it over with no explanation. I also didn't like the way it was trashed. But that's okay, you've got your needs, I've got mine. But all my life I've worked hard to avoid being disposable."

"What?"

"You know, the kind of convenient person whose only function is to be there, and who can be replaced by any moron. I don't want to be that in my work. I don't like that in friendships either. Especially friendships. Now I'm beginning to wonder which of those I am to you, and I don't like either choice!"

"Biz, what are you talking about?"

"Oh shit, Devlin! Our *friend*, Cowan of Funny Boys, Inc., called and asked me to relay the message that he called you and . . . Let's see if I can get this straight: That he'd gotten a call from your mutual friend who's getting upset because he hasn't heard from you and you should call. If that makes any sense."

"Don't worry. I understand."

"Don't worry? Is that all you can say?"

Devlin sensed that the sooner he stopped talking, the better. "How about thanks?"

She slammed the phone in his ear.

twenty-one

Devlin called the FBI number from a pay phone a block from Police Headquarters. "What the hell are you doing passing messages to me?" he demanded when Bequai came on the line. "Your job is to sit and wait!"

"What the hell are *you* doing? It sounds like you're roping Matella into some drug deal. How does that fit into your homicide work?"

"Look," said Devlin, "don't crowd me like this. We made an agreement, now stick to it. If you push me over the edge, I'm dead and he slides. Is that what you want?"

Bequai grunted.

"Are we agreed?"

"All right, agreed. But when can I get something to work on?"

"If you send a clone to the Baltimore police lab and ask for Dennis Garn, he'll get a gram of cocaine that passed down Matella's chain to me."

"How strong a chain? Can we use it to tie him up?"

"Not yet, but it might come in handy to whip somebody else with, and that's a start."

"Look, if you tell me what you're doing, I'll only offer suggestions."

"One, we don't know each other that well or trust each other that much. Two, even if we did, I'd be afraid spreading this around might blow it up in my face."

"Thanks for your vote of confidence," complained Bequai.

"Oh, one other thing: Your clone should use the code name Agent Bozo, but show Garn his real I.D. and follow as much standard procedure from there as you want in order to make a good case. But he walks in there straight off the street, no Departmental liaison, no muss, no fuss, no tracks."

"Agent Bozo?"

"Yeah."

"You're an asshole, Rourke."

Devlin ached to take his sportcoat off during the hot walk back to the Department, but he didn't want any citizen flipping out over the .38 Devlin wore on his hip.

There was one call Devlin hadn't made, one call that turned into a series of five calls before he found the person.

"Dr. Herman Weis speaking."

"Sorry to interrupt your tennis game, Doctor, but this is Police Sergeant Devlin Rourke in Baltimore."

"Ah yes, I've been expecting your call. InterDec informed me that our friend is in your city. Has he struck yet?"

"No, Sir."

"Well, if the ad ran when they said it did, you shouldn't have long to wait."

"Do you think he'll follow his regular pattern?"

"As much as he can. However, the only part of the pattern we know is the ad-murder, ad-murder syndrome."

"I've read your report. I wanted to talk to you because we'll probably get together later in the case, if you're willing to help."

"Sergeant Rourke, my entire career has been devoted to putting mangled minds back together again and turning their owners back out into the real world. For once, I'd give anything I have to see one particular mind welded inside a steel cage."

"Can you give me your impressions of this guy? Not a clinical diagnosis. Tell me about him . . . I don't know, from the guts."

"He is without question a man. I'd say a mature man, a highly organized man. If he weren't so organized, if he weren't mature and fairly bright, we'd have found out something more about him by now. I'd say he's a loner, although he may work surrounded by people. Perhaps he was never married, certainly by now he is divorced or widowed. I'm sure he's not homosexual, though he may have aberrations which include homosexual acts. He's a man used to being entrusted with power, perhaps a great deal of power, and exercising it fully, almost without question. Whatever he does for a living, he is quite good, one of the best in his field. He's probably admired by his fellow workers and his peers. But he is aloof—possibly charming, possibly friendly in a controlled and manipulative fashion, but aloof.

"He's come to think of himself as more than human. Hence the religious, Biblical ads. I think he sees himself as not quite God. Possibly a reincarnation of some sort of divine being. An angel is how he referred to himself once . . . the Reaping Angel. He believes he has a divine link and a divine mission."

"A specific, finite mission?"

"Yes, I know what you're thinking. He could finish his mission before we find him. There is that danger. But I'm assuming his mission is on such a grand scale that he'll be busy for some time. Consider: he is superior. Would he have less than an incredible mission?"

"Does he have a religious background? Strong church upbringing?"

"Not necessarily. Certainly some exposure, but the argument cuts both ways on that one, and is thus inconclusive."

"How long has he been crazy?"

"Perhaps all his life. Like a baseball player reaching his prime, though, he may not have realized it as anything other than a natural state of being, and by the time he started killing, he was way beyond questioning himself."

"Would anyone notice?"

"Probably not until it was too late."

twenty-two

No one was waiting for Devlin when he got home at 8 that night. No one ever was.

"Another Saturday night and I ain't got nobody," he sang to himself.

He looked around the apartment. A third-floor one-bedroom dwelling in a neighborhood called Charles Village—old people, college students from the nearby university. Quiet. Except for the electric bugs outside his window and the traffic on St. Paul Street, a one-way shot to the heart of downtown Baltimore.

The white living room facing St. Paul bowed out in a large bay window—his tower. He'd placed a rolltop desk running out from the tower to catch the sunlight. The wall directly opposite his front door braced his couch. A large, brown-toned photograph of a wild mustang struggling through a snowy field in a blizzard hung above the couch. The photograph had been a present from a distant cousin out West who Devlin sheltered when that relative journeyed East. Opposite the couch, to the left of the front door, sat his stereo console and a TV he'd been storing for a friend for three years. The small fireplace to the right of the door wasn't much, but it worked. A narrow hall ran from the living room to the back of the apartment. The first door on the right was the bathroom, the first door on the left the bedroom. The second door on the right was a huge closet, then the hall emptied out into the kitchen.

Devlin tossed his sportcoat on the couch and unwound his tie as he headed towards the bathroom. He stopped, turned around, walked to the bay window and turned on the air conditioner. He'd eaten dinner—a forgettable sandwich a kind patrolman brought up to the Homicide squad room. Now he had only two pressing thoughts beyond the woes of his life, profession and predicament. The first thought was a shower.

Twenty minutes later he slipped his now-clean, always lean body into the pair of blue running shorts he wore around the house for decency's sake. You never know when someone might come calling. He checked with his special 24-hour police answering service. No news yet and yes, they would call him at home. He glanced at the TV guide from Sunday's paper. Nothing he wanted to watch.

"Well shit," he said, "why not get stoned?"

He was too tired to sleep anyway.

First he put the water on to boil. Nothing went better with the cocaine aftertaste than coffee cut with milk. He thought he still had milk, but checked the ice box to be sure. Better to find out now than disappoint himself while stoned.

Next he crossed to the stereo. Unlike marijuana, cocaine doesn't heighten perceptions of its users. Music doesn't sound better or more esoteric. But music was one more experience, and the coke high cries out for experience to command. He pulled out several albums, settling finally on Keith Jarrett, a solo jazz pianist who commands his instrument, moaning and groaning and thumping it to his own will until the music becomes the man and the man the music. Absolute fusion, absolute sweetness, absolute ego. The perfect sounds for a coke stone. Devlin picked the "Koln Concerts" album with a white record jacket that wouldn't work for his other purpose. He found a book with a dark cover, laid it on the table, and fetched his pewter box where earlier in the day he stashed the cocaine given him by Kibler. He also brought a single-edge razor blade from the bathroom. Not the same type of razor blade he used for shaving, but a blade that was legally non-incriminating. He stopped in the bedroom for a dollar bill and his buck folding knife.

As Jarrett's piano tinkled in the background Devlin thrust the knife blade deep into the baggie, drew forth a mound of white powder and carefully tapped it on the dark book. With the razor, he finally chopped the mound until a circle of white dust approximately the size of a half dollar waited on the book. As he chopped, the alkaline, chalk-like odor of cocaine drifted up to his waiting nostrils. The razor divided the snow circle into two thick, inch and a half lines, big even for average quality cocaine. Two to four lines of average coke gave a good stone for perhaps 30 minutes, maybe more. Devlin estimated he had the equivalent of six "average" lines drawn out in two rows. If Dennis were right, the quantity of those lines should be far beyond average.

He rolled the dollar bill into a thin tube, looked down at the two crystal lines running across the book like railroad tracks without ties, and said, "Here goes nothing."

Jesus.

He took the dollar-bill tube from his right nostril. He'd barely lifted his left forefinger from blocking his left nostril while he snorted up one line like a vacuum cleaner with his right nostril before the rush hit. An electric wave shook through his body as the insides of his nostrils and his sinuses burned with the acid-like fire of cocaine absorption. He took two deep breaths, fought back the impulse to sneeze, then lowered his head to the book on the table again, this time with the dollar tube held in his left nostril and his right nostril blocked. He snorted deeply, the tube following the white trail in front of it like a hungry green elephant's trunk searching the sand for a peanut.

Jesus again.

He leaned back. The stuff was far better than he'd imagined, far better than he'd thought possible. The fast, instant rush came like a shot of bourbon hitting the bottom of the stomach, jarred his head, tightening, tightening—then burning free. He felt the thick alkaline taste in roof of his mouth, the cocaine postnasal drip. His front teeth went numb as the powder settled through his body like a fine white cloud, tingling, tightening, energizing.

He walked to the whistling kettle in the kitchen, humming along with the music. He wasn't giddy; the coke didn't do that. But he felt . . . He felt tremendously alive. He felt incredibly in control. The coke's intoxication danger is its tendency to enhance belief and perception beyond ability and reality. He had to know his limits to avoid going beyond where he really was.

Or he'd end up nowhere at all, with no way back.

twenty-three

Monday morning the phone jarred him awake, sending his pulse racing.

All Sunday he'd read. His only nonprofessional reading had been the color comics; Peanuts, Doonesbury, The Phantom, Prince Valiant, Gasoline Alley and Spiderman—in which Kraven the Hunter was duping the people of New York into believing Spiderman was an alien from outer space instead of a man doomed to a double identity. The rest of the words absorbed by Devlin's tired eyes dealt with real death and madness. His badge convinced the librarian at Johns Hopkins University that he didn't need a student or faculty I.D. to solicit her help. He skimmed everything he could find on psychopathic killers. A book on Jack The Ripper written by a London policeman. A novel based on Son of Sam by journalists who'd communicated with that madman while the killer was still at large. Articles in psychiatric and psychology journals. Magazine and newspaper clips on San Francisco's Zodiac Killer, L.A.'s Hillside Strangler and Skid-Row Slasher. He studied the case of 32-year-old Theodore Bundy, a former law student who earlier had been sentenced to the electric chair for the bloody night in 1978 when he'd broken into Florida State University's Chi Omega sorority house and beaten two coeds to death. Bundy was a suspect in other violent crimes across the vast road map of America, for like Reaper, Bundy believed in mobility. Devlin even pursued *Helter Skelter*, Curt Gentry and Vincent Bugliosi's study of Charles Manson's "family" of murderers whose targets ranged from a screen star to President Gerald Ford. Finally, bleary-eyed and mentally numb, Devlin went home to a deep, exhausted sleep.

Which the telephone's blare ended.

"Hello?"

"Devlin? Did I get you up?"

"Lisa?"

"*Well*. We're doing so fine we need to ask which woman is calling. I didn't think you'd forget my voice so soon."

"Or how cheerful you can be in the morning. How are you?"

"Good. On that little chore you asked me about . . ."

"I'll call you at work in a bit."

"Gracious! Could I be interrupting something? Waking someone else? Devlin, I'm glad for you, I *really* am! I'll probably be at home, not the office."

She hung up.

His heartbeat slowed back to normal.

Then the alarm clock screamed.

Parking had been tight the night before. He'd ended up two blocks away, by the hospital. After showering and dressing, he used a pay phone in the hospital lobby to call Lisa.

"That was quick," she said. "I hope it was good." Before he could reply she continued. "Look, Dev, I hope you realize I'm . . . that my bitchy little teases are just jokes."

"I know that, Lisa."

"Does she treat you as nicely and kindly and as gently as you deserve? And as passionately as you like? Is she smart? She'd have to be smart or she wouldn't be there. Is she pretty? I hope she's beautiful. You know I know I am, that's just a fact of life for me, like I'm blond, my legs are skinny and I have an ugly mole and some cellulite on my ass. But I know how deeply the rest of how I look affected you. You didn't believe a beautiful woman could be attracted to you. You're not a gawky kid any more, Devlin. The pimples are all gone. Your lean isn't skinny, it's sexy and strong and so wonderful when you think of all those droopy paunches around. Believe it or not, a lot of wonderful women would appreciate that amazing brain you have. And your dumb sense of humor. *If* you gave them a chance. Obviously you're giving someone else a chance. Is she terrific, Devlin? I really, really want her to be as terrific as she is lucky."

"She's terrific," said Devlin.

"You know, even as latently, irrationally jealous as I am, I'm happy. If I knew I wouldn't be a bitch, I'd love to meet her."

"That probably wouldn't work out."

"No, it probably wouldn't. You'd be so nervous! *That* might make it worthwhile."

"What did you find out?"

"One of us is always business when the other is ready to giggle. Well, you understand this is guess work, what I could piece together with the Yellow Pages, my social contacts, and my amazing knowledge of real estate in our fair county?"

"That's all I could ask, Lisa."

"No, you could ask for more, but you know what you can get. The church bells narrowed it down to three areas:

"The Whitecrest Road area of Towson. There's a big Episcopalian church there, with a new bell they bong every chance they get. The sound reminds all the parishioners how rich they must be if they can afford that sound.

"The second area is off North Charles Street, Aspenhill Lane to be exact. It's a dead-end development not far from where you live, high above the rush and bustle of busy Baltimore, secluded in its own park-like environment. Twenty houses, tops. Mucho posh. Old money as opposed to the new money of Whitecrest Road. One block from the junction of Aspenhill and North Charles is a huge nunnery, the motherhouse of the Sisters of Marseilles combined with some cloistered order. Cement walks and stained glass windows, plus a huge tower with three old bells they brought from France. The sisters ring out loud and clear every quarter hour.

"The third area is the Upper Lawton suburb just outside the Beltway. It's the new money, the managerial class and doctors and lawyers whose daddys didn't do more than work in the Mill. Everybody is mortgaged to the hilt, and nobody stays there long. They're either on their way up or on their way down.

"There are numerous houses such as you describe in each one of those places, lots of lawyers, a judge or two, a couple state legislators. Does all that help?"

"Lots, Lisa."

"I hope so. If I can do anything else, call. And be happy, Dev. This hurts to say it, but do a real good one with that lucky woman. For me."

"Good-by Lisa."

"Good-by Devlin."

"Do you have any idea what you're asking?" said Bequai when Devlin called him a few moments later.

"Some."

"All the members of the Bar in three neighborhoods with indistinct boundaries—"

"Hearing distance of those church bells."

"—cross-checked for their clients with O.C. or political corruption cases or any other known associations with O.C. members, activities or organizations. Do you know what sized task that is? Probably half of those legal eagles qualify for that criteria. Are you playing some sort of silly hunch or do you have something you're looking for? Something specific?"

"A rathole."

"I'll get right on it."

As he walked across the concrete sidewalk to the main doors at Police Headquarters, Devlin realized he had another problem: his feet hurt. The Federal shoes didn't fit. He knew he had a blister on the back of his right heel, probably one or two more on his left foot. The soles of his feet felt like they'd been beaten with a billy club. What was the name of that Spanish torture? The *bastinado*? He'd be limping in a few hours, barely able to walk by evening.

"Son of a bitch!" he thought to himself as he shuffled by the desk sergeant. He had no time for shoe shopping. That meant back to the running shoes in his desk drawer.

A woman about Devlin's age sat just inside the squad room door, a pretty woman who would have been exceptionally pretty, even beautiful, if she gained back about ten pounds on her slight frame, her too-thin face. She had rich auburn hair expensively cut to look natural, and widely spaced brown eyes. Her wide mouth opened to ask Devlin a question, but then retreated to a timid smile. Her suit was expensive. She gave an overall impression of refined gentleness and pained, determined pride. That last impression kept her from seeming out of place in a room devoted to violent death. Devlin nodded to her, noticed her both as a detective and as a man, but shuffled to his desk intent on shedding the painful shoes. She nodded back. He noticed he was the only other person in the squad room. Even the Captain's cubicle was empty. She was probably a witness or a next-of-kin in some other cop's case. He stole another glance at her thin, finely shaped legs as he sat down, wondered if her skirt was fashionably slit.

The federal shoes were stashed in the laundry drawer, the running shoes were waiting on the floor beside his desk, and he was massaging peace back into his feet while studying the previous night's incident log, looking for any sign of the Reaper, when Detective McKee walked into the room, smiled at the woman, and said, "That's Sgt. Rourke, Ma'am."

Devlin looked up in time to find the woman almost beside his desk and Paul McKee winking at him over her shoulder.

"Sgt. Rourke?" she asked, her voice low, husky.

"Ah . . ." He quickly stood, kicked the running shoes out of sight under the desk even though she'd probably watched his intimate shoe shuffle. "Yes, what can I do for you?"

"I'm Barbara Austin."

"Barbara Austin?"

"Jimmy Austin's mother. The boy who was murdered in Denver. We talked the other day."

"Oh! Yes. You're in Baltimore."

"Aren't we all?"

"But why did you come?"

"You told me you were making routine inquiries, that no murder like my son's had taken place in Baltimore. I called your switchboard and found out you hadn't lied about the Baltimore murder, but I still didn't buy a 'routine' inquiry. I finally got the Denver police officer who handled my son's death to tell me you had some theory about a mass murderer named the Reaper. How you think . . . How you think he's moved here now, will kill some child here now. I had to come."

"I appreciate your concern, Mrs. Austin, but you didn't need to do that. There's nothing you can do here."

"There's nothing I can do back in Denver. Except sit and wait, count the hours and minutes since July 7, 1977, when Jimmy disappeared. Or count the hours until someone like you calls me on the telephone to tell me it's happened to some poor family again, or that finally this . . . person has been caught. If there's nothing I can do, well, at least I can do it here and feel less helpless. If I can't do anything, at least I can be somewhere."

"I understand," said Rourke. A uniformed policeman wandered into the squad room. He leaned against the wall, pretending to talk to McKee but actually eyeing Devlin's visitor with the practiced undressing analysis of a lifelong lecher. The Captain was back in his cubicle too. Devlin knew the squad room would mysteriously grow much busier. He briefly thought about pulling a chair beside his desk to talk with her, but the discussion would be awkward enough without a gawking crowd and the sounds of detectives working the phones or typing reports. There was a witness interrogation room just across the hall, a tiny closet with a table, two chairs and bright lights. That would be worse than here.

"Look," he said, "could I buy you a cup of coffee?"

"I'd love one. Denver is two time zones behind us, and this is usually the hour I'm just getting up."

"Fine. Just let me give this to Detective McKee," he said. He pulled a piece of paper from his desk, and carefully obscuring what he wrote, jotted brief orders. "If you'll go that way," Devlin said, gesturing towards the door. As she walked away he noticed the sway of her slim, rounded hips. He hurried after her, handing Paul the note as he passed his desk. "Take care of this right away, would you?"

"Devlin!" he heard Paul hiss as he followed Mrs. Austin down the hall.

"Later Paul," he called back. Right after he pressed the elevator button, he knew what Paul wanted: he'd forgotten his shoes. His stocking feet suddenly felt very naked and very large. He curled his toes in tight over the cool tile, hoping she hadn't noticed, hoping nobody would notice. Not likely, but it was too late to do anything but hope.

Half of the round tables in the second-floor lounge were empty. He sent her to one while he walked to the vending machines with her coffee order. He heard a policewoman snicker, but knew better than to look around. He stepped close to the machine, and in so doing put his cloth-shod left foot in a cooling spill from someone else's purchase. His sock soaked the brown liquid from the grungy floor like a sponge. *Fine*, he thought, *just fine*. He made his way back to their table, only twice spilling hot coffee down his hands and on his feet.

"Where are you staying?" he asked after they'd sipped their coffee in uncomfortable silence for a minute.

"The Raleigh Hotel," she replied. The Raleigh is Baltimore's classiest hotel, and is about nine blocks from police headquarters. "I got lost walking here. I've never been to Baltimore before."

"I've never been to Denver," he said.

"This building," she said, her brow wrinkling briefly. "I

know it's new, but it smells more like a museum than a police station."

"You mean you miss the earthy odors of urine, cigarette smoke and sweat? Me too. They keep this place clean. There are no cells in the whole building. That contributes to its lack of classic ambiance. Plus it's new, like you noticed. Except for the uniforms, guns, labs and communications equipment, it could be just another big bureaucracy. Even the pain here seems antiseptic."

"Is there a reason that tall skinny man keeps frowning and staring at you?" she suddenly asked.

Devlin looked over his shoulder towards the vending machines. There stood Jeffrey Stern, Attorney-at-Law. Their eyes met. "Damn," sighed Devlin as Stern walked toward them.

"Sergeant Rourke." The greeting was cold.

"Counselor."

"We citizens aren't keeping you too busy, are we? Your new assignment must be quite arduous if you're already taking a break this morning."

"The hardest part is dealing with horseshit from supposedly smart people."

Stern bristled. He glanced at Barbara. "I'd respond in kind, Sergeant, but there are some levels of communication decent people avoid."

"Why go decent on me after all this time, Counselor?"

Stern snarled, but he stalked away without saying another word.

"Yes," said Barbara, "I definitely think he's a fan of yours."

"You know how these groupies are, throwing themselves at you. I try to be as gentle as I can with them, but some-times . . ."

"You just have to be stern," she said.

"True." He smiled, looked across the room. The lecher cop entered the lounge. He stood in front of a candy machine pretending to debate his selection, but his eyes were on their table.

"Look," said Devlin, "I've got to go check something on this Reaper business, and this is not the best place to talk. If you'd like, you can ride along with me."

"That would be fine. But there's one question I think I should ask."

"What?"

"Don't you think you need some shoes?"

They laughed all the way to the elevator.

twenty-four

"What we've done," explained Jackson Bricker—more to Barbara's attentive and attractive eyes than Devlin's professional interest, "is develop parallel programs. We have a program on each of the victims—age, weight, height, clothing worn at the time of death, address, race, eye color, hair color, parents' occupations, even the number of letters in their names and their birthdates. Zodiac signs. Shoe sizes, for chrissakes!"

He glanced at Devlin's blue-sneakered feet.

"The computer will sort through all the victims, looking for common denominators. We didn't just stop with their lives either. We've got programs on their cities. Take Denver and . . . and your tragedy. We plugged in altitude, weather for a month before and a month after the "incident sequence"—the time from the first ad that ran before the prostitute murder to until after the death of the child. We stick in population demographics, major industries, ethnic characteristics, economic indicators, political demographics.

"I borrowed a guy from the math department who used to work as a cryptologist for the National Security Agency. He converted a couple of their methods, adapted some of his own, and created a program to analyze those newspaper ads. If there's a message or a code pattern buried in them, we'll find it."

"I hope your machine works," said Devlin.

"Oh the machine will work," insisted Bricker. "It'll do just what it's been set up to do with what it's got."

"When?"

"We flip the final switches some time tonight," replied Bricker, "9, 10 o'clock, the last of the programs will be double-checked and fed into the machine. As soon as that's done, I feed in the master program telling the machine what to do with the data. Then it goes to town."

"When will it have something to say?"

"Sometime tomorrow. Of course, I'll recheck the process at the end and analyze the data, but that should only take two hours after the machine is through."

"You've got the 24-hour number, my home and office phone. Call me the second you've got something."

"Thank you for explaining all this to me," said Barbara as they left the room where white-smocked data processors typed line after line of facts and figures into clicking computer keyboards.

"My pleasure," said Bricker. "My pleasure, indeed."

"You know," said Devlin as they drove away from the University, "I understand you wanting to be here in case something happens, but it might be a while."

"Do you really think we'll have that long to wait before he kills somebody?"

"No," answered Devlin truthfully. "But even so, the hotel, your food, the plane ticket . . . You're running up a hell of a bill."

"You trying to get rid of me, Sergeant?"

"Devlin. I thought we agreed, Devlin."

"Devlin, are you trying to get rid of me?"

"I'm trying to save you additional heartache that you pay for with resources that might be useful later."

"In other words, you don't want the divorcée to end up flat broke on top of all her other problems."

"Something like that."

"Thank you for your concern, but you don't need to worry. My husband, my ex-husband, James Austin, III, came from Houston oil money. We are tied into *the* Austins of Texas, but it's an extremely long rope. Our Austins aren't big Texas money. A few million plus some cattle ranches."

"Small potatoes."

"Really. My parents were middle-class factory workers in New Hampshire with a bright daughter who won a scholarship to a fancy school and 'landed' a fancier husband. It actually wasn't much of a landing. We crashed into each other. I thought all his Western easiness and secure wealth was what was real and he thought all my earthy East coast of-the-common-people roots was what was real. In those days, what was real was extremely important. And relevant, of course. "Relevant" was the big word then. Plus we both thought the other one was sexy.

"Skipping up a bit, Jimmy's death was the force that cut the last cords. Big Jim is still and always will be a kind, generous, sweet man who'd have been a successful lawyer in his own right even without the head start his family got him. I probably clear more in monthly alimony payments than you net in half a year. That doesn't count all the joint savings and investments we split, plus little Jimmy's insurance. So you don't need to worry about me starving to death. This is the first time I've ventured anyplace besides Denver or Texas in a long time. It's no vacation, and I'm not enjoying it, but I'm well past affording it.

"Which reminds me," she said as he pulled up in front of her hotel, "can I buy you dinner after you get off work this evening? Your wife or girl friend or whatever too?"

"It's just me."

"See? Baltimore won't crimp my budget. Come on: it's better than me eating in my hotel alone. I'll thrill you with the rest of my life story and you can tell me yours, too."

twenty-five

"One thing has haunted me all this time," she told him as the waiter poured their after-dinner coffee. For the first time that evening she refused to meet Devlin's eyes. They sat at a small table in Baltimore's best and one of its cheapest and most informal seafood restaurants. "More than all the grief and pain of his death, more than the sight of his body in the morgue.

"It's the door. I *know* I locked it! And the windows weren't cracked enough for someone to open. Not with him inside, not with enough people passing by who'd hear Jimmy scream as someone forced the glass—which no one did. He would have had to disobey me, unlock the car door, let . . . let that person take him. I know I locked the door. Such a small thing, really. A button pushed down. But it makes all the difference in the world. I carry enough of the big "G" for Guilt around with me not to have to worry about that door, but I can't get it out of my mind."

"Probably wouldn't have made any difference if you'd taken Jimmy with you," said Devlin. "We're pretty sure he was being stalked. The Reaper would have gotten him another time, probably at school when you weren't around and the teacher was distracted. The door makes no difference. But knowing that takes faith, belief, and getting those takes time."

Devlin wanted to sound more positive in his reassurance of the woman in the simple black suit—*black for fashion*, he thought, *not for mourning*. She wasn't that strung back in time and morbidity. He thought Barbara Austin was quite a lady, and he now knew for sure she was Barbara Austin. The note he'd scribbled to Detective McKee in the squad room when they'd gone for coffee had been a command for McKee to request a telecopied print of her driver's license from the Colorado Highway Patrol. The picture matched. The woman was indeed Barbara Austin. Barbara Melby Austin, to be exact. She allegedly weighed 127 pounds (which he doubted, seeing her thin frame). He felt The Big G for Guilt. Intellectually he knew he'd been right to be sure she was who she claimed. This was too tight a game to chance a fundamental error. Yet still he felt The Big G. He had no claim against her privacy.

"He'll kill a prostitute first, won't he?" she asked. Her explanation of The Big G had led them from an easy evening of light conversation and gentle laughter back to where they'd started and why they'd met.

"Yes."

"Where will he . . . find her? No, don't look at me like that. I'm beginning to know your crafty mind. *Why does she want to know? What could she do with that knowledge?* I don't plan on setting myself up as a decoy or an avenging angel in disguise. Besides that being absurd, I banished such melodramatic thoughts two years ago and hooker is a role I could never play. Despite what some of my snobby coed 'friends' thought when Jim and I got married, I never have been nor will I ever be for sale. I just . . . I want to know as much as I can."

"He has a number of options. There are a couple of houses, but he'll probably stay away from them. Outcall massage service, maybe. But I'm betting he'll pull someone off the Block."

"The Block?"

"Our tenderloin district. If you hadn't gotten lost walking to the police station, you'd have gone right through it. It starts across the street from Headquarters."

"Convenient. Is it . . . terrible?"

"More sad than anything. And seedy. I'll show it to you from the car, if you like. It's on the way back. Sort of."

"I'm not sure I can make it back. My body and mind are exhausted, though my spirit wants to stay up. You're the nicest cop I've talked to since a Massachusetts highway patrolman lectured me about the dangers of carrying marijuana in my glove compartment where it was visible when I had to get my registration for a speeding ticket. His lecture was tough tongue-in-cheek. He 'dropped' the evidence upside down on a windy highway. When the grass blew across the pavement, he informed me the lost and damaged evidence meant he couldn't make his case. He suggested I drive on, and be more careful in the future. No threats or tit-for-tat innuendoes, just mercy for a poor scared college girl who could see her life going down the drain on a drug bust because she'd been careless.

"I'd like to learn more tonight, put off that dreary hotel room, but I'll need to drink a ton of coffee to keep from drifting off on you, and even that's no guarantee."

Devlin leaned back. The idea was crazy, of course. He didn't want to take this woman through the sewer streets of Baltimore, to mix her alluring integrity in with the tawdry falsehood on the Block. Neither did he want her to leave him any sooner than necessary. For a moment with her he'd forgotten the Reaper even though that madman was responsible for bringing Barbara to him. He'd forgotten the fire-green eyes of Matella when she smiled at him. The schemes of the Lieutenant, Jeff Stern's vengeful traps, all took two steps back from his life. This idea he had was crazy, of course. She'd be offended or frightened or suspicious of ulterior motives (which he knew he had but which he tried to supress) or disappointed or indignant or a thousand other terrible things. And he exposed himself to such danger. In the very least she was bound to say no. It was such a crazy idea.

He did it anyway: "Have you ever tried cocaine?"

twenty-six

"Every time I do this I feel like some drug-crazed junkie in a 1950s scare movie," said Devlin as he chopped out eight lines of cocaine on the book. Duke Ellington played softly on the stereo while the tea kettle creaked and groaned against the rapidly heating burner on the stove.

"I smoked a lot of grass in college," said Barbara. She sat on the couch not far from him, her hands tightly clasped in her lap. Her voice betrayed her nervousness. Her eyes were locked on his chopping razor and the white mound he'd taken from the baggie. "I dropped speed for tests, and the doctor forced some Valium on me after . . . after Jimmy. My husband and I did mescaline once at the ocean, but I've never done this. When I've gone back to Houston to visit . . . the wives our age in the type of Houston society the Austins *naturally* moved in . . ."

"Naturally," interrupted Devlin as he dexterously drew out the lines.

". . . Naturally. The wives used their gold spoons in little gold vials every chance they got, sit around the pool and do it. They'd ask you not to do it when their children were around, but in front of their maids, at parties . . . Anywhere but in front of the kids and the mothers and fathers they plan to inherit from, it's up the old gilded nose. I guess their husbands do it too. They were the ones who bought it from God knows where. Some of our friends would take us up to Aspen when they came to Colorado to ski, and there was as much white power being used inside the cabins as there was on the slopes. I was always . . . leery, a little afraid of it. Besides, *those* people used it, the golden gods, the beautiful people, the chic set and the nouveau riche, and I didn't want to be like them. Maybe that was kind of dumb, 'cause I know from Jim that our car mechanic was always raving about it, and he was as redneck a Colorado hippy stomping cowboy as you can get.

"Are you sure it'll be okay? That I won't . . . do anything or get hurt or anything?"

"Sure I'm sure. But if you don't want to, don't. Don't."

She looked at him and shrugged her shoulders.

"Look," he said, "if you can't trust a cop, who can you trust?" He bent down, snorted two of his lines, then laid the dollar tube on the book beside the remaining six. The tea kettle began to hiss.

"You're right," she said. "Who can you trust if you can't trust you?"

She bent over, imitating his blocked-nostril, concentrated snort. The first fast rush had burned through him. He heard the crackle of her panty hose as she moved. He glanced at her, carefully coaching her through her first two lines. He saw the softness of her smooth, long white neck, the steady fine line of her chin where she would never sag. He heard her stifle a sneeze. She sat back, and he knew the first rush was roaring through her body. The tea kettle whistled. Energy coarsed through him. He walked from the room, leaving her alone while he went to make their coffee.

She was pacing back and forth, concentrating on her reactions, her arms crossed over her small breasts when he came back with the steaming cups.

"Look, I'm not sure this stuff is working on me." She walked as she talked, occasionally waving her arms in a natural though emphatic gesture.

"I mean, I felt that bang when I snorted the lines and was a little dizzy for a second or two, but then, well, I mean I felt a little tingly too. But I'm not stoned, if you know what I mean. I mean, the music sounds the same, not quite as peppy as I'd like maybe, but nice, but not *nice* nice, I mean. You know, not stoned nice where all the notes sort of leave you ringing and hollow, floating around the room. Is that for me? Thanks. Oww! The cup is hot." *Slurp*. "Mmmmn. That's really good,

nice taste, blending in the mouth with that chalky kind of not
quite yechy taste, you know? The roof of my mouth is
. . . . dead and my teeth are numb, like at the dentist. But I'm
not stoned. Are you stoned? I mean *really stoned*? I mean,
maybe I'm a little high, a little tingly, but that's not stoned, is
it? I mean look at my eyes, how do my eyes look? Do they
looke stoned?" She quickly walked to the bay window as if to
look down to the street but really to check her reflection in the
glass. She didn't spill a drop of coffee, coming or going. "I
mean do my eyes look stoned?" The black pupils of her eyes
were the size of nickels, but Devlin said nothing. He hoped
the numbness of her mouth wouldn't cause her to accidentally
burn her soft red lips, her smooth long tongue. "My eyes feel
the same, I feel the same. I'm not giddy or anything. I feel
good, sure I feel good, but I felt good before. I'm not tired
anymore, but we had two cups of coffee after dinner and now
this cup here. This is good." *Slurp*. "My teeth are numb, but
that's all. I mean I really feel good, really tight, really in
control, really real, you know what I mean? Really real, not
stoned at all."

She paused for breath and looked at him for a frantic second,
unsure of what to do or what to say next. She glanced around
briefly—at the apartment of the man she barely knew, at the
book with four waiting parallel powder white lines. She itched
her right ear with her little finger, a cute little right ear she
found in the thick auburn locks with a cute little right finger.
She sniffed, then she sniffed again. Her eyes fixated briefly on
the coffee table, then they roamed back to him, big as nickels,
and she said, "I'm stoned, aren't I?"

"You're stoned."

"I'm really stoned, aren't I"

"You're really stoned."

"Oh shit."

twenty-seven

Devlin was not sure what was talking: his conscience, his frustrations, the fears he felt for the horrors he knew. Perhaps it was just the backlog of all the words he'd dared not say in the last few days breaking free at last. Perhaps it was just the cocaine. No question that the sharp white hot powder energy underlined his words. They'd done the two more lines each after the first two, then two more each for the road. He'd dipped his wet finger in the precious white powder bag, then smeared the equivalent of a skinny line on her gums so she would know that sensation too. Perhaps she was why his mind flew that night, the warm waiting person who sat beside him in the moving car, her nickel eyes wide and intent on the sharp colors around them and on his words.

The Block. Actually the area is two blocks long, boundaried by Commerce Street on one end and Gay Street on the other, two blocks of two dozen or so topless bars, massage parlors, adult bookstores and special peep-show movie theaters, flashing red neon lights, strolling males, anxious brash visitors to this tenderloin turf where the only natives are the nasty-looking old men and their unshaven scruffy younger versions who hawk tired lines about the magnificent quality of the wares inside: "Check it out! Check it out!" A dozen seedy white winos of varying ages ply for handouts. One of them is a dwarf. Disco music blares from open bar doors, and occasionally a female creature in commercially cut sparse clothing walks from one establishment to another, eyeing pedestrians, eyeing cars, an empty smile on her lips. The Block is small, sad, an end unto itself. The only amazing thing about it is that so much of mankind's worst could be packed into such a small corner of his world.

Devlin was male, and somehow he felt that made it

necessary to explain all of this to the woman who sat beside him, perhaps to justify it, as if he were somehow responsible.

"Sometimes when you've bottomed out, a place like this is where you end up," he said, "where you try to lose yourself and your blues in the stench and deceit and decadence of the whole thing which is worse than even you think you are. Lose yourself, and maybe lose it all forever and never get it back. One guy told me he found it all again in a place like this. Maybe for some people who come here this shallowness and disappointment compared to the fantasy or the desperation that drove them here creates a gap, such a glaring discrepancy that they get jerked back from the edge. I don't know. I don't know if anyone thinks when they find themselves walking the streets of a place like this. Thinking would be too ugly a process. They just pretend, and try to survive."

Barbara shook her head. "But it's all for men. Maybe that's another sick part of it: it's all for men. So one-dimensional. The whole thing screams 'put your penis in here and that will solve everything.' What does a woman do, where does she go when she bottoms out?"

"I don't know," said Devlin. "I've never been a woman."

twenty-eight

The phone rang three times before Devlin reached through Tuesday's predawn darkness to grab it. "Yes?"

"Devlin? It's Jackson Bricker. You told me to call you right away."

"What do you have?"

"Nothing."

"Are you crazy?"

"Stunned. Mad. Disappointed. But not crazy. There's no common link. Nothing in the data. The children are children and the whores are whores. No race, sex, city, numerical, ethnic or age pattern at all. Nothing. Zip."

"Are you sure?"

"I'm triple-checking, but yeah, I'm sure."

"Thanks, Jackson."

"No thanks yet. I know this is a pisser of a way to look at it, but maybe . . . Maybe Baltimore will provide some clinching data."

"That is a pisser of a way to look at it, Jackson." Devlin hung up. As his hand passed before his eyes he saw the radium glow of his watch: 5:32. Almost light. His hand went back to the sheets. And the empty space beside him in the bed.

He'd gone to bed happy even though he'd gone to bed alone. The computer angle had seemed a solid bet. Something which by all rights should have provided a key to the Reaper. With that key, with *any* key, he felt confident he'd be able to unlock the man's life and catch him.

And then there was Barbara. They'd laughed and talked as they had gotten stoned together. He sensed her easing up with him, discarding some of her load. That made him feel proud, lucky. He hadn't wanted to say good-bye to her the night before, but he hadn't known what else to say. There was no reason for him to delay when he let her out at the hotel—especially after touring the Block, a depressing journey which crushed all thoughts of honest physical intimacy. He'd promised to call her the next day; she'd promised to be there. He guessed that was as close as either of them had come to a commitment in quite some time. His hand wandered across the empty sheet. He'd come home alone. Gone to sleep alone. But the hope he'd felt for that future and the hope he'd felt for his dilemma with The Reaper et al. sent him to bed happy.

Now the computer had failed, and he'd accomplished little more than making it through yesterday. Today was uncertain, tomorrow risky.

He got up, went to work.

The memo on his desk was from the Commissioner's Lieutenant:

> *Sgt. Rourke:*
> *It has come to my attention via the persistent complaints from Jeffrey B. Stern, Attorney-at-Law and President of the Baltimore Better Government Citizens Committee, that your conduct as a police officer leaves much to be desired. While many of Mr.*

*Stern's comments and charges have been vague,
inflammatory and probably unsupportable—such as
his charges of persistent sloth—he has one specific
allegation which supports his overall complaint. He
alleges that you have been seen dressed in inappro-
priate clothing for an on-duty detective—to wit, blue
sneakers and on at least one occasion, stocking feet. I
informed Counselor Stern that if this were true, you
no doubt had an excellent reason for violating the
dress regulations spelled out in the General Orders.
If your attire is as Counselor Stern charges,
Sergeant, I suggest—strongly—that you alter your
personal appearance to conform with accepted
practices.*

Which, as far as Devlin was concerned, made it absolutely
necessary to wear the blue running shoes whenever possible.

At 9:15 Captain Goldstein called him into his office to ask
what he'd accomplished so far.
"Nothing, Sir," replied Devlin.
"That's not good enough," said his commander.

At 10:03 an irate Biz called him with another referral
message from Bequai via Cowan. She was even less pleased at
being used this time than she had been before. Twenty
minutes later, when Devlin called Bequai from a phone booth
in a drug store, the Federal agent wanted to read him a list of
thirty-seven members of the Bar who owned homes in the
areas described by Devlin. Bequai had yet to identify which of
the thirty-seven might have O.C. connections.
"Then why call me with their names?" asked Devlin.
"I thought some of them might ring a bell with you," said
Bequai. He started reading the list: "Barber, Harold; Van
Buskirk, Sheila; Holloron . . ."
"What do you think I am? An encyclopedia? Just send me
the list in the mail."
"What have you got on our man?"
"Nothing."
"Even the encyclopedia beats that."

At 11:15 the phone on his desk rang. Kibler's friendly tones
came over the wire. "Hey Buddy! How you doing?"

"Terrific. I'm busy now. I'll call you when I have time."

"Oh sure. We just get a little anxious when we don't hear from you regularly. We worry. Maybe an accident or something happened to you. Baltimore's a rough town. But we'll wait for your call. I'm sure you'll have good news for us soon. Although as long as I got you on the line, how *are* we doing?"

"Terrible. I've got nothing."

"Zero isn't a good score this late in the game, friend."

At 12:32, just after part of the soggy submarine sandwich Detective Perry had been kind enough to bring him from a deli fell into his lap, Devlin got a call from Jackson Bricker at the computer center.

"It's final and official," said Bricker. "We got nothing."

"At least we're batting a 1000," said Devlin.

twenty-nine

The only good thing about Tuesday was that Barbara agreed to have dinner with him at 8 that night. He sponged the submarine stain from his pants as best he could, straightened his tie, and picked her up at her hotel. They drove through the ethnic neighborhoods to a cheap, delicious Italian restaurant. She wore a frilly summer dress of golds and browns that set off her eyes and accentuated her lithe form—and the fact that she wasn't wearing a bra. The retreating sun took much of the day's heat with it. She had him smiling within a minute, laughing within two. Halfway through the fried mozzarella cheese appetizer the headwaiter summoned him for a phone call.

"Yeah?"

"Sgt. Rourke? This is Central Dispatch. Our orders are to inform you of any female or child homicide reports."

"Yeah?"

"We got one."

thirty

The neighborhood is called Otterbaum or Federal Hill, depending on who you talk to. Shrewd real-estate developers have their eye on it for future exploitation. But that night, in that particular section, revolving blue lights from two parked prowl cars lit up a still-mean street a stone's throw away from the successful inner-city homesteading project. The scene was but a five-minute drive from the Block. Most buildings in this section were boarded-up brick shells destined for destruction. The only one with any current function was the church on the corner. A chain link fence topped with barbed wire surrounded that scruffy center of Presbyterianism. The center of all interest that night was the vacant lot between the church and the row of crumbling brick skeletons.

Devlin braked his car to a stop around the corner from the address he'd been given. As he jogged towards the small crowd of waiting men, carefully watching where his feet fell, his last civilian thought was to hope Barbara had no trouble getting a cab.

"Oh! It's you, Sergeant," called a uniformed patrolman who stepped forward to challenge the figure coming through the darkness. "Didn't expect to see you. We already got two Homicide guys here."

"Who?"

"Cooper and Smith."

"Shit!" Of all the Homicide detectives, the only two whose work Devlin didn't trust and who he didn't like were Detectives Cooper and Smith. "What have we got?"

"It's pretty grisly. Black female, young, snazzy-dressed hooker type. Some boyfriend cut her throat."

"I'm in charge of this one now. Me—just me. Me before anyone, including the Commissioner. That's the way this is

run. Pass the word. Nobody talks to *anybody* about this but
me."

"Yes, Sir!"

"Run up to the corner, stop all traffic—foot and vehicle. I
don't want any more messing of tracks than this army has
already done. Hold the meat wagon back there too. The only
people you let through are the technicians. And send your
partner around the block the other way to do the same thing.
While you're at it, call for two . . . no, three backups. When
they get here, have the senior officer in the group start them
searching those deserted buildings. Tell them to be careful not
to botch up anything they find. They're looking for the
obvious, passed-out drunks, anybody hiding. The technicians
will comb through there as soon as it's light.

"You!" Devlin called to another uniformed cop as he neared
the group of men standing at the edge of the vacant lot, "you
and your partner start a circle pattern out from here. Get the
license plate and vehicle description of everything on the
street within four blocks of here, understand? If you see
anybody, detain them until you get full I.D. and explanation of
what they're doing. If they can't give you something that
makes sense, cuff 'em and call for back up. Be careful, and
don't miss a thing."

"Hey Devlin!" called a blurry white man of forty in an ill-
fitting double-knit suit: Detective Smith. "What you doing,
boy? This is our squeal. Besides, we all been told you're
detailed to some sort of special assignment."

"This is my special assignment. And you two no longer have
this one. You done anything?"

Detective Smith looked at Detective Cooper, his counter-
point in appearance in all ways except Cooper was black.
Cooper shrugged.

"No," said Smith. "We just got here too. The way I get it,
some wino who works cleaning the church found her. He
called the cops, broke into the sacrament wine and chugged a
whole bottle before the uniformed unit got here. He's passed
out now in the preacher's office, and I mean *passed out.* The
preacher is with him."

"Loan me one of your radios, will you? I came from off-
duty."

"Sure."

Devlin informed the Dispatcher he was on the scene, then turned to the two detectives.

"Look," he said, "you two can split if you want." Devlin tried not to offend the two men, but his mind was racing with the job at hand. They weren't offended. He'd let them off the hook on a boring, routine case coming between them and retirement.

"Hey, no problem," said Cooper. "We'll keep you company until the technicians arrive. Show you what we got."

It was that time. Devlin turned and walked through the high, dusky-smelling green weeds. Cooper loaned him his flashlight. Devlin cautioned them about footprints. He knew their subsequent exaggerated care was for his benefit and their sarcastic amusement, not the desire for good police procedures.

What had been a woman lay surrounded by weeds 19 feet, 7½ inches from the edge of the sidewalk in the dark shadow of the church.

"Pretty sight, ain't she?" asked Detective Smith.

No, she wasn't. Maybe she had been once, before she turned professional. Maybe she'd even been a kind of tawdry pretty when she was alive, only a few hours before. Now she was just a shocking, pitiful, dead piece of meat. The crime search analysis and the autopsy discovered that she'd been killed there, probably after being knocked unconscious. The Reaper brought her here, dragged her stunned form face down through the weeds from a car, bent over her, lifted her head up by her Afro, and drawn his razer-sharp instrument across the ebony blackness of her throat. The shock of sudden death startled her unconscious form enough to make her twist and flip around in dying futility. Now she lay sprawled on her back. The electric blue dress with the neckline plunging to her navel and the hem that ended at mid-thigh was soaked with a dark stain beneath Devlin's flashlight beam. Soaked well past her small breasts. The swirl of her skirt revealed cold, rubbery legs almost to her pantyline. She wore no stockings.

"Hey, did I tell you that great whore joke I heard?" Detective Smith asked Detective Cooper as Devlin slowly played his light beam over the corpse before them.

"No," replied Detective Cooper, "I don't think you did."

The dead woman's hands lay spread eagled from her sides, palm up. The lifeless fingers curled inward.

"My wife found this old record album by some broad named Belle Barth, a real gas. You're going to love it: *There's this guy, crotchety old fart. One night he and the missus are at home. He's doing his books, mumbling, cursing, swearing.*"

Devlin raised his flashlight beam to the woman's face. If this thick-lipped, droopy-eyed, saggy-cheeked corpse showed any expression, it was one of resignation.

"*What's wrong with you?*" *this guy's wife asks.*

The blood had dried around the gaping wound, exposing the torn cartilage, the slashed windpipe, the muscles and tendons for easy viewing. Devlin played the flashlight beam along the body, stopping it suddenly when the light glistened off a small object. He started to reach for it, then stopped. The camera crew first, then the technicians to bag it.

"*I've worked all my life,*" *says the husband.* "*Worked, worked, worked, and I've got nothing to show for it. Nothing. And you haven't helped at all.*"

Devlin shone his beam around the corpse in an ever-widening spiral.

This really pisses the wife off. "*We've had a full life,*" *she says.* "*The kids got a good start. We've got our health. What more could we ask? And besides, what could I have done to help more? I was raising the kids, making sure you had three meals cooked for you every day, cleaning house. Now is the only time I could work, and what can I do? I'm 70 years old too!*"

A vehicle stopped in the street behind them. Two doors slammed. A moment later, cautious footsteps approached the three detectives: the civilian technicians, the crew responsible for all crime scene searches, for preserving and protecting any physical evidence from the elements, the public, and clumsy police officers.

"*Well,*" *says the old man,* "*you could become a whore.*"

"Hey Devlin!" called a new voice, interrupting the joke. "How you doing?"

Devlin turned: Ken Urtz. He'd been lucky enough to draw the best technician and crew.

"Fine Ken. Let's talk before you get going."

So anyway, continued Smith, getting back to the serious business of a good joke. *The old lady says,* "*A whore?!*" "*That's right,*" *says her husband.* "*A whore. You could do that, earn some money, help out around here for a change.*" *She thinks a*

moment, figures what-the-hell? "Okay," she says. "I don't
know if it'll work, but I'll do my best and give it a whirl."

"My, my, my!" exclaimed the lab technician when he saw the
reason for his presence. "Somebody did a job on her."

*So the next night the old lady gets all duded up, gussies her
face, puts on her slinkiest dress, and goes out. The old man, he
just sits there, mumbling and doing his books, feeling sorry for
himself. She doesn't come home that night, nor the next
morning.*

"Take a look at this, Ken," said Devlin.

*Along about noon, she staggers in and boy does she look a
mess, like a truck hit her. Her hair is all matted, she's all bent
over and limping, disheveled, her clothes twisted every which
way.*

"It's . . . a button," said the technician as he stared at the
object on the ground spotlighted by Devlin's flashlight. "Fake
brass, plain flat face." The small gold circle lay a few inches
from the dead woman's shoulder.

"Not off her dress either," added Devlin. "Let's hope it came
off the guy who dumped her here."

*"So," the husband says, looking up from his books, "How'd
you do?"*

"We'll see. I wish it had rained today. That would give us
better time-frames to work with for things we find."

"Pretty good," says the wife. "I made $28.10!"

The photographer popped his first flashshot. A pale explosion sliced through the blue darkness.

*"Ten cents!" screams the husband. "Who gave you ten
cents?"*

"Everybody gave me ten cents!" she says.

Detectives Cooper and Smith roared. After they'd laughed
for 30 seconds, Cooper said, "You need us around here
anymore, Sergeant?"

"No," replied Devlin, "I don't need you here."

Devlin watched as the photographer worked his way around
the corpse. Each shot burned the scene into his mind with a
crisp brilliance. All the other photographs of the Reaper's work
had seemed unconnected to him. Now here he was, on the
scene of yet another entry in the killer's scrapbook. Perhaps his
blue-sneakered feet would show in some of the photographs.
He'd been in such pictures before, almost a hundred times. All
of them were different, and he knew he'd never grow

accustomed to the sights and sounds and smells of violent death. Steeled, yes. Accustomed, no. If he did, he'd be like Detectives Smith and Cooper. They were so detached from their work they barely went through the motions. That was never his problem.

Indeed, perhaps he was too close to it. For all the gore he found, for all the disgust he felt, to be there was so exciting! To be there, to look and think and discover, to hunt and find and chase down the why and who and the how was what made this ultimate expression of intent so fascinating. He shook his head. Broken weeds lined the path where the whore had been dragged. Devlin glanced back once more at the butchered corpse, then carefully paralleled the path out of the lot, his eyes rolling over that ground, looking, backtracking. *This is the way it starts*, he thought, as flashbulbs popped white through the blue-black surreal time around him. *This is where it starts*.

The trail ended at the edge of the lot. He swept his flashlight beam over the sidewalk. Perhaps the lab team could find scrapes where her high heels dug into the concrete. He played the beam out further, down to the gutter. The first police car on the scene stood over where the killer would have parked, possibly on top of any tire marks the killer might have left. It figures, thought Devlin. The kind of error which wasn't an error until after it had been committed. The officers answering the radio call had no reason to exercise evidentiary caution until they found the body. They were responding to a babbled phone call from a drunk. How could they know? He walked to the edge of the sidewalk, squatted, and shined his light under the cruiser. The broken asphalt showed no discernable tracks. The weather and the surface were wrong, so the prowl car made no difference. He stood, still swinging the beam on the road. The shaft of light moved from behind the rear bumper, along the sandy, gravel-filled gutter, past the rear tire, under the rocker panels and mud stained white body to the black front tire, around it to . . .

To nothing astonishing. Perhaps to nothing significant, he thought. But perhaps. He bent closer, leaning on the front of the cruiser to examine the small square splotches of tan. Paper. Torn, clean pieces of manila folder-type paper. And at least on the sides he could see, blank.

"Ken!" he called, and the technician joined him. "What do you make of these?"

"Paper."

"I know. But I doubt that any of us dropped them. There's been a slight breeze all day. See how they're fluttering, even shifting a bit? They couldn't have been here long."

"I wonder if they're all blank."

"I hope not. Stick here and guard them. Pick them up as soon as we've got a shot of them and they're diagrammed in. I don't want some cop moving a cruiser over the top of them."

"Right."

"I'm going to question the wino who found her, though I bet that's a waste of time. And could you do me a favor?" The technician nodded. "You're on a different channel than these radios. I don't want to . . . Have the dispatcher find Detectives McKee and Perry. I don't care where they are, on duty or off. There's no other homicide cooking in the field. If there is, tell Central to switch it to Cooper and Smith. I want McKee and Perry to help me door-to-door back there where the lights are. And tell the dispatcher to call Vice. I want their top whore men down here right away—before we move the body. If they don't know her, they might know where to start finding out. See if you can give them a facial shot, an instamatic without the cut showing, then send them to me. I'll line them out hitting the bars. If you get any flack, buck it to me right away."

"Devlin . . . You're calling out the first team on this one. I mean, murder is murder, but this is just one dead whore. Some John or pimp or competitor killed her, and that's that."

"I know who killed her, Ken."

"Hey, then this will be an easy wrap, right?"

Devlin walked into the church without replying.

thirty-one

The plastic jar rattled as Devlin shook three white tablets into his hand: 500 milligrams of Vitamin C each. On top of the 200 milligrams in the compound tablet he'd popped earlier, there'd soon be enough citric acid coarsing through his blood to convince a coroner he was an orange. He didn't dare catch a cold now, and since his night's sleep consisted of two hours on the Captain's couch, he needed all the help he could get.

Better living through chemistry, he thought as he washed the bitter chalky tablets down with cold coffee. A uniformed officer dropped a stale sandwich from the lounge vending machines on Devlin's desk, then recoiled slightly as Devlin breathed his thanks on him.

"I don't blame you," Devlin said. His mouth was sour with the long night. "I wouldn't stick around me either."

Thank God for the telephone, thought Devlin. His first call was to Jackson Bricker.

"Hey Devlin, how you doing? Little late for you to be starting work, isn't it? Damn near 9:30. Were you out celebrating last night? Was that terrific Texas woman with you?"

"Jack, he got the whore."

Pause. Then, "Oh shit. Last night?"

"Yes. I'll be sending stuff over to you as it comes in. Program it and . . ."

"And pray. We'll be waiting."

We'll need the alleged power of prayer, thought Devlin. The woman was black, young, still unidentified and dead. Beyond that he had only the vital statistics concerning the state of her body and health and a precise technical description of how her throat had been cut. He studied the autopsy report for a half hour, finding in it only basic data similar to the other Reaper murders.

Beyond that, he had only two useless clues.

The first clue was the button. The technical reports indicated that it probably came from the assailant's clothing. One shiny fake brass button, gold in color, no insignia, no distinguishing marks, no manufacturer's I.D. or number. At 9 A.M., police officers under the direction of Detective Perry began hitting all button, sewing and garment stores in the city, armed with color photographs of the button and questions Devlin assumed would conclude that the police had discovered a button from any one of a million garments, male or female. The crime lab was checking through their extensive records, and a priority query was into the FBI for a similar search.

The second clue was the handful of torn paper, small jagged sections of tan parchment with a consistency akin to a file folder. The pieces of paper were blank on both sides. When laid together, their jigsaw showed an incomplete pattern. The missing pieces no doubt were the ones with some sort of writing. Given the lab reports and his own intuition, Devlin assumed the squares were from a commercial parking lot, the remnants of a ticket stub used for a receipt. But why would the Reaper tear up the stub? Devlin made a note to check with the psychiatrist. Odds were that the Reaper was a man of compulsive habits, one of which could be tearing up paper he was through with. A minuscule, inconclusive bit of trivia. But something. Something. The product of a habitual person which someone might have noticed. Somewhere. Perhaps those pieces of paper would help fit together the puzzle of who the Reaper was. A second team of policemen, this one under the direction of Detective McKee, was checking with everyone who worked at a parking lot in Baltimore in the last 48 hours, showing them a picture of the dead prostitute, asking if they'd seen her or a customer who'd ripped up the receipt they'd given him into tiny little slips, then taken them away. The lab was processing each piece of paper, looking for fingerprints, fiber patterns, anything which would help narrow down the place at which the paper had last been whole. Devlin doubted these efforts would net anything.

The phone rang.

"Detective Rourke? This is Currier, Vice. We've got a tentative I.D. on your dead lady. One of the guys thinks she is Shelly Desmond, 25, worked out of the Flame right across the street from headquarters on the Block. Street name of Crystal DuBouis. Fake accent, claimed to be Creole French from New Orleans, but really came from Beltsville just outside the city. We busted her once a few years back when she first hit the streets, but she's picked up some savvy and now works that bar. Sometimes she strips, but mostly she tricks. We rousted her two months ago when a conventioneer complained she boosted his wallet. He backed out when he found he'd have to go to court and admit he'd been where she could lift it."

"Get her file up to the Medical Examiner, check her prints and photo against the body. Do you have a home address?"

"One-three-seven-six Marborough, number 2. Basement in the bottom of a flat row house in the ghetto."

"Got it. Get over to the Flame. If it's not open, find somebody who runs it and start the questions. All I want you to find out is if they've seen her in the last five days, and whether she's got any friends or a pimp or a boyfriend. Lean as hard as it takes to get that. If they got anything, sit on them and radio me. Also make sure of the I.D. right away. I'm going to hit that apartment with a lab team now, and I don't want to be wasting any time on the wrong whore."

Devlin returned to the squad room precisely at noon. By the time he'd reached the apartment, Currier had confirmed his identification of the victim. But whatever Devlin might have wished for from her mildewed, dank basement home hadn't materialized. There's been a bed with grimy sheets, a telephone, a stack of beauty magazines, a small closet with the glitter clothes of her profession, plus a few pairs of jeans and some simple blouses and sweaters, two chairs, an icebox containing two souring bottles of wine, some moldy cheese and half a quart of milk for a cat who meowed as it he hadn't been fed in days. Devlin put the cat outside, free to fend for its own fate. Shelly a.k.a. Crystal possessed an assortment of expensive stereo components Devlin assumed were stolen. She owned 17 soul-disco records and a portable black-and-white TV which barely worked. Three posters covered the walls. Two depicted horse racing, one advertised a soul rock concert at the Civic Center from the year before. Her bathroom contained a wide selection of cosmetics and two months of birth control pills. The bedside bureau yielded her underwear, G-strings, two bags of what smelled like mediocre grass and a handful of assorted pills. A man's suit, some shirts, a pair of shoes and some dirty underwear filled one corner of her closet. The dust on the closet shelf outlined a suitcase which wasn't there but hadn't been gone long. After the print team dusted several likely areas, Devlin searched the apartment. If she'd kept a trick book, it wasn't there. Her only papers were some copies of the documents outlining her brushes with the law, a postcard from someone named Ty in Atlantic City that had been mailed 10 days earlier, and an expired driver's license. He found no money. When they'd rolled the corpse over at the scene of the crime, they'd discovered a small disco bag dangling from a strap round her waist. The bag held no I.D., a make-up kit, four condoms, a pack of cigarettes, and $185 in old bills.

Crystal didn't leave much of a legacy.

She also probably hadn't turned the Reaper's trick in that apartment. Devlin had no reason to know that, but if they'd gone there, why had he bothered to kill her elsewhere? Besides, if the Reaper were white, he wouldn't have felt comfortable in that neighborhood, a fact Crystal would have worried about when she plied her wares.

The phone on his desk rang.

"This is Currier again, Sergeant. We don't have much for you. She shacked up, off and on, with some guy named Tyrone Wallace, a pickpocket grifter who sometimes ran numbers. Nothing special in the street, but she liked him enough to let him blow lots of her trick money on the ponies. The word from the bartenders at the Flame is Ty has been in Atlantic City for a month, scoring off gamblers. I put out an APB on him and called Atlantic City. They'll probably tag him for us.

"Nobody at the Flame remembers much beyond her being in there for yesterday's noon crowd. From what they don't say, she turned a trick in the back room, but it sounds like it was a regular who's been coming in there for years, two, three times a month, to get his rocks off.

"Crystal had one good friend, another hooker who works there most of the time, dancer type named Jade."

"You've got to be kidding."

"Hey Sergeant, they're the ones with the names, not me. Jade is really Deborah Jones. She's also called D.J. She wasn't there or at her home when we went calling. I left a man parked out front of her apartment, but I'm betting that as soon as we left the Flame, she got a call somewhere and she's making like smoke in the wind. We'll run her down, eventually."

"Eventually might be too late. You know that 24-hour number I gave you?"

"Yeah, we left it all over the Flame and her apartment for her. She won't call, though. It doesn't work that way."

"It just might. Check in with it every half hour for a message from her or me. If she calls and you can't find me, go sit on her until we link up."

Delvin depressed the receiver button, then lifted it to call Kibler.

"Our friend has been waiting to hear from you," said Kibler. "We understand there was a development last night."

"Then I don't need to waste time telling you about it," said Devlin. "I need to find a whore. Her real name is Deborah Jones. Sometimes she calls herself Jade, sometimes D.J. She works out of the Flame bar. She took a powder and I need to ask her some questions. And I need to hear some straight answers from her."

"I think that can be arranged. What should she do?"

"Call that number I gave you. Leave word where she is, then sit there until we get to her."

"No problem. Our friend Tony should be able to help us. Anything else?"

"Yeah. The dead girl had a boyfriend named Tyrone Wallace, a pickpocket who's probably working Atlantic City. He should turn himself into the Atlantic City police as soon as possible. He might have some answers to some questions I haven't thought up yet."

"No problem. We have lots of friends in Atlantic City."

"I'll bet you do."

He hung up just as Captain Goldstein beckoned to him from inside his glass cubicle. Devlin frowned. The Captain wasn't alone, and the other man looked like the Deputy Commissioner.

"You look terrible, Sergeant," said the DC.

"Yes, Sir."

"And you smell pretty foul. If you're not going home, have a patrolman go out and pick up a clean shirt, some underwear. Hit one of the showers in the building. Might clean your mind as well as clean your body."

"Yes, Sir."

"Don't worry. I'll spring for the shirt."

"That's not necessary, Sir."

The DC rubbed his eyes. He'd gotten more sleep in the last week then either Devlin or the Captain, yet he was tired too. "Sit down, Detective." Devlin lowered himself into the room's only empty chair.

"The prostitute who was murdered last night. The Reaper?"

"Yes, Sir."

"Christ." The DC shook his head. "And that means he's probably picking some kid to kill now, right?"

"Yes, Sir."

"You don't have anything more than what the Captain knows?"

Devlin shook his head.

"That's great. One down, one to go, and we don't know enough to get any further than the file cabinet. If you can't manufacture something out of thin air, all we'll end up with is another corpse and a second chance. Only this time it'll be a kid instead of some no-count whore.

"You know how many kids there are in Baltimore under the age of 12? I had Research run it down this morning. Just under 128,000. And if he strays into the suburbs. . . . It might not be our jurisdictional worry, but that's no consolation.

"When I first heard about this Reaper crap I thought it was somebody's angle. I wondered how that foundation got a hook into both the Mayor's and the Commissioner's office at the same time. How you figured into it all. I decided it wasn't your angle, that maybe you were just a name they came up with, maybe after the press you got for nailing that councilman who bagged his wife, or the security guard at the girls' school who knocked off those three girls. I didn't like the whole deal, but there really wasn't any reason or much of a way to say no, so I figured why not play it out? See what comes of it. Nobody could get hurt.

"Now I got a corpse out there. You're our best man, Devlin. We don't tell people that, we don't even tell you that, but you are. You got everything I can get out of the Department to back you up."

"I appreciate all of that, Sir."

"We'll see how much you appreciate it when this is over. If it doesn't come out right, somebody might need to hang for it. That might be you. I'll cover you if I can, but I might not be able to do more than save you from getting kicked out of the Department. They might ship you off to limbo, strip you of rank or gut your badge. I'll be able to keep them from chopping off your head, long as you don't do something real foolish. I wanted you to know that, to know the worst that can happen if you blow this, so that you won't worry needlessly. You're smart enough to know the mess you're in. I wanted you to know it won't be terminally terrible."

"That's a big relief, Sir."

"That's one problem solved. We got another one. There's been a lot of talk about this Reaper stuff around City Hall. I've tried to keep a lid on it, but I don't know. If it gets out that some creep out there is stalking a kid, not only might we lose him, we might have more people hurt in the panic than he'd kill in his lifetime. This is a tough town. Some guy with kids thinks a stranger is the Reaper, he's liable to smack him with a lead pipe first and call us a distant second. And all the home-grown creeps and weirdos, they'll ooze out of the woodwork. We don't need them and their kinky problems.

"So far we haven't had any rumblings from the press. I don't think the story will leak out of here. But the Mayor's office is a fucking sieve. And he and the Commissioner aren't the best of friends right now. If the Mayor thinks he'll take some heat for this, he'll dump it over here in a hurry. I'm trying to stop that whirlwind from starting up. But once word leaks out, we'll get a whole mess of bullshit flying that does nothing but gum up your job and make headaches for everybody."

"I understand, Sir."

The DC glanced out the window. The heat of the day shimmered over the city beyond the air-conditioned glass.

"You know what bothers me most about this Reaper?" he asked, then answered his own question. "The intimacy. I can handle random kills. I can handle that there's craziness in the world. But this guy . . . Son of Sam shot strangers. He used a gun, stood back and blasted a face who didn't know him, who didn't contribute to her own death, even innocently by knowing him. But our Reaper not only kills, he betrays. I mean, we know he tricks the whores. And we assume he somehow tricks the kids into trusting him.

"And how he kills them! A hand they trust puts something cold and alien to their throat, then slices their life and integrity away. He makes my flesh creep.

"Have you thought of using the media to contact this Reaper?" he asked suddenly, shifting tacks.

"Yes, Sir, but I've rejected it. So far he doesn't know we know he's there. I prefer that edge."

"Hmph. I agree. But at some point we might need to use the media in order to keep the media from running away with this and fucking up the Reaper without our assistance."

"We'll chance all that when the time comes, Sir. I'd like to be the one to make all those decisions."

"Devlin, you have to live with them, so you get to make them."

thirty-two

After his conference with the DC and the Captain, the detective stole a two-hour nap, then spent 20 minutes under the shower on Headquarters' second floor trying to convince his body to wake up. The patrolman he'd sent out for fresh clothing hadn't returned. Devlin saw no point in putting dirty garments on clean flesh as he walked through the halls.

Devlin was holding his grungy shirt in one hand, his underwear and socks in the other, wearing only his pants and the blue running shoes as he rode the elevator up to Homicide when that machine stopped on the 6th floor. The doors opened, and there waited Jeff Stern, The Avenging Attorney. Stern blinked at Devlin's half-naked form, blinked again, stared so long he forgot to get in the elevator. The doors closed. Devlin was too tired to care.

The patrolman brought him a shirt suitable for hot weather wear—off-duty hot weather wear. The red cotton pullover wouldn't be the Lieutenant's idea of proper attire for Baltimore detectives.

But it beats naked from the waist up, thought Devlin as he pulled the shirt over his head.

The anonymous man's call came through on the 24-hour line

50 minutes after Rourke returned from the shower: "The chick Jade what you want will be waiting for you at the Flame, half an hour."

Which gave Devlin enough time to study her rap sheet and bring Vice Detective Currier into headquarters. "How the hell did you find her?" Currier wanted to know.

"I knew somebody who knew where to look."

"You really think she'll show?" asked the stocky vice detective in the grey suit as they walked across the street from Headquarters and headed into the Block.

"If she's got any sense."

The Flame lurks just around the corner from the main Block area. The air-conditioned atmosphere has the smoke and liquor smell common to all such bars. The Flame isn't an elaborate establishment. A simple "C" bar hooks around the front wall, out of which juts a small dancing stage backed by a huge mirror. The bar opens at 11 A.M. and shuts at 3 in the morning. Little effort is devoted to cleaning during the hours the establishment is closed. Some woman—any woman—is usually dancing on the stage during business hours, grinding out simple routines designed around her ability to undulate and take off the scant costume she wears. Blue and red strobe lights played on the lean black woman in the bikini underwear and high heels who pranced her stuff to throbbing disco music as Devlin and Currier entered the bar from the afternoon's outer world. The five male customers seated at the middle of the bar didn't even glance their way. Devlin found it impossible not to look at the dancer, at her long legs sleek under the colored lights, high heels clicking, her stomach muscles rippling as she unfastened the scanty bikini top and dropped it to the pit between the bar and the stage. Her breasts were small and rode high on her chest with tiny, dark brown nipples evenly set on chocolate-brown flesh. The lights made her lean face with its fine jaw line, thick lips and wide set eyes seem close to beautiful. Devlin had expected her to be more . . . repulsive. His lack of revulsion bothered him. She wasn't supposed to seem that good. Not to him.

"That's Linda," whispered Currier, who'd seen her several hundred times before. She was of little more interest to him than a bar stool. "She's a speed freak."

The woman bartender had been dead on the inside for three score and more years. The saggy flesh holding physical life in her short body was pale and putrid even under the flashing red-and-blue strobes. One continuous wrinkle etched all the ugliness she'd seen into her face. Her eyes were hollow—void of color, of life, of concern. Devlin believed he could put his revolver to his temple and blow his brains out in front of her and the most she would do would be to call for a janitor to move the mess out of the paying customers' way.

"So?" she asked Devlin as she shuffled towards them. Currier stood behind Devlin where she could not see him at first. He moved next to Devlin, leaned on the counter.

"Where's Jade, Dorothy?" he demanded.

Contempt oozed from the old woman, but she changed neither her expression nor her tone. "In the back corner."

The heavily made-up girl nervously smoking on a stool in the deepest bar shadows was barely old enough to legally enter any bar. She was white, dyed-black hair contrasting her pale flesh, dumpy and terrified. She obviously knew Currier. Devlin felt no need to flash his badge. He wondered if Currier felt the girl's relief that the police had indeed come for her, and if the vice cop was curious as to who had frightened her more than the representatives of law and order whom she'd been dodging only hours earlier.

"You shouldn't have hid from us, Jade," scolded Currier.

"I wasn't hiding!" she insisted. "Honest. I was just around."

"*I was just around!* My ass, bitch! You wasn't around because you was hiding. Now we know that, you know that, so let it be the last bullshit we hear from you. You're in enough trouble already. . . ."

"What for? I didn't do nuthing!"

"You hid, didn't you?" snapped Currier. He leaned close to the small woman. She shrank back from his accusatory finger, her brief rebellious assertion of innocence shattered. "You ran when you was supposed to come! You pull any more crap like that, and I'll have your ass on the shit list so long nobody will see you but the big mamas in Detention Hall. You don't want to go round with them bitches, you do what's right."

"Yeah, okay."

"What?"

"I mean, 'Yes, Officer Currier.'"

"You remember that," hissed Currier, jabbing his finger toward her once more. "You remember that. And you tell us whatever we want to know. No bullshit. No lies. No little teases 'bout what you think we want to hear, 'cause you can't think worth shit."

"Deborah," began Devlin, speaking just louder than the juke box's pounding rhythm. "I'm sorry about Crystal."

The woman sniffled. Her lip trembled. Devlin thought the grief was genuine, not just a show or a fearful reaction to what could have happened had she taken her murdered friend's trick. "She was a great friend, a great kid. We picked our stage names together."

"I never knew her. But I'm going to catch the guy who killed her. And you can help."

"I don't know anything."

"Don't bullshit us, bitch!" snapped Currier.

Devlin cut short this attack with a sharp gesture. Both cops knew the game. Mom-and-Pop, hard guy–soft guy. Currier, in keeping with the image he cultivated to survive on his beat, would play the battering ram, the vicious, vindictive angel. Devlin would keep him in check, sympathizing with the target of aggression. Jade's role was to crack, probably to Devlin who offered her relief from the battering ram. He was sure she'd been around long enough—hell, seen enough television—to understand the game. But even so, she'd respond to it more than to any straight line of questioning. The added, unseen edge of Tough Tony Cardozo's hand would also pressure her. Devlin's only worry was that she was indeed ignorant.

"You may know something you don't realize, Deborah," continued Devlin, deliberately using the name from her past innocence. "Try and think, remember, answer my questions. And don't worry. I know you're a whore. Currier knows. The Judge knows. Everybody knows. But right now, I don't care, so Currier won't care. Nobody else will care either. You have my word on that. Nobody is here to bust you.

"You say you don't know anything. You mean you don't know who killed her, right? Did she have any enemies, any old boy friends, any pimp or ex-pimp, anybody who might have been mad at her?"

"She didn't have nobody but Tyrone, and he's as tough as a housefly. Besides, he's in Atlantic City. She didn't have no other personal men. She said she'd never had a real pimp. Nowdays we all kick in a per . . ." Deborah realized she almost mentioned the one thing which she knew would get her killed. Currier frowned. Devlin was ready to cut off his questions. He didn't want the vice cop prying into Cardozo's protection racket. Not yet. "We all kick in some of what we make turning tricks here to . . . well, to the bar. We make the customers buy a bottle before we take them to the back room. $35, some cheap wine or fizzly stuff, whatever the girl normally drinks. And . . . Well, you know," she said, nodding towards Currier. "You busted enough of us."

"But nobody in the business was mad at her, right Deborah? None of her friends?" continued Devlin. She nodded quickly to him, the both of them grateful they'd avoided a dangerous aspect of her business. "So it had to be a customer."

"Deborah would go out with a John," said Jade, "if she'd turned him once or twice before. She didn't have a good enough apartment to bring guys to in the afternoon for extra bucks, so she wanted to score other ways. She'd charge them more than the $50 in the back room, and they'd have to take her to their place or rent a room somewhere's instead of coughing up $35 for a bottle. She was just thinking about finding a motel where she could get kickback for regular business. But she hadn't gotten around to that before . . ."

"Okay, so she had no regular hot bed. When was the last time you saw her?"

"Day before yesterday: we were both here in the club. I had a bad couple days, she was doing good. She was really up. So happy. And then a thing like this . . ."

"Had she had any weirdos? Any freaky things happen to her in the last two, three weeks? Any new steadies, especially anybody kooky?"

"No, not really."

"What do you mean, not really?"

"Just . . . Well, she *was* doing a regular, a guy who came in for the first time a few days ago, maybe last week. She turned him in the back room three, four times. Big tipper, she said. Easy. Nice guy. Not a creep."

"Is that who she would have gone with last night?"

"Maybe. I don't know. She said that guy told her he wanted an all-nighter this week. He really dug her, she said. Had big bucks."

"What else did she say about him?"

"Not much."

"Do you know who he is?" prodded Devlin.

"I don't know, I tell you!" insisted Deborah, her angry rebellion flaring again. "Why the hell should I? Why should she? He was just another sucker."

"Maybe not quite. So maybe she didn't tell you much. But she might have mentioned something. If she turned him three times, she'd spent enough time to pick up something besides his cash. You were her best friend, he was becoming a big customer of hers. What did he look like? What was he like? What did they talk about? She must have mentioned something."

"Nothing that makes any sense."

"Deborah," explained Devlin, slowly, emphatically. "What doesn't make sense to you isn't important. I'll worry about making sense of it. You tell me whatever she told you about this customer."

"Well . . . It wasn't much."

Devlin nodded.

"He was an older guy."

"How much older?"

"Pretty old. At least as old as you."

Devlin closed his eyes. Age was a blurred reference point for her. She was 23 and stupid. Anyone with more years was old. Anyone over 30 probably qualified as ancient.

"Anything else? A description, maybe a name he gave to her, a story he told her, anything peculiar?"

"Well . . . See Crystal was black. I got nothing against blacks, but sometimes she'd talk black talk and I couldn't understand her. You know, that street corner jive. I mean, I talk it too, but the black people, they talk it differently, you know what I mean? Besides, she was a little spacy on top of all that. I mean, Crystal was not your most down-to-earth person. A good kid, a good friend, but a little out there."

"So?"

"So the only thing she said about him, besides him dropping a lot of cash on her, was that he was . . . What was it? She called him 'Old Cloud-head' or said he had his head in the clouds or something. I didn't get it, but you gotta be cool and play like you do."

"Clouds? Cloud-head?"

"Yeah. Maybe not the head part, but she said something about him and clouds."

Devlin kept at the whore called Jade for another half an

hour. At one point, the hollow-eyed bartender put two whiskey-filled shot glasses in front of the policemen. As she watched, Currier casually, carefully pushed them back to the edge of the bar. They toppled over the edge, crashing into the sink below. One of the customers turned to look, but the rest of them concentrated on the fat blond woman in the wrap-around white negligee huffily prancing her stuff on stage. The dead woman behind the bar didn't change her expression when her hospitality was rebuffed. Later Devlin would question this creature about the man who'd paid for sex with Crystal on her small, dingy back-room black vinyl couch.

"I know nothing about that," she insisted, her voice empty of emotion. "The girls come and go, they buy a bottle and borrow the office. Why bother to watch what they do? There's nothing to see. Crystal was as popular as any of them, more popular than most, more than that chunky tub Jade. So she had a good week, I couldn't tell you. All I look at is the money crossing the bar. And it don't make any difference how hard you lean on me," she intoned, her empty sockets lingering on Devlin. "The answer is what the answer is."

On stage, the blond dancer had stripped to her high heels. She staggered, bent down, grunted, and after 30 awkward seconds completed a leaning handstand, her hands braced on the stage, her high heels spread wide against the mirror. Upside down and reflected, all her inverted sags bouncing out of rhythm with the music, her grotesqueness was beyond anything Devlin had previously known. He looked back at the shadowed corner where he'd left the grease-painted Jade, then back into the hollow-socket eyes of the crone behind the bar. There'd be no more answers here.

And as Jade said when he pressed her about the meaning of the cloud reference, "I can't make any sense of it. But then, that's your thing, isn't it?"

thirty-three

The reports from the field teams contained nothing useful. The button was common, untraceable. The bits of paper were bits of paper. Perhaps they'd come from a parking lot stub, perhaps not. No parking lot attendant remembered a man and the woman in the photograph. No one remembered a customer neatly tearing up a parking stub. Perhaps the Reaper used the lot another day, thought Devlin, and parked on the street when he'd picked up Crystal. Perhaps, perhaps.

And now he had a vague reference to clouds which might not even be real.

The phone rang when he was about to leave for home.

"Devlin," said the man, "what the hell are you doing? I leave town on the first vacation I've had in three years. I get two measly weeks at the beach, leave some summer intern reporter to knock out the vital statistics stories from the police blotter. When I come back, all I hear is my favorite is up to his ass in stories. But he hasn't called me. I want you to know I'm hurt, Devlin. Deeply, personally hurt."

"Bleeding, I'll bet."

"All over my nice tan. Disgusting. So I think it would be a good thing if two old friends got together real soon, like before another deadline time, and had a little chat to bandage up the hurt."

Devlin closed his eyes. Gary Ebbenhouse of the *Star* was the best crime reporter in town, good enough to find somebody who'd give him a story tied into the Reaper. The public-affairs office could defuse the rest of the reporters, the TV guys looking for good visuals rather than good stories, the reporters from the town's other papers. But Ebbenhouse would poke here and there until he pieced something together. Devlin didn't dare risk that. "I'll meet you in George's park in . . . 25 minutes. I'm on my way home."

"Boy, would I love a soft job like yours."

The small memorial square circled by traffic called Mt. Vernon Place sits a few blocks from the Block and hundreds of miles from the Virginia colonial farm which gave it its name. A white marble statue of the first American President with wooden teeth presides over the square from atop an equally white tower which resembles a Moslem minaret more than an American memorial. Baltimore built the first monument to George Washington, financing the 1810 erection through a lottery. A gothic, five-story-high, steepled Methodist church waits silently a few steps away from George. The church's three heavy, dark-chocolate doors are closed. The Peabody Conservatory of Music sits across George's square. This elegance is home to begging winos and a milepost for Baltimore commuters.

Gary Ebbenhouse resembled a model in a cigarette commercial as he sat on a grey concrete bench waiting for Devlin. The reporter's sport shirt daringly plunged down his hairy chest to show off a tasteful gold necklace and emphasized his flat stomach. He had a $20 haircut, a picture-perfect macho mustache and a deep tan that obviously went beyond where the bulge of his bicep disappeared in his tight shirt sleeve. His perfect white teeth smiled at Devlin.

"You look like shit."

"You're a hard act to copy."

"You should get out more, go to the beach."

"Sincere advice from a man who's only taken one vacation in three years."

"I'm trying to change my ways. I'm getting too old to chase ambulances and squad cars and fire trucks all night, then pound some sense into my typewriter during the day. They got young guys with master degrees from Columbia, all this great knowledge about Chi Square analyses of public opinion, who know how to run the VDT machines we got plugged straight into the computer-run presses. Those guys wear suits and ties all the time, fantasize they're Robert Redford and Dustin Hoffman in *All The President's Men*. They hang out in parking garages. Go to parties with young lawyers. Snort cocaine. But they never get dirty. Hell, all I can do like that is wear this little gold chain I got from some chick named Eileen who won't ball me anymore. I don't even have a chic gold spoon for it. Want a joint?"

The reporter lit a crudely rolled cigarette, took a long, deep hit to make sure it was going, then passed it to Devlin.

"I used to be a rebel on the paper, you know? When I first started, nobody wore jeans, everybody wore a tie. Nobody liked doing cop stories. Everybody wanted to go to Annapolis and do the statehouse bit so they could shift over to the Washington bureau and ball the President's secretaries and write columns about the importance of Senator Suck-Ass in the Florida primary. Now all of a sudden I've become respectable. I mean, it's chic to wear jeans—preferably designed by some New York faggot. Christ, it's either that or the Chi Square's three-piece jobs. I'm considered a character, a kind of acceptable standard if you want to 'get into' that kind of thing. You know how I overheard one of the hotshots who's on his way to Annapolis describe me? 'Quaint.' Fucking *quaint* and I'm not even 30 like you."

"Time is cruel, Gary."

"Yeah. And like today, when I don't wear jeans, when maybe I feel like showing a different side of the old man, I get looks like I finally either came around or sold out. That's a hell of a draw, ain't it? Quaint, convert or coward. Hard to be a purist.

"That's what I told Stern. He can't get it through his head that you and I and he are all different cards from the same deck. He keeps pestering me with crap about you. He wants your ass. He claims you're in trouble with the Commissioner's office, which I figure means Lieutenant Lackey. I told him so what. Then he told me you had some special assignment, some crooked game or bureaucratic boondoggle. I figured he was blowing more bullshit. . . ." The reporter paused for a deep toke on the joint, passed it back to the detective. "But then somebody else mentions it when I call around to my sources to let them know that Bull is back in town.

"Then the intern who was covering for me mentions that last night some whore got killed after deadline. At least, the police flack told us about it after deadline. Convenient, huh? When I check it out for a two paragraph wrap-up, I find out that not only are you working the case, but you bumped Abbott and Costello off it, then called out the fucking cavalry. All I can get from my sources is that it's something special, and all I can get from the public-affairs office is that it's something routine.

"Now I don't mind calling any flack a liar, especially when I can throw in a few facts to back me up and do it with my clever golden prose which still sneaks by the publisher. But I'd like to get the story straight, seeing as how it involves my old friend Devlin, plus I'd like a bit more: background stuff, plus if you need to have it in to cover your ass, an on-the-record 'no comment.' It will round out what I'm doing anyway, and we can tailor it like it came from someplace else."

Devlin took a deep drag on the joint, then passed it back to the reporter who did the same. As tired as he was, the dope hit him like a two-ton marshmallow, easing him back, slowing him down, making him woozy with intensified sensations and a desire for sleep.

"We've known each other what, five years? Ever since you came by my old place to wheedle stuff out of me on the Vice Squad bust, right?"

"You were just a patrolman, but the word was you were smart and straight."

"And I fleshed out what I could for you. Then and maybe a hundred times since."

"You give the Baltimore public righteous service. More than their money's worth."

"I've run maybe 50 names through the computer for you, given you inside poop on hundreds of cases beyond what the Public Affairs guys want, even helped you with O.C. stuff when I was on the task force. We've played pool together. I struck out with chicks you scored when we met them in bars. I'd say we're friends as well as professionally related."

"I can feel where you're headed, Devlin. All that's solid. But I got nothing if I ain't true to my job. You know that. You got my markers. But I got my job."

"I'm not asking you to kill what you *should* print. You're right. There's something more to this than one whore dying. But if you treat it any differently now, there's going to be a lot of blood spilled that I might be able to stop otherwise. I won't be able to prove it, but it'll be on your head, from your typewriter. When I can, I'll give you stuff that'll burn the pages right off the presses. But now not, nothing now. Do your two paragraph follow-up with a noncommital 'police are investigating' tag. She was a whore who got killed and dumped. Do that.

If you can somehow steer other reporters that way too, do it. Do it for me, do it for you, do it for the public. Write the story you should print, not the one you could."

"That's a lot of noble horseshit. Don't tell the public, the truth might hurt them. Kind of runs contrary to common sense and the democratic theory, don't it Devlin?"

"Most of the time. But theories get twisted in the street."

"So maybe some sunshine will straighten them out."

Devlin took a final drag on the joint, passed it back to his friend. He was tired. Maybe if he weren't so tired he could think of another way. But he was tired. He watched as Gary sucked the joint down until it was a stub. A woman passing by sniffed the air, but overrode her impulse to look at them. The sun glared off George's Arabian tower.

"I can't stop you from going for your story, Gary. But it's wrong if you do. And it's important, so important that if you do that, you'll never get another story or any help from me. I'll put out the word so that even if I take a fall, most of your other sources around town will dry up too. You'll be the last reporter to hear of anything. When we can, we'll slip stuff to one of those hungry Chi Square types, and pretty soon you won't be the best boy for the investigative beat anymore. And like you say, you're getting old."

"Maybe you can dry up some of my contacts. So what? I'm too mean to scare with chickenshit, Devlin. I've been down to zero before."

Devlin sighed. There was no other way.

"You'll be down to minus, Gary. We'll bust you for a misdemeanor possession of marijuana. Maybe tack on a felony trafficking charge. I'll bust you myself, with my own deposition."

"I'll take you down with me."

"Never happen. Not in my town. Not on my force. I already got the groundwork wired for something else. It'll be clean and cool, no matter how much heat your paper puts out. I'd hate myself, part of me would die doing it, but this . . . this is big enough I'll pull that trigger."

The two men sat on the bench for a long time, a long time *stone* time and a long time *real* time. The glare from all of George's whiteness burned Devlin's eyes. If only things were always that clean, that crisp.

"Shit, Devlin," said the reporter. "You must really be out there with this one. Really out there."

"All the way."

"You've never given me that "God and Motherhood greater good" crap before. You've never tried to trade or play tough. You've been straight and true. A friend. You didn't need to come on heavy like that, flash your badge and gun."

"I needed you to know I'm dead serious."

"That's what I buy, Devlin. That you're serious. That your brilliant little Sherlockian brain is right.

"So okay, I'll play this your way as long as I can. But because you're serious, not because you think you can beat me down. Because I trust your brains and your integrity. Even with that fuck job you spun out. And because I know you'll come back with double my pound of flesh when this is over. But you gotta know that's an awful big marker you made. And you gotta know I'll hit you like a hurricane if you're fucking me."

thirty-four

At 9:30 the next morning the third ring of the telephone woke Devlin from his first deep sleep in too long. He grabbed the receiver, tumbling out of bed and checking his watch in one motion.

"Yes?"

"Just what I wanted to hear. This is Barbara. They told me at your office that you were more dead than alive when you finally went home yesterday afternoon. When was the last time you ate?"

"You mean a real meal?"

"Or something resembling one."

"Well, there was that salad we had in the Italian restaurant before I got the call. And I had a handful of stale coconut from the box in the frig when I got home last night."

"I figured. I'll be over in an hour to cook us breakfast. Don't be a bore and be gone when I get there. I had to use my huskiest stage voice to get the address and phone number out of Detective McKee."

Devlin started to protest, but she'd hung up. "Damn!" he swore, even as he knew his anger was insincere. He called the hotline. No progress from any of the teams, nothing new, no messages.

He called Bricker at the computer center. In precise, cold terms, the computer man explained how the data from Crystal's death had proven as inconclusive as all the other murders.

"You don't sound quite so excited any more," said Devlin.

"Your lab included pictures with their reports."

Devlin showered, shaved and dressed in slacks and a shirt. He pulled on his blue running shoes. They still made him smile. Why wear a tie this far down the road? he thought. The Baltimore *Star* claimed the thermometer might break 100° by noon. And reported that an 11-month-old Michigan girl had drowned in a bucket. But the Reaper hadn't claimed a child in Baltimore. Not yet. Devlin's air conditioner hummed steadily after 18 hours of continuous use. The hell with utility bills. At least his apartment was pleasant. The long sleep had refreshed his body, his mind and his spirit. The first cup of coffee warmed him. When he felt a slight caffeine tingle, the thought smiled at him seductively. Why not? He went to his stash, cut two inch-long lines of cocaine, snorted them down. He put the stash on his desk, not quite out, not quite away, casually within reach. Just in case. He heard Barbara knock and call his name. She'd taken three steps into the room, fresh and cool-looking in her blouse and wide skirt despite the heat and the climb up three flights of stairs with a stack of groceries when Devlin smelled her expensive musk perfume and sneezed.

"Let me guess," she said. "It's not a summer cold."

He followed her into the kitchen, an embarrassed grin on his face. "I'm really not that hungry," he said as she spread food out on the counter.

But she forced a Danish pastry on him anyway. On her request, he cut her two lines. While she snorted, he made them each a fresh cup of coffee. Then he snorted two more big lines and cut a third for her. They sat stone still, concentrating on holding their noses closed—but lost it and sneezed for a chorus that ended in laughter at what the neighbors might wonder.

"My God!" gasped Barbara as the laughter eased. "Another woman's been murdered. Another child is probably doomed. And we're sitting around stoned and laughing!"

"We're still alive."

He'd meant it to be only a passing straight line, but she threw it back to him seriously, as if she'd been waiting for just such a chance.

"First time in what seems like forever that I've felt like that. When I came out here, I was . . . Well, since 1977 it's been like drifting through a fog, one vague place to another, pushed along by . . . by a kind of duty. Jimmy's murder turned me numb. I mourned him, but I was numb. I didn't feel it. I mourned out of duty. I plodded on through my marriage out of duty. When it fell apart, I followed my husband's lead out of duty, divorced him out of duty. Went on living in Denver out of duty. Let a couple of men roll me around out of duty. When you called and I figured Jimmy's death might not be over, I came out of duty.

"Coming out here cleared most of the fog away. I had something to *do* with my duty. Before that, duty had been something to avoid doing anything else. Two nights ago, when they called you at dinner and that woman was dead, all the fog got blown away, the duty with it. That night, while you were gone, I lay there in that hotel room and cried, cried for real for the first time. Cried for Jimmy. Cried for all the others too. I quit mourning out of duty, quit mourning myself, and buried my son. That night I looked in the mirror for the first time in five years, really looked. I saw a 34-year-old woman who could be striking if she gained back about 10 pounds in the right places and smiled like she used to. She's smart and can do things and she's no better or worse than anybody else can expect to be. And she's alive. For the first time in a long, long time, she's alive."

She'd been sitting on the chair, facing him where he sat on the couch. Somehow she'd undone her cuff buttons without him noticing it. Perhaps they'd been unbuttoned all along. Her eyes locked on him, beautiful black nickels of light in rich brown rings. She unbuttoned her blouse from top to bottom, spread her arms wide as she opened the cloth and dropped it on the chair. Her breasts had once been fuller, heavy with milk and youth. They sagged slightly, had lost some of their weight, but they were still soft, wonderfully rounded, deep and thickly white. Her nipples were brilliant pink nickel buttons, blood swollen on wide crimson aureolas. She took a sliding step across the space between them, and was kneeling before him, their eyes level, their mouths level. Devlin's heart slammed at his chest and his hands shook, the cocaine racing his tight nerves, his hunger. Barbara licked her lips and whispered, "Be alive with me."

Then she kissed him, full and deep and probing, their lips mashing together, their tongues searching each other out. They kissed again and again and again; she broke away, moaning, panting slightly, kissing his cheek, frantically kissing back to his ear, to his neck, around down the front of his throat and she kissed him as she unbuttoned his shirt, down, down his chest as she kissed him, down, down, down.

thirty-five

"You do that very, very well."

"Then we're evenly matched."

They nuzzled on his bed, cooing and sighing, occasionally giggling softly. Finally Barbara said, "Was it the coke?"

"No. Maybe you'll think so sometime, but no." He kissed her, his body taut even in the afterglow.

"Why are you so worried about this case? Worried more than normally?"

"What makes you say that? You've never seen me work any other case. Maybe this is how I always am."

"I don't think so. You're spending too much energy keeping yourself together. You're tense all through, all the time. You're the type who conserves energy, who goes along at an easy pace until the right moment, quiet on the outside, carefully complete on the inside, then *bingo!* Roar it all out, focus it right where it has to go. You're more than you seem and exactly as you are. You're a paradox, a lovely, wonderful, sexy, sexy . . ."

"Hey! You keep that up and I'll be more than a paradox!"

"We can hope. Now, where was I? Yes, I remember. *Here* . . ."

"Mmmnnnn."

". . . and *here,* talking about my paradox. You're an incredibly diverse man, yet so single-minded when you once get going."

"I keep meeting people who think they're the detective, not me. What makes you think you know all this stuff?"

"We older women have these ways."

"You sure do. God help us all when you reach 60."

"Why can't you relax, focus all that energy? You're obsessed, but not with merely finding the maniac. That's not the right way to be obsessed for this game."

"How can I be obsessed in a *right* way? I've got one murder that might or might not be but probably is tied to all the others, to your Jimmy's. I've got three clues: A dimwit whore's memory of a jive conversation which she didn't understand in the first place and which may not refer to anything meaningful in the second place. I've got a pile of carefully torn paper slips which might have no connection to the murder and which could have come from a million places for a million reasons. My most solid clue is a button, a simple, shiny fake brass button. Button, button, who doesn't have this button? Any one of a million people who might be innocent. I've got those terrific clues, a whiz-bang computer that comes up knowing nothing, a not-too-bad police force with nowhere to look and everyone to protect. All I know about my adversary is that he is highly resourceful, highly mobile, a brilliant planner, bold, efficient. And crazy. Or at least we *assume* he's crazy. This whole game is running to a clock and a set of rules only the Reaper knows. Which of Baltimore's 128,000 children is running on that clock too?

"And then I've got . . ." He paused, knowing better than to voice the truths running through his mind. "I guess I am obsessed with the case. But I've never had one like it. I can't focus with a motive or a reason or a fugitive or an alibi to break. I have to be obsessed with and focus on something unreal, something I can't see. It's like being stoned: What you feel isn't real, but it is. That's this case."

"What else?"

He looked at her, feigning innocence, but she neither bought his silent arguement nor looked away. He sighed.

"I had a special friend once. She's still a special friend, but she's gone. As she'd say, I'm in a bit of a tight with this one. A bit of a tight. Extenuating circumstances. I don't know if I've got all it takes to hold all the sides who've put me in the center, but I've got to play like I do. Everybody has to believe I can do it. Especially me. Or I can't."

"Will you tell me more?"

"No."

"Any reason for that?"

"Yes."

"Will you tell me the reason?"

"No."

"Can I help at all?"

Devlin smiled. "Well . . . I need . . . a friend. Someone who doesn't want to put me on the line or in the center."

"You got it. But I'd like to be something more than just another one of the guys."

"Well . . ." he sighed with exaggerated deliberation. "Okay."

They smiled. Devlin rolled on his side, kissed her lightly, and raised up on his elbow as he said, "Now *this* friend should get up and help you fix that breakfast so he can get back to work keeping from being crushed. Besides, he's hungry again."

She stopped him from moving off the bed with a firm but gentle hand pressed against his inner thigh.

"Me too," she said.

thirty-six

"Look, I've *got* to go." He freed himself from her embrace. They stood at his apartment door, he with his blazer in hand, fully clothed and ready to meet the world, her clad only in one of his completely unbuttoned shirts which hung to her mid-thigh. Her auburn hair was tousled, her makeup-free face was puffy and whisker burned, and he'd never seen her look more lovely or desirable.

"I know," she said, pouting slightly. "Duty calls." He frowned, and she said, "You know I didn't mean it . . . *that* old way. You go ahead. Catch that creep. Get out from the middle. Take care of yourself. All of the above. I'll probably hang around here for a while. I'm not a bad housekeeper and you sure could use one. Besides, it beats staying around the hotel. I might even hit your stash."

He smiled.

"I'll see you tonight. Now scoot!" With a final kiss and a slap on his ass, she sent him down the stairs feeling better than he had in months. Which was irrational, of course, he thought, given the total situation.

Which hit home to him half a block later far harder than he needed. The black limo parked across the street from Devlin's apartment had telephone antennas, mirrored windows, and its motor running. *No doubt to keep it nicely air-conditioned*, thought Devlin as he walked towards his car. The driver's window snaked down with an electronic hum, revealing a hard man in a summer suit Devlin had never seen before but recognized immediately. He broke into a sweat.

His first thought was for Barbara. He had to keep them away from the apartment, away from her. They might know she was there, they might even know who she was and where to find her at a later date. But if she didn't see them, there was no reason to concern themselves with her. Unless they wanted to

133

use her as another level against him. But Matella must know there are limits beyond which I'll rebel, thought Devlin. He's not irrational.

"He wants to see you." Somehow Randy had come up behind him. From where, Devlin didn't know. His senses had been dulled by the morning's sweetness. That couldn't happen again. With as much nonchalance as he could muster, Devlin turned and stepped away from the mountain of a man in the white country-club suit who loomed behind him. Devlin kept his right arm cocked slightly, close to his body, with his little finger hooked to be sure the blazer would move aside in case . . .

"After spending a few hours staring at your freaky form I don't wonder he wants some relief."

Randy's massive hands opened and closed, opened and closed. "Don't be stupid, cop. I would crush you before your gun cleared your holster. And remember, he might turn me loose on you someday. I wouldn't need to make it easy. He's got no love for inferior life forms."

"You'd never know that from his hired help."

The hands opened and closed, opened and closed. Then the head looming far above Devlin's eyes nodded towards the limo. "Let's not keep him waiting. His patience has its limits."

"Mine too!" Devlin stalked across the street, the giant shadow silently, effortlessly gliding behind him.

The car's electric rear window slid down. Kibler sat closest to the street, but beside him Devlin saw Matella's white head of hair.

"Hey Buddy!" yelled Kibler. "How you been?"

Devlin ignored him, just as he forced his mind to ignore the menacing shadow at his unguarded rear. The detective thrust his head toward the open car window. He rested his left hand firmly on the slot where the glass had disappeared. His thumb touched metal, and he pushed. Perhaps a print on the car sometime in the future might help. Keep pressing, thought Devlin, keep pushing. Or roll over and die.

"Well Sal," he called to the elegant man in the back seat. The man's expression didn't change at the sound of his irreverently abbreviated name, but Kibler blinked and Devlin felt the hulk behind him stiffen. *Press on, jerk the chain.* "Nice of you to drop by. I'd invite you upstairs, but we just had the building fumigated for vermin and I'd be afraid for your health.

"You know I should bust you." Devlin jerked his thumb back toward Randy, but his eyes never left the green fires burning in the old man's face. "We've got a leash law here in Baltimore: dogs, donkeys and dumb apes, and you're letting him run around loose."

"It's wonderful to see you in fine spirits," said the old man in cultured, controlled tones. "And that you're managing to relax in all this hot weather we've been having. Things must be slow at the office."

"Damn right they're slow, and they don't get any faster with you taking up my time and hawking me!"

"We haven't had a progress report from you since you found the murdered prostitute."

"She's still dead. I predict no change in her condition."

"You'd do well to remember that that is an extremely permanent condition. What have you learned?"

"Nothing new. You know about what the other whore told me, or you're less efficient than you seem. You probably also know that the computer keeps coming up with zilch. I'm sure your wires into the Department have you fully informed on the zeroes we've been getting on the other stuff. All the standard police work is still churning, and still churning up nothing. So far, we're going to play it like it comes."

"I was hoping for a bit more than 'standard operating procedures' from a man of your alleged caliber, Detective Rourke."

"I've played straight with you, Matella, but you keep jerking me around. You do that too much, you'll jerk me off of what I need to do, then neither of us will like what happens."

"I've never tolerated disappointment, Sergeant," said Matella.

The old man leaned back in the seat. The shadow behind Devlin moved as Randy walked around the car, climbed in. Kibler smiled encouragingly, then the mirror window slid up. Devlin stared at his own reflection as he backed away from the car. The driver slipped the limo into gear and it purred away from the curb, down St. Paul Street toward the center of town. Devlin glanced at the license plate, but he assumed it was false. He watched the limo move out of sight, effortlessly sliding through traffic. He looked at the sidewalks, the buildings, the parked cars. No one seemed to be staked out watching him, waiting. No silenced gun whispered the old man's anger. Devlin walked to his car, unlocked it, slid behind the wheel. The motor turned over without igniting a bomb. His memory flashed on Randy's huge and powerful hands opening and closing, opening and closing. He looked down at his own hands—strong, but nowhere near as strong as the muscleman's. So far he was still pulling if off, still alive. And he'd told them nothing. His fingers gripped the car's steering wheel until his knuckles were white. He released his hold, and stuck his hand out in front of him. It trembled, but not from post-cocaine rush.

thirty-seven

"So what did you do today?" asked Barbara as she lifted the covered saucepan from the counter to the burner. Devlin wanted to tell her that wasn't the way to cook corn on the cob, but he knew enough to keep his silence.

"More of what I've been doing since this started . . . what? A week ago?" he replied. "I've been over all the reports on all the killings two more times, looking for correlations or nuances the computer might have missed. I've been over all the interviews and evidence on Crystal's murder. I even went back to the vacant lot hoping for inspiration. I should have gone back to the Flame, but I couldn't stomach that again so soon. Did you know I've made little index cards on all the killings, like flash cards kids used to use for vocabulary lessons in school? I take them with me wherever I go. I'll pull them out, shuffle them in a different order, try to find some facts or pattern I've missed. Change the environment, change the thought pattern, maybe come up with something new.

"Hell, I even met with four Bibical scholars: one Jewish, one Catholic, one Protestant, one academician. I've got them working on all the ads, looking for something, anything. I keep checking back with that shrink Herman Weis in New York, too.

"But mostly I wait. Sit around and wait. That's the hardest part, that takes most of your energy. Sitting and waiting can beat you down faster than all the gumshoeing in the world."

Barbara stacked some dishes in the sink. She glanced over her shoulder to where Devlin sat at his small kitchen table. "You need to free your mind while you wait. Give it a rest. Percolate all that grey stuff. Let it go on its own rather than forcing it. Maybe after dinner we'll see if we can't find a stimulating but relaxing activity for you."

"You're always trying to fatten me or fuck me!" joked Devlin. "Which way do you want me to die?"

"I'm merely trying to bring you up to a new balance." She moved towards him. He pushed his chair out from the table, and she lowered herself to his lap, kissed him gently. She ran her hands up his lean sides: no love handles, no hint of a paunch. She held his face between her hands and kissed him again. "And I wouldn't worry if I were you. Your teeter-totter can take a lot more . . . weight."

He smiled and pulled her mouth down to his.

"Ah-ah!" she said a moment later, breaking the embrace and standing. "Something might start to burn."

He smiled.

"Amuse yourself while I finish dinner."

Devlin scooted his chair back to the table. She had his plate on the stove, forced to dish up his corn and fried fish directly from there because he owned no serving plates. He barely possessed dining plates. He reached across the table, and pulled the glass salt and pepper shakers to him. He slid them back and forth between his hands, absentmindedly at first, then with more studied concentration, as if he were playing some soccer-like game with his hands as the goals and the shakers as the balls. Barbara set full plates on the table. He joked with her as they ate, teasing her about bringing new luxuries like serving dishes into his life; she countered with cracks about his skeletal lifestyle. They talked and teased, laughed and joked. Yet he couldn't concentrate on this fascinating woman and the easy time surrounding her presence. Something lay in his mind, something just below the conscious thought level bothered his concentration, something that kept reaching up and scratching at his thoughts, demanding attention he couldn't focus. His hands kept returning to play with the shakers.

"Salt and pepper!" he cried suddenly.

"What?"

"Salt and pepper: that's what you call somebody with grey-flecked hair, right? Salt and pepper."

"I guess so. I never use the expression myself. Kind of a quaint phrase that's fading from our culture. Hair dye has helped its demise. You don't need to worry about that, or about baldness."

"Hair. Hair." Devlin sat silently as his corn stopped steaming. Then he softly whispered: "Holy shit. Holy shit!"

thirty-eight

He didn't dare chance any of the phone booths in the neighborhood or any pay phone he'd ever used before. He drove aimlessly for half an hour, carefully checking his rear-view mirror for any tail. The sun hadn't set, so he had a good view of what went on around him. Perhaps for the first time, he thought.

Nor could he risk billing the number to any police department credit card, his home phone, or the special 24-hour Reaper line. His biggest risk was that there was a tap on the phone he was calling. That was one chance he had to take. At least the man he needed to reach had given him his home phone number. If Devlin's luck held, he would find him there. He dropped 15 cents into the pay phone slots, dialed 0, then tapped out 212-434-2565 on the shiny metal squares. The operator came on the line.

"Operator 719. May I help you?"

"Yes, please. I'd like to charge this to my home phone. Area code 301-656-6787."

"And what is your name please?"

"Biz Grey. It's an unlisted number, billed to B. Grey. If you want my address . . ."

"That won't be necessary, sir. Thank you."

The maid answered on the third ring. At least it sounded like a maid. And then the man he needed to talk to came on the line.

"Hello?"

"Dr. Weis? This is Devlin Rourke, the Baltimore detective."

"Sergeant, I hope this is good news for once."

"It's not really news sir, not yet."

"Thank God. I thought he'd killed the child and we'd lost him again. Until next time."

"We might be closer than we know, Doctor. I realize you're busy, but there are a few things I want to run by you."

"You can have all my time you want, Sergeant."

"Could the Reaper be playing out some kind of crazy, ironic cosmic joke?"

"I beg your pardon?"

"Bear with me. This is hard, and I can't tell you too much, but . . . Could he also be flaunting his power, sort of combined with proving it?"

"You mean acting out a deep-seated insecurity, possibly combined with a history of highly competitive victories? Proving to the world he has it?"

"Or *still* has it?"

"Well . . . yes."

"Does that contradict anything we know?"

"Sergeant, craziness is the ultimate contradiction of reality. Anything goes within those boundaries. A crazy man can believe that he is pretending to do crazy things, believe he's in control of his pretense, and all the while be wrong and really be out of control and truly, truly crazy. His delusions can be more real than he admits even to himself."

"So he could be playing a game he thinks he created for his amusement or . . . or whatever, and all the while the game is playing him?"

"Yes. And no. Craziness is the ultimate paradox, simultaneously complex and simple."

"One of the things which has bothered me is that the Reaper has never made any direct contact with either the authorities or the news media. The ads don't count, especially if they're merely a ruse. . . ."

"What?" shouted the psychiatrist. "What are you . . ."

"Bear with me, Doctor. And please, don't challenge me yet: we can't work that way now.

"But whether the ads are a ruse or part of the ritual—or both, if you're right about the complexity here, they don't count as contact with the outer world. They're one-sided, with no possibility of feedback for the Reaper from the outer world—and he's not so crazy he wouldn't recognize that. But most mass murderers these days flaunt themselves to get feedback. Son of Sam, for example. Christ, even Jack the Ripper sent letters to the authorities. But nothing from the Reaper."

"It's a point, Sergeant, but you've got to remember any criteria is almost impossible to establish. Not only do we not know enough about such madmen in general, we don't know enough about the Reaper. Perhaps such contact is planned somewhere down the road, perhaps he's waiting until he's killed 30 people because that's the number God told him to begin confessing with."

"I understand, Doctor. But isn't it possible that the Reaper who—no matter what—is a supreme egotist, who already thinks of himself as God or God-like, who's probably a man accustomed to power and the rewards and attention it brings, would want some recognition, some . . . I don't know, some sense that somebody out there knows about his mission and cares? Perhaps, if you will, somebody to deliberately, knowingly outsmart, to flaunt his power to?"

"Of course that's possible, but we have no data. . . ."

"I don't want to worry about such data. If it's there, I think I've already got it."

"I'm afraid I don't understand, Sergeant."

"I'm afraid I might, Doctor."

Devlin hung up. He pulled his change from the return slot, reinserted it, and dialed 656-6787. The phone rang and rang and rang and rang. And rang. Logic dictated that he should hang up, that more than 20 unanswered rings meant no one was home to answer. But Devlin wasn't motivated by total logic just then. He was hot, he could feel it, he could feel the energy flowing around him with him, his own natural stone. He wouldn't give up and hang up. He couldn't, he refused to believe Biz wouldn't be there when he needed her. Not tonight, not when everything was finally flowing. He could feel it all racing, and such small considerations as her not being home simply weren't real.

"Goddamn it! This better be some emergency!"

"Hey . . . Biz! Are you always so cheerful when you answer the phone?"

"D . . . D . . . Devlin Rourke! God*damn* it! I've had it with you and Danny the G-man! I'm not going to be your messenger any more!"

She slammed the receiver down so hard the click hurt Devlin's ears. He winced, then worried briefly that he didn't have any more change. But his karma was true, the energy was right. He called her again.

"Listen, I'm sorry!" he blurted before she had a chance to yell in the receiver. "But this is important. Really important!"

She groaned in frustration.

"I mean, I wouldn't call you if it weren't important business, would I?" He paused, but she didn't reply. "I know how busy you are. I . . . Did I disturb your dinner or work or something?"

"Or something? Or something?! Yeah, or something!"

"Oh." The detective automatically asked, "What?"

"If you must know, I'm getting laid."

"Oh."

"What the hell is that supposed to mean: 'Oh'?"

"Nothing . . . I just . . . Oh. I mean, hell, it's only 8 o'clock."

"So?! So what?! What's so strange about 8 o'clock, huh? Don't you have any romance in your soul? Do you have a soul? And what's so strange about getting laid, huh? Aren't D.A.'s supposed to have sex either? We already know they're not supposed to be women, and if they are, well, they're probably all fucked up and can't be *real* women. I'm not such a bad catch. I'm not so ugly or cold. Of course, Baltimore's greatest detective hasn't noticed that, has he? You and your damn blind blue eyes! You're not the only man, you know! Lots of men find me attractive! So what if Henry isn't as cute as you? Or as lean as you or as tall or has as much hair? He's sweet and gentle and kind and not bad in bed, all those things you probably could be if you tried and weren't so cold and dumb and all cop all the time!"

"Ah . . . Sorry to bother you at a time like this, Biz, but this really is an emergency."

Her groan changed to a resigned sigh. "What the hell do you want from me?"

"Could you call Danny at home? His number is 483-1442. Have him call me from a pay phone? Don't mention my name. I'm at 372-9648. And have him do it right away? This is important."

"If I do, will you promise never to bug me again? Ever? Either of you?"

"I'll try."

"Oh . . . All right! You've crushed the evening this much. A little more won't matter. Besides, I'm used to it. Why change the way things happen between us now? And afterwards, you can remember this generosity as my classy way of telling you to fuck off."

"Thanks a lot. Oh . . . Biz, there's one other thing."

"I said fuck off."

"Well, see, I've already done it. I charged a long-distance phone call to your home phone. I'll reimburse you. I hope you don't mind."

"Don't mind? Devlin, that's a federal fucking crime!"

"Don't worry: I've got friends in high federal fucking places."

thirty-nine

The pay phone rang 45 minutes later.

"Danny, what I need you to do is have Bequai find out where Matella was during 8 separate blocks of time, the first one in November 1975, the rest spread out since then."

"Why don't you ask him yourself?"

"Because if I do, he'll push me too hard to know why I want to know, and if you ask him, coax him and court him, that'll buy me more breathing room."

"Listen Rourke, don't fuck around with Bequai. That man's Albanian. Came over on the boat with his folks. The way he grew up, what he learned over there, plus what he's been through . . . Albanians don't take a fucking lightly. I've seen you slide safe through more shit than any man alive, but don't fuck with this guy."

"He doesn't give me much choice."

Devlin waited, but his friend wouldn't speak.

"Come on, Danny. The most he can yell at you for is helping me, which is what he ordered you to do in the first place."

"What do I tell him when he asks why you want all this stuff?"

"Tell him I said to fuck off, no questions if he wants any answers."

"Christ, Devlin! I can't tell him that!"

"Then you'll think of something more suitable and equally effective. Pretend the last letter in FBI stands for 'Initiative'."

Danny's voice grew cold. "You know, Devlin, you're a hard friend to have."

Devlin looked through the smudged glass encasing the phone booth. Night wasn't far away. The browns of Baltimore's low townhouses were about to fade into darkness. A few long, fluffy clouds hanging high over the city glowed blood red with that day's death. He looked at their crimson wisps, and remembered the pure white locks above Matella's fire green eyes, pure white hair, as white as a cloud should be. "I try, Danny," he said. "I try."

forty

"Hey, how we doing, huh? How we doing?"

Devlin looked at the Duck's eager face—his broad smile above his neatly pressed blue uniform, all ready for another day's hard work. Devlin wondered what the Duck had been doing in Central Headquarters' hall first thing in the morning. "We're doing fine, Sergeant," Devlin told him. "Just fine. And you've been doing a terrific job."

"I've been trying so hard!" explained the Duck. "Whenever I can, whenever I'm not handling some other assignment, I go places I figure you aren't. Sometimes I even go in plain clothes, though to tell you the truth, I'd rather wear my uniform. Like yesterday: I knew you were working out of Headquarters here, so I went to the Stadium where they were having a baseball game. Not only did I do *our* job, I beefed up *their* uniformed security. How's that for showing initiative?"

"Mind boggling. Who won the game?"

"I forget."

"It's good to see you haven't lost your standards."

"Thank you, Sir!"

Devlin checked his desk and the dispatcher for messages. There were none. As he put down the telephone, Detective Perry yelled to him, "Hey Devlin! The Commissioner wants to see you right away!"

The summons probably wasn't from "the Commissioner," but from "his office." Which probably meant the cagey Lieutenant. Which meant there was no rush. Devlin bummed a cup of coffee from the detective who kept an electric coffee-maker in the closet. He glanced at the morning paper, concentrating only on the comic page. Devlin shuffled his index cards, ran through them one more time. Nothing new occurred to him, so he jammed them in his pockets. They fit, but what with his notebook, pens and pencils, his evidence bags, his spare bullets, his keys, his folding knife, a small pocket lens he sometimes carried, and a handful of change for telephones, it was a tight squeeze. As he rode the elevator and walked down the long hall to the Commissioner's office, he let his mind roam over thoughts of Barbara, of her soft, eager flesh, of the round tautness of her high-tucked bottom. He followed the secretary's pointing finger, opened the wooden conference door next to the Commissioner's office . . .

And there sat Bequai.

forty-one

"Where's your army?"

"Close by. Where the hell have you been and what have you been doing? And what the hell is the cocaine and those checks on Matella adding up to?"

"One, I've been waiting to hear from you. Two, I've been busy. Three, the cocaine might turn out to be evidence. Four, until you tell me how Matella checks out and where he was on those dates, I don't know what it's adding up to."

"Neither do I, and I don't like hunting blind. Especially when I'm not sure about my hunting partners."

"You can never be sure, Bequai. But I don't see how a man in your position can be any more sorry."

Bequai's tough guy aura broke. *Much more quickly today then before*, thought Devlin, who wondered if the increasing case of that transformation meant that Bequai was nearing the end of his strength.

"I can be sorrier," disagreed the FBI agent sadly, "not much, but a bit. You and whatever game you're playing is the closest I've come to Matella since the bomb went off. Back then, all I had was his name and the knowledge of what he was doing. That wasn't much. Today I don't have much more.

"And you don't seem to be adding to it. I've hung on all these months in that drab cell of an apartment, chopping away at other creeps, hoping to cut them into rungs for a ladder leading to Matella.

"The Bureau is as tolerant and helpful as I've ever seen them. But they're still a bureaucracy, they're still chained to the old days when J. Edgar used to dummy crime statistics that had little actual relationship to the Bureau's job and activities, use them and plain old implied blackmail to keep his franchise. Back then, we didn't admit organized crime existed, let alone a man like Matella. But the Bureau protects its own

and hits the people who hit it. But, after a while, they have to
be concerned about more than revenge on a puff of smoke we
barely see.

"Oh, they give me men. I've got an army to protect me. And
clerks for paper work. But then it gets tight. I have a few men
in the field, and I can borrow agents from other field offices.
But my 'army' is mostly a headquarters corps.

"Like your list of lawyers in those neighborhoods. If I could
swear it was a high priority with a direct yield, I could pop
whatever you're looking for out of it. But so far, all I've got is
names. About 30 percent of my people are working on tracing
O.C. connections. That they haven't finished the task yet tells
you something about how many troops I got.

"And now you ask me for time checks on Matella, some of
them going back to the period when he was 'retired'. Those
dates mean nothing to me. And you're going to love this: We
can't help you. Don't look at me like that! I know! If he's so big,
why don't we have him under 24-hour surveillance?

"One, because not everybody believes in Matella. I can't
come up with enough believers to commandeer the troops.

"Two, he's the cagiest, slipperiest man I've ever seen. Much
of the time he sits in that Brooklyn barbershop, even
occasionally cutting some customer's hair, giving them an old-
fashioned shave. His shop does a steady business. He sits
there. Him and a goliath muscle freak named Randy, who is
listed on the IRS forms as a hairdresser and general barber's
assistant. Sometimes one of the *consiglieres* from one of the
Families drops by, sometimes it's a Don, but that's rare.
Matella's accountant, guy named Kibler, he drops by a couple
times a day. Kibler is his main errand boy. Delivery men come
by. Paper boys. Salesmen. Half the people who go through
there are probably messengers, couriers. We gave up photo-
graphing them all, let alone tailing them.

"You know how hard it is to get a tap these days? We don't
even try, not even an illegal one. You know what's upstairs from
Matella's shop? A private security firm specializing in electronic gear and counter-surveillance. The best in the city. Legit.
We know it's a front. Just like we know that as part of their
lease to the corporation which owns the building, a corporation which Matella owns, the security types run constant
checks on the barbershop and its six telephone lines. We can't
get a bug near that place without them knowing it.

"But suppose I could get the men. Suppose we could find a way to stake out that shop, move into that tight little neighborhood that Matella has wired to the teeth, to sit there and watch him. He disappears. He shakes any tail we put on him. We put an army on him, he puts a bigger army on the streets. Delivery vans back out of alleys to block our cars tailing him. A fat lady once jammed a revolving door on a department store he'd just entered. Our guy was stuck in it for 10 minutes. Smooth, subtle, and unbeatable. The same thing with Randy and Kibler. They know all the dodges. Besides, Matella doesn't always travel with them. He's like a ghost. Sometimes he supposedly slips around the country, meeting with the various Families all by himself. That keeps them on their toes, keeps him independent, harder to pin down.

"So I can't tell you where he was on those dates. If you could tell me where he *might* have been, I could feed his description out to the airlines, the bus companies, the local police departments, hotels, you name it. The Bureau can track down trivia like no machine on earth. And that would be something concrete I could sell them on to get the manpower. *If* you tell me some places, some reasons. I know you still won't give it all to me. I'm not asking for that. But with a little more, I can help you a lot."

Devlin thought a moment, then said, "I can't give you any more."

"Hmph." Bequai breathed deeply, then stood. Devlin saw the grim agent solidify before his eyes again. Bequai nodded to the world beyond the clouded office door.

"For the record, I came to Baltimore because the Bureau has you listed as one of the area's top homicide specialists. I wanted to get your opinion on a Bureau plan to list all such experts in a publication distributed to all police departments. The Commissioner bought that cover because he's used to dumber things coming out of Washington. He insisted I take as little of your time as possible, so I'll be going. By the way, you're against the idea."

Bequai moved towards the door, his walk changing from a shuffle to a stride as he steeled himself again. He turned, looked at the detective one last time before he left.

"I keep having to trust you more and more," said the FBI agent. "And liking it less and less."

forty-two

The phone message on Devlin's desk told him to call David Dugan immediately for an urgent message. Devlin had never heard of David Dugan, nor did the detective recognize the number. But he hit the appropriate numbers on his telephone before he sat down.

"Advertising, Baltimore *Star*."

Devlin's grip tightened on the receiver. "Mr. David Dugan, please."

"This is David Dugan."

"This is Sergeant Rourke, police department."

"Oh yeah, hi. I've never talked to you, but you talked with my boss, Mr. Hines. He's gone to the beach for his vacation, but he left strict instructions for me to call you if that customer mailed in another ad for the religious notice thing. You know what I'm talking about?"

"I know."

"Well, it's here."

forty-three

"How many people have handled this?" asked Ken Urtz. The lab technician used a letter opener to point to the single piece of paper on David Dugan's desk.

The puzzled ad man glanced nervously from Urtz to Devlin

to the other lab technician to Detective Paul McKee. They surrounded his desk. His small office was tucked in the far corner of the large display advertising room. Beyond his glass walls a dozen men and women sat on high stools behind elevated tables, pasting ad copy to pictures and drawings. D.D.—as he was known in Baltimore ad circles—hoped they didn't know these men were from the police. Not that he'd done anything wrong, mind you. Or that he was ashamed to be seen talking with policemen. But like most citizens, D.D. found himself trembling inside as his outside tried to calmly talk with the cops. He had an irrational fear that somehow these policemen would discover he stole candy from an open bin at a grocery store, or that he fudged his expense account and cheated on his income tax, that he snuck off to a Pikesville motel with the dyed redhead from circulation two or three times a month (whenever he could hide the room money from his budget-conscious wife).

"Well . . ." D.D. said, trying to explain what might have happened. Not that he knew. He certainly hoped he wouldn't be held accountable for any mistakes that had been made! Why had his boss left him in charge of this one? "Let's see. It probably came through the mail room, got sorted there. The pick-up boy might have touched the envelope too. Mrs. Perkins opened it, and as soon as she saw what it was, she brought it straight to me. I . . . I didn't know better, you understand. I handled it a bit. Then I called you and it's been sitting there ever since. I didn't touch it after I talked to you, Detective Rourke, just like you said."

"Where's the envelope?" asked Devlin.

"Ah . . . I guess Mrs. Perkins must have thrown it in . . . in the outer office trash, I guess. She's the big woman in the purple pants outfit."

Devlin nodded to McKee and the other lab technicians. They turned and headed for the purple hunk of flesh in the main room.

"Is this . . . Is this important?" asked D.D.

"Yes," said Devlin.

"Well we don't have to run it if there's going to be any trouble! I mean, I don't know what we'd do about the money if the man who placed it never came back, but . . . We don't have to run it."

Devlin moved behind the nervous man to where he could read the typewritten message on a plain sheet of white paper.

> Dear Sir:
>   In accordance with the agreement signified by Job Order 4017, run this ad as before, as soon as possible. The cash payment has been made. Let the words be red.

Beneath the letter was a felt tip, black inked "R."

"I wonder if that 'red' is supposed to be some kind of pun or something," said D.D. "He never paid for colored ink."

"What do you think of the signature, Ken?" asked Devlin.

"Could be the most we've got yet. If he handled it that much, maybe he left a print. Mr. Dugan, we'll need to fingerprint you and anyone who might have touched this. And get your blood types. He might have sweated on it."

"Of course, of course."

They all stared at what had been bought and paid for.

> And Behold, He that sits in the clouds, He that thrusts in his sickle to clean and harvest the earth shall not rest until his work is worked, yea, even till all the false prophets and betrayers have been taken before the heavenly throne. The Flock of the Lord shall be gathered and fed, and sheltered from the storm, from the first to the last. And even as the children of Levites were cleansed and shaved, that the children of Israel might be saved with them, so shall the children of the Flock be cleansed and saved and gathered, like grain for the harvest falls for the Reaper.

"Boy is he nuts!" said Urtz, whom Devlin had told about the Reaper.

"Well," rationalized D.D., attempting to justify his paper taking the ad which caused this disruption he didn't understand, "Baltimore is a very religious market.

"Look, Sergeant Rourke, we don't have to run the ad. I mean the publisher told me to cooperate with you on whatever you needed, just like he made me promise not to tell any of the news people about your interest. As if I'd talk to *them*: they think they run this paper!"

All the contingencies, all the possibilities Devlin had mulled over with his superiors, with the psychiatrist, with his own conscience rolled through his mind as he stood staring at the message from the Reaper. The Reaper killed the children between 2 and 17 days after the ad ran. Maybe the appearance of the ad started the Reaper's clock. Maybe it started when he mailed the letter. Maybe by delaying or even denying the ad they could stall or prevent a child's murder. Maybe they could do that and still catch the Reaper. Maybe the Reaper didn't give a damn about the ad or what they did with it. And if his secret theory was right . . .

"No," he said, "run it, same as before, nothing special. But hold it up a bit. Instead of tomorrow, run it . . ."

"The man would have been informed there might be a 24-to-48-hour delay after receipt of the ad copy."

"And he'll assume that if he mailed it in Baltimore, it got here today. So run it . . . day after tomorrow.

"I'm going to assign two police officers to you. They're here to handle any calls, any walk-ins you have regarding the ad. We should have done that before, but better late than never. I don't think you'll have any, but just in case. Detective McKee will bring them over in about an hour. Keep it quiet. No one is to know who you don't have to tell. Make up some cover story for them."

"Anything you say."

"I wish."

forty-four

The reports came back in two hours.

The lab report showed no unidentifiable prints on the paper. Perhaps the Reaper wore gloves. The scrawled "R" yielded nothing either. The letter and ad had been typed on an IBM Selectric typewriter. Such typewriters have a small ball impregnated with raised letters instead of the old-fashioned typewriter keys. The ball "element" was removable, a featherweight device interchangeable with every IBM Selectric typewriter in the world. It was possible that the police could find the correct typewriter, but if the Reaper had removed or switched the element, they would never know it.

Detective McKee had two plain-clothes officers taking ads at the *Star* counter. A back-up unit of two more plain clothes cops in an unmarked car parked within sight of the door.

The Biblical scholars and the psychiatrist were studying the latest Reaper message. The initial reaction from all of them was one of interest without insight.

Jackson Bricker called to tell Devlin the computer was digesting the Reaper's latest public notice.

Devlin leaned back in his chair and stared out into nothingness. Not quite nothingness, because for the first time since he'd been plunged into the Reaper madness, he knew where he was headed, and he had an idea of how to get there. The lab be damned, the surveillance be damned, the gumshoeing be damned, the psychiatrist be damned, the Biblical scholars be damned, the computer be damned, he knew where he wanted to go and nothing they could come up with would help him.

forty-five

Timing was the trickiest, deadliest factor.

He called his friend on the force, his buddy from the Task Force days who'd first told him about Tough Tony Cardozo. Devlin risked the phones being tapped: the person who'd get those reports would understand what they were doing soon enough.

"How can I find Cardozo this time of day?" Devlin asked, looking at his watch: 3 P.M.

"Are you crazy?" said his friend. "You want to see him, meet him?"

"That's right."

"Without a warrant and a SWAT team to help you serve it?"

"As quietly as possible."

"You are out of your mind. He'd rather rip a cop open with his bare hands than make a thousand bucks any day of the week."

"Can you help?"

"I'm not even going to ask why."

"You don't want to know and I wouldn't tell you."

His friend paused, then quietly said, "You're one guy I never figured to apply to Tough Tony for a place on the pad."

Devlin's voice grew cold. "Shame on you if you don't still figure that."

"Look, are you serious about this?"

"Dead serious."

"Don't use that word, it makes me crazy. I might be able to tell you where to look, but you gotta remember: for the Department, Cardozo doesn't exist. We don't have anybody keeping tabs on him unless they're nuts like me. Or unless they want to know where their next pay envelope is coming from. I *might* be able to jab it out of a guy who maybe it's not wise to let know that *I* know enough to jab him for this. Understand?"

"Yes."

"Is this a big thing, worth it?"

"I gotta say yes."

"Is this another of your gonzo seat-of-the-pants plays?"

"I wouldn't put it that way."

"You're out on a limb, right?"

Devlin didn't answer.

"I just hope I don't crawl out there with you and saw it off as I go. Hold on; this may take a couple minutes."

The phone line buzzed with that peculiar deadness of being on hold. Devlin watched the second hand sweep around the clock once, twice, three times. He wondered what games his friend was playing with what crooked cop, and what the cost would be. The phone clicked back to life.

"You might try Dockman's Laundry and Dry Cleaning about an hour from now. They don't know you're coming, and I can

keep a lid on that until then. But they're always nervous-type
people down there when Mr. C. is around, you understand?"

"I understand."

"Look, you know I'll help you if I can."

"You've done it all, all you can."

"Don't fuck up and get your ass shot off."

"Never happen."

He hoped.

forty-six

Devlin drove through the residential neighborhoods of
identical flat stone townhouses with their white polished
marble three-step stoops looking for a smile on the pedestrians' faces. It was too hot for humor. The only happiness he
found radiated from one home—a painted plaster bust of Elvis
Presley someone had enshrined in one of the townhouse
windows. Elvis's dead grin cheered Devlin not at all.

Dockman's Laundry and Dry Cleaners sat in the buffer zone
between the industrial harbor area and Baltimore's Little Italy,
a cramped two-story building penned in by large warehouses
on either side. Heavy security grates caged the smoked glass
windows, making it impossible to see into the building. Devlin
parked three blocks away and around a corner. A man who
looked too healthy to be a derelict despite his shabby clothes
watched him from a doorway across from the laundry as Devlin
made his way down the street. A third warehouse stood
opposite the laundry. Devlin saw a second figure watching him
from a third-story window in that building. A longshoreman
who whittled silently sat on a deserted building's stoop three
doors down from the laundry. The whittler paid more attention
to passing cars and pedestrians than to the block of wood in his
smooth hands. Devlin's blazer stuck to the back of his shirt. He
glanced at the cars along the hot, shadowy street. Even their

unlit headlights seemed to watch him as he walked closer, closer, closer to the laundry door.

He needed to ring to enter. The admission buzz was a long time coming.

It was even hotter inside the laundromat than in the street. None of the three blurry men waiting behind the counter looked like tailors. Sweat ran off their foreheads, trickling down towards their eyes. They fought the urge to blink. All had their hands out of sight behind the counter.

"What do you want?" asked the skinny one on the far right.

"Tell Tony he's got company he needs to see now," replied Devlin. He casually, slowly slipped out of his blazer and slung it over his shoulder. The men refused to react when they saw the gun clipped to his belt.

"Tony who?" asked the thin man.

"Tough Tony, your boss, asshole," said Devlin evenly. "Tell him a representative of civilization has business with him." The heat of the room would account for the stains spreading out from his armpits and down his back. The three men wouldn't know how much of that moisture came from nerves. "Go tell him now. This heat bores me."

The thin man stared back at Devlin, then lifted the telephone receiver from its cradle on the wall. He mumbled for a few seconds, then listened. One last grunt, then he hung up the phone and said, "You can come in."

"Lucky me," said Devlin. One of the other goons lifted a portion of the counter so Devlin could follow the thin man back through racks of neatly pressed garments, back through the pressing boards and sewing machines where real tailors busily plied their trade. The laundry had recently won a special cleaning contract from one of the major shipping firms, a contract the laundry had been underbid on by three other companies. A tailor pressed down on a huge industrial iron. Steam hissed. Boiling air tumbled across the crowded room to sting Devlin's flesh. He pretended not to notice. He followed the skinny man up a narrow flight of stairs in the back. The two men who'd guarded Cardozo the first time Devlin met him, waited at the top of the stairs. They relieved the detective of his gun, patted him down quickly but competently, then pointed him towards a heavy, closed wooden door. Devlin thought about knocking, but decided to ignore all decorum.

"I didn't fucking believe it," said Tough Tony Cardozo. He

stood behind a massive desk, his powerful squat body straining the buttons of his expensive shirt. His tie hung loose from the open collar. Devlin felt the comforting rush of cool air from a window-box air conditioner behind Tough tony. They were the only two persons in the room. "Did you lose the phone number we gave you, cop?"

"I couldn't be sure who'd get the message, and I decided you would be glad I didn't risk that."

"I would, would I?"

"Interesting phrase. Almost a palindrome. You wouldn't know what that means, but it's a word or phrase which can be read backwards the same as it reads forwards. Cambodian rulers loved palindromes. What you said doesn't quite make it, though."

"What the fuck is this? G.E. College Bowl? I got no time for word games from a fuckin' smart-ass cop. You got your job to do, now you come messing around here. I want to know why. If I don't like what I hear, Matella will be real mad at me for running his new pet through the steam-cleaning machine."

"Matella is the reason I'm here. Because he's kind of a palindrome, a forwards-backwards puzzle. And because of that, you're on the line."

"If you don't start talking American, you're going to learn to talk without any teeth."

"You know what Matella has me doing, and why, right?"

"The crazy killer thing. Sure, I know."

"You don't seem excited about helping out."

"I'm real fucking sorry his grandkid got cut. But that don't have anything to do with us. Nobody thinks he's slipping on account of it, so I figure it's one of those rough things in life. But he can push a problem too far sometimes. Tell him I said so. I don't give a fuck."

"You should, he put you here."

"I got here," Tony said. And he smiled.

"And you want to stay. So that means whatever Matella does in Baltimore puts you on the line."

"So? They know what Matella is doing. It ain't bad for business."

"It would be if he were stuck in the middle of it."

"You ain't got the balls or the brains to pin him anywhere, anytime, or anything."

"He might already be stuck, waiting for me to stick a label on him."

Tough Tony cocked his head.

"He's quite a mystery man. Moves around where he wants, when he wants. Sometimes with Randy or Kibler, sometimes without them. He could have been a lot of places a lot of different times. Done a lot of different things. And he's the kind of guy who'd like to . . . at least to have somebody know how good he is."

Cardozo smiled. "You gotta be crazy. I know where you're going thinking like that, and you gotta be crazy."

"I don't have to be, the Reaper is."

Cardozo laughed, a sharp, snort, guttural whoop. He started to say something, then laughed again. "You think . . . That old man, all he's done, getting his jollies off of penny ante . . ." The beer keg man laughed again.

"It's a strange world, and palindromes aren't the only crazy kind of thinking games around."

"So," said Cardozo after a final bout of laughter, "That's what you think."

"That's what I think might be solid . . . maybe."

"Just because."

"No. Just because I got something."

Cardozo cocked his head. "Maybe you'd like to tell me without I should have to pop off your kneecaps."

"Maybe I wouldn't. Maybe trying to change my mind would be the dumbest of all plays."

Baltimore's crime czar smiled. "But a fun time could be had by some. So what does all this thinking you've been doing have to do with me. You got the job from Matella."

"You're the one responsible for Baltimore. You're the company rep on the scene who can be charged with an error, who's supposed to be in command. I don't think the Commission or Council or whatever you call that little clique that put you and Matella where you are laughs at errors. They play pretty rough ball."

"So?"

"So there's an easy way for us to know. Here's a list of places, approximate times and dates. You got the contacts. Tell me if you can place Matella in two or more of those places. If you can rule him out, fine. If not . . ."

"If not, what makes you think I'll bring it back to you?"

"You don't dare handle a problem like this yourself. If you decide to let it slide or take me out, somewhere down the line it'll come out that you knew a nut was managing the firm, and you let it go on. If you try to handle him yourself, the Commission might think you're pulling a coup. You'll need me to convince them. You'll need official action."

"No way in hell we're going to let Matella walk into any prison where you could bargain with him or any nut house where you got doctors with them talking drugs. Even if he's bonkers, his mouth is connected to what's in his brain."

"There's a way we can cut a deal to make everybody happy. That's the key. Everybody happy on this one, or we all lose. But you lose the most."

"This kind of puts you out on the line."

Devlin smiled. "I'm already there."

"You know, cop," said Cardozo, "you're stupid, but you're not as stupid as I thought."

"You'll do it?"

"I got your list. You know where to find me. You know how to leave. Get out, before I suggest we talk a bit more about why you thought all this bullshit up."

forty-seven

As soon as he turned the corner off the street of the laundry, Devlin ran to a pay phone. The eyes of Tough Tony Cardozo could still be on him, but he didn't dare waste any seconds.

"Yeah?" said the gruff voice that answered Devlin's call.

"Find me Kibler," ordered the cop. And after the rerouting clicks, his "friend" came on the line.

"I don't have time to talk," said Devlin, "and you don't have any time to waste. Meet me right away. Same place as you made the delivery. Only don't bring Randy or any of the other goofballs. This is just you and me."

Devlin drove three blocks, then pulled to the curb. No

other car appeared. He changed from his running shoes to the ill-fitting but electronically equipped wing tips, checked to be sure the pen was in his jacket pocket. He hadn't dared wear a bug into the laundry. If Cardozo had people skillful enough to put a bug in Devlin's shoe, they were skillful enough to find another one hidden there. Such a discovery would have doomed Devlin. But at a meeting with Kibler, he might still get away with it.

The heat and humidity reflecting off the windless bay pressed down on Devlin as he waited for Kibler. He'd been only 15 minutes away when he called. His shoe change took only two minutes. Kibler arrived 10 minutes after the policeman.

"The thing of it is, Joe," Devlin explained, sipping from the cup of Coco-Cola Kibler had brought him (Devlin wondered if that present had been a subtle tease), "I've got a delicate problem. One that only you can help me with, so I'm hoping we can work out the details today."

"I always do what I can to help a friend," smiled Joe. "Like when you called and wanted to meet me, I said maybe he needs something again. So I stopped at the burger palace and bought a couple of cold cokes, brought them along because I know you must get awful thirsty pounding the streets and all. It's hot as hell out here."

"Sure is. See, the thing of it is, Joe, I've got this . . . oh, I don't know, kind of a wild idea. But it's itching me, driving me nuts, and I can't keep going if I don't get it scratched. Mr. Matella, he wants you to help me on this, like he wanted you to help me when you brought me the other coke, the two ounces which, by the way, were excellent, excellent."

Devlin paused, but Joe only smiled.

"See what it is," continued Devlin, "I have to eliminate all suspects. And this one idea I got, silly as it seems, says Matella just might be the Reaper."

Kibler dropped his coke. "What the hell are you talking about?"

"It's logical, psychiatrically sound," continued Devlin. "He puts me out to hunt him down. Half a dozen plausible psychological explanations. Plus there's this scrap of information, not really a clue, that I've got running around in my head. No need to bother you with it."

"Friend," said Kibler, "before I met you I thought there was only one madman in my life."

"That may still be true, but he may be a great deal closer to you than you'd imagined."

Kibler stared across the bay to Fort McHenry for a full minute. "You didn't tell me this to give me nightmares," he said at last. "You want something from me."

"That's right."

"What?"

"Here's a sheet of times and dates, the dates and places of all the Reaper murders. I want you to find out where Matella was on those dates. If they coincide, we'll figure out what to do."

"Now I know you're crazy. Why would I betray him like that? Especially for such a flimsy excuse as your logic and your unshared information? I'm not crazy too."

"No," announced Devlin, all the easy lilt gone from his tone as he picked up the heaviest hammer he had, "you're not crazy—you're caught.

"By me. You gave me cocaine in an attempt to bribe me. You did so on orders from Salvatore Matella, but that makes little difference unless we're talking conspiracy. I've got you. I taped that transaction. Plus," he lied, "I have our touching exchange scene on film, video surveillance. I've got Randy and that gunsel chauffeur too, if I want them. And all the legal groundwork laid. And all in the hands of some heavy law-enforcement types who'll come after you with an army bigger than Matella's if I should happen to meet with any kind of an accident. They'll hit you with murder too.

"And even if the charges don't stick, how happy will Matella be with you? You blew it, you got caught in a simple, straightforward, legal police trap. How could he trust you? How much could anyone in the Mob trust you? Alive.

"So you see, *Buddy*, any way you look at it, you're in a bit of a tight.

"I don't want your ass. I don't want your boss—unless he's who I think he might be. In that case, we both want him put down. Everybody does. You play with me, you help me nail him or exonerate him, and I'll let you walk. If not, you're now in the center with me."

Kibler stared at the hard police detective in front of him.

"I believe you mean it, buddy. I believe you think all of that is real." The errand boy of organized crime looked out over the

Bay. He glanced at the sheet of paper Devlin passed to him. Almost absentmindedly he folded it, stuck it in the inside pocket of his lightweight suit. He turned back to Devlin. "But the only thing you said that makes any sense to me is that I can walk. And walk away I shall." He strolled past Devlin's Camaro to the Ford with rental car plates which had brought him. Before he slid behind the wheel and drove away, he patted his pocket.

Devlin watched the Ford roll away. *I might have done it,* he thought. *I just might have done it.*

He'd planted a seed in both Cardozo and Kibler. If they told Matella, and if Matella/Reaper decided to kill him, his two chief aides would worry and wonder, maybe intercede. That worked even if Matella were not the Reaper, but merely angry and vindictive.

Kibler hadn't tumbled any further into trouble for the tape recorder. Devlin knew his case was shaky on the basis of the previous tape, but Kibler probably couldn't reconstruct the conversation well enough to feel secure. Plus the bluff about the photographs. That barb must have sunk in. Now Kibler was out on a fine line with almost nowhere to go. If Matella were the Reaper, or got angry at him for being sloppy and getting taped, Matella might kill Kibler. Kibler would think twice about going to him with the truth. And if he did anything but risk a full confession, he was forced to conceal Devlin's play and his own predicament. That in itself became treachery. And that gave Devlin yet another hook into Call-Me-Joe Kibler.

If. If everyone is as logical as me, thought Devlin. As thirsty as he was, he didn't want the few remaining ice cubes from Kibler's second Coke gift. He looked around the vacant lot, the run down buildings. Not a garbage can in sight. The heat lay on top of the Bay in front of him like a shimmering glass mirror. He rattled the ice in the cup. Suddenly he felt victorious. He was moving, maybe even scoring. Perhaps, just perhaps, he was winning. His hand crumpled the cup into a ball. He glanced to his left, he glanced to his right. He squinted out to the Bay. The nod, the wind-up, the pitch—a wild curve that veered hard to his left, then plummeted straight down, bouncing off the rip rap far short and far wide of where it should have gone.

I still can't make the Orioles, he thought.

forty-eight

"I can't see you tonight," Devlin told Barbara when he phoned her from his office.

"Are you sure?"

"I'm sure. And do me a favor?"

"I hope it's fun."

"It's probably unnecessary. Stay in your hotel, don't talk to strangers, and lock your door."

"I love it when you're reassuring."

"Don't worry."

"That's what they all say, then they go and fuck up. Don't be one of them, Devlin. Call me when you can, but please be around to call me."

"Have I ever let you down?"

He didn't even make it home. He saw Randy leaning on his Camaro in the municipal parking lot as soon as he walked out of Headquarters. The boldness of the move startled him. He had no idea what it meant, but he wanted to back himself up as much as possible. He could always bust Randy, right there in front of Headquarters. An army of fellow officers was but a whistle away. But . . . But there were too many buts. He joined a group of uniformed officers he knew who were walking his general direction. He made a point of checking the time and date with them, and of nodding toward "that big fellow sitting on my car, a guy named Randy—faggy name, isn't it? Randy's a New Yorker involved on a case. Shady guy the Feds have their eye on. He probably wants to meet with me." With that implanted in his fellow cops' minds, he felt he at least had a bargaining chip or someone who would remember him after he was gone. He walked to his car.

"The van is waiting around the corner, cop," said Randy. "You're going for a ride."

"Anywhere with you, handsome," purred Devlin. "As long as it's round trip."

"That depends on the ticket you've bought."

They took him to the same office in the same house in the same van wearing the same hood. The drapes were closed again, so he had the same limited view. Matella sat behind the same desk. Kibler sat on a corner of it, smiling his same sad smile. Devlin sat in a new chair. Outside he heard full-throated dogs bark at each other, then fall silent. He glanced at Kibler, who nodded to the piece of paper Devlin had given him. It lay before Matella.

"A fellow should always play the best game around," explained Call-Me-Joe almost apologetically. "And he should always play straight with the team he makes."

Devlin felt the fire-green eyes of Matella pulling at him. The detective slowly turned his own gaze to meet them. Their grim stares locked and held. Until Matella laughed.

"An extraordinary deduction!" exclaimed Matella, humor dancing behind the fire in his eyes. "What led you to it? The mere hypothesis of a powerful man slipping into homicidal megalomania then somehow developing a death-wish syndrome, and loosing a weapon of his own creation to bring about his own destruction? A fantastic, incredibly imaginative idea! One with sound psychological precepts, or so you inferred from Dr. Weis in your late night phone conversation."

So they did have the doctor's line tapped, thought Devlin. *Or did the doctor belong to them too?*

"Wasn't all that a rather bold leap to make purely on speculative deduction? Perhaps you were engaging in a bit of wishful thinking, eh?"

Now or never, thought Devlin. *If I've missed, if I'm only wrong, then at least I have some defense. And if I've hit home, Kibler has another bit of evidence supporting me. Maybe I can woo him to my side after all. Or at least start him scheming to destroy Matella after . . .* Devlin broke his chain of thought, told them about the whore's "cloud" references, about the links he'd made from it to Matella's hair.

"An imaginative deduction," said Matella. "A clever, courageous move following through. I like that. The attempt shows your reputation is well-founded and that you have not been idle. Merely incorrect."

The door opened behind him, and Devlin wondered if

Matella used a foot button to summon someone. An angry slab
of flesh stomped past his left side. Tough Tony Cardozo looked
down at Devlin with a lifetime of rage, but his words were
clear, crisp and void of emotion.

"Like you told me, Mr. Matella, I checked out where you
was during the times on the list he gave Kibler."

Gave Kibler? What does that mean? thought Devlin as
Cardozo cleared his throat. That the only assistant to report
treachery to his boss had been Kibler? That Cardozo had not
told Matella he too had been approached? If that were true,
then Devlin had a lever against Cardozo. And Cardozo thus
had one more reason to destroy Devlin.

"Two of the times are blank and you won't fill them in for me.
Two other times, you was in the same city as when a hit was
made. One was the New York whore killing, which is where
you live. You left town before the kid got it. The other time
was the Kansas City kid killing. You were there briefly,
overnight the night before, and left that next evening. So you
could have killed only 4 of the 16, whereas if you was the
Reaper, you would have killed them all. Like you said, for
three of those occasions, we can give Rourke hotels and
airlines he can check. He could find people who saw you who's
got no reason to lie."

"So you see, Detective Rourke," said the *consigliere tu
consiglieri*, "I cannot be the Reaper. But at least you are
working. I applaud that, and I forgive your misguided efforts—
including your childish attempt to blackmail Mr. Kibler. That
was a shameful thing to do to a man so nice. And ineffective.
You weren't the only one taping those sessions. Our tape shows
you do not have sufficient evidence to get an indictment, let
alone a conviction. That is without addressing the interesting
question of entrapment on your part. As for your alleged
photographs, Mr. Cardozo assures me that the area was
completely secure and free of any outsiders, especially policemen with cameras. And Mr. Cardozo is an eminently trust-
worthy, capable man."

Cardozo didn't blink.

"Now as much as I've enjoyed talking with you, you must be
on your way. You'll need your rest. Day after tomorrow, the
Reaper's ad appears. Don't look so surprised. We have one or
two friends at the *Star* whom I alerted to certain developments

in which I was interested. And you needn't worry. Your security from leaks on their part is also part of Mr. Cardozo's responsibilities. Good night."

Call-Me-Joe Kibler walked Devlin to the van. The detective felt terrible. He'd tried a play, and not only had he been wrong, he'd executed it ineptly. It was little consolation to know that there was one less likely suspect as the Reaper, for he did not doubt that if he pursued the packet of information handed him wordlessly by Cardozo, he would find an alibi for Matella. It was still less consolation to know that a new, puzzling link had been forged between Tough Tony and himself.

"Don't be upset, Buddy," consoled Joe before they put the hood over Devlin's eyes and drove him away. "I'm not mad. We're still pals. Mr. Matella, he still likes you. Hell, he admires your spunk. You showed a lot of flash even though you made a bad play and blew it." He paused while Randy roughly adjusted the hood. Through the blackness, Devlin heard Kibler say, "Just don't blow the whole ball game."

forty-nine

The first phone call was to the 24-hour Reaper number. Nothing had happened while Devlin had been out of touch. He closed his eyes, exhaling his relief. They'd let him out in an alley three blocks from Police Headquarters and his car. He'd walked to the nearest pay phone.

The second call went to Bequai's hotline. One of the clones answered. "Tell your boss our friend is still in Baltimore," ordered Devlin, "and that the house he's staying at has a couple of big dogs living there too."

The third call went to Barbara. "Hey," he said, "Guess what? I'm not dead."

After he calmed her, soothed her, even teased her a bit, she
agreed to let him sleep alone. He hung up. He noticed his
hand in front of his face as he lifted it off the black receiver. His
hand. Shaking.

fifty

Devlin was on his way to a Saturday afternoon meeting with
the group of Biblical scholars, thinking about the current news
of another fugitive mass murderer, Dr. Josef Mengele, wanted
for the systematic murder of 400,000 men, women and
children at Auschwitz. Simon Wiesenthal, the Nazi hunter,
had posted a $50,000 reward for information leading to the
apprehension of the man known to millions of branded victims
as The Angel of Death. The electronic squawking of Baltimore's police radio on the seat beside him jerked Devlin's
concentration from the jungles of Paraguay to the steamy
streets outside his moving car where another mass murderer
with a heavenly name hid from those who would punish his
sanctified slaughter. On that quiet, overcast August Saturday
in Baltimore, Maryland, U.S.A., a strange man had been
reported lurking in the vicinity of the last-known whereabouts
of a just-reported lost child. One foot patrol officer was on the
scene with the mother. The child had been out of sight for only
15 to 20 minutes. He'd been playing in the park, his mother
reading on the bench. When she looked up, he'd been gone.
He was bound to turn up. Millions of children disappear like
that every day all over America, then reappear in the darndest
places, unharmed. Why, his mother, concerned as she was,
probably would have found him without incident, but she
happened to mention it to a passing policeman, who, because
Devlin had so arranged, immediately radioed in the report of a
missing child. Probably routine. Nothing to get excited about.
After all, The Reaper's second ad wasn't even scheduled to
appear until the next morning.

And yet.

And yet.

Devlin grabbed the hand-held radio from the seat. He was six blocks away from the park, probably as close as any other unit. He contacted the central dispatcher as he jerked the car to the curb.

He ordered the officer on the scene to stay with the mother until he arrived.

He ordered every available backup unit to the scene, leaving it to the dispatcher to spread them out in a net surrounding the park. The officers would detain any male and child, or any single male. All officers who could be spared from the cordon were to search the park. Devlin ordered the dispatcher to alert Homicide.

He jammed the gearshift into reverse and whipped the unmarked sedan into a tight, crying-tires turn until he faced the direction he came. He slapped the magnetic blue light on top of the cruiser, hit the siren, and raced towards the park.

By now the mother was worried. She'd heard the radio calls. This lean detective bounded out of an undercover car after it screeched to a halt on the footpath. She heard other sirens wailing in the distance, closer, closer, closer, fear coming her way. Coming to where her little boy had been merely missing, was not presumed . . . Her throat tightened as she choked back her terror, her panic. The uniformed patrolman held her arm in a reassuring but tight grip. What was wrong with one missing little boy?

By now Devlin was infected with crisis urgency: "Please tell me exactly what your son looked like!"

"He's just a little boy!" she insisted. "Just a little boy. With brown hair and blue eyes and a T-shirt and jeans. He's just a little boy!"

"Where did you last see him?"

"He was playing . . ." She began to disorient. Devlin touched her hand, lightly. She looked into his blue eyes and started to chew her lip. She couldn't talk. But she could point, point to the center of the park, point toward the swan pond.

"Some kids told me they saw a strange man down there," said the uniformed cop. "I was going to check it out when she stopped me."

Most of the park was rolling hills. Tennis courts and basketball backboards lined the edges. Jogging paths looped through the rolling fields. All the open areas, like the grassy field where they stood, surrounded a three-block-sized, oblong swan pond that cut through the park, the only area with thick forestation. The public bathrooms were over there too. And isolated toolsheds. The trees rose proudly out of the lush green grass on that summer's day. Birds and butterflies flew into the foliage. Flew in, and vanished. If . . . if anything happened, if anything waited, it would be in the darkness of that small forest.

Devlin listened. Sirens filled the air. By now, the first units would be in position. Cordoning the area would take time. Perhaps too much time. He hated to do it, but it would be easier than interfering with the dispatcher's dispersal of arriving units.

"We can't wait for backup," he told the young officer holding his almost hysterical charge. "You take her, and work your way through the woods from the left side of the pond. I'll do the same from the right. Most of the buildings are on my side. Keep a hold of her, radio a backup to you as you move. Doing something will help keep her calm. Now go."

He didn't wait to see if his orders were followed. He reached the swan pond in thirty seconds, panting only slightly from his run. He passed a mother walking a carriage, two senior citizens jogging, a doddering old man shuffling along with a cane who was far, far to decrepit to be of any danger to anyone. He jogged around the edge of the swan pond. Those elegant white birds looked at him, but when he threw no crumbs they lost interest.

He heard no sounds from the park bathroom. The woods around him hummed with the barest whisper of a wind, the quietest of sighs as leaves caressed leaves. Occasionally laughter and the *pong!* of a tennis ball drifted to him from the distant clay courts, or a bird whistled, an insect chirped. But no sounds came from within the two redwood stained shacks marked "MALE" and "FEMALE."

Logic and custom sent him to the men's room first. He jumped in, let his eyes adjust to the light. The smell of disinfectant and stale urine ruined the green foliage aroma he'd just left. The bathroom seemed deserted, but he had to be sure. He pushed open first one, then the other stall: empty.

Next he did the same to the women's room, carefully holding his badge before him like a vampire hunter brandishing his protective crucifix in a graveyard. Devlin had no time for any properly outraged woman whose privacy he'd invaded like a dangerous pervert. The badge was meant to forestall such a problem, but it wasn't needed. That small room, with its three dirty stalls, was empty too.

Where could they be? thought Devlin as he moved through the woods. Already he was thinking of a "they," not just a he. Not just a small, lost little boy. But a they. A victim and a Reaper. *A live victim*, he kept insisting to himself. *We're in time. He's still alive. Say it enough and it'll be so.*

The edge of the forest waited just ahead, on the other side of the hill. But between Devlin and that edge was a decrepit rain shelter. Little more than a lean-to with a back wall and a sloping roof. This shelter sat on the highest point in the park, a nice view for looking at the city. The shelter waited at the edge of the woods, its board back to Devlin now 50, now 45 feet away. He remembered there was a picnic table in the shelter, an ordinary heavy wooden picnic table, slabs of wood with cracks between the planks where spilled lemonade would trickle through to splash on the legs of careless picnickers. He remembered too how one of Baltimore's many Protestant churches used the lean-to as the rally point for their Easter sunrise service. He'd seen the church service one Easter when he'd been a patrolman briefly assigned to the park beat. Devlin was not religious, not in the denominational sense of the word. If pushed, he labeled himself a karma agnostic, or if he were feeling flip, a druid. Yet he found something divinely beautiful in a white-robed minister offering ritual as he stood in that lean-to, the fiery sun coming up behind him in the trees, Communion chalice held high in his hand, the cup of red, red wine glistening with the morning rays above the picnic table, the simple picnic table draped in a virgin white altar cloth.

The voice whispered through the trees to him when he was but 30 feet from the lean-to. He stopped, tried to make out the words, but he couldn't. He turned off his radio, cutting his link to the outside world, not daring to let its crackling announce his presence or drown out the sounds he strained to hear. Through the limbs, through the leaves and bushes, he saw the back of the lean-to. From this angle he'd normally be able to see the picnic table. But this was not a normal day. A battered piece of . . . cardboard, it looked like cardboard, leaned against the open side of the lean-to forming another wall.

Perhaps it was an old refrigerator box dragged there by kids. Kids love to play with old refrigerator boxes; they make great forts. And when a box is too battered to serve on its own anymore, when the flat cardboard is leaned up against an opening—by kids—it makes a nifty wall, further insuring the great and treasured intimate privacy to house children and their wild imaginations. Beyond a doubt, kids placed that cardboard wall there. Children. Sweet, innocent, laughing children.

But it was no child's voice which drifted towards Devlin. The voice was strange: insistent, intense, not quite decipherable, with an eerie resonance. The words rolled to Devlin with a forceful, compelling cadence. He quickened his pace while trying to move even more silently. He now used only his left hand to part the underbrush. His right hand rested on his gun butt.

Fifteen feet away, almost free of the trees, he understood the words. A hissing voice, strained tones, urging, arguing, demanding:

All the sinner show have sinned, yea, the righteous who have fallen, all the lambs and the Children of God shall stand before the throne of eternity on Judgement Day, there to . . ."

Devlin raced through the trees. A branch pulled his radio from his pocket, but he ran. A rose bush tore across his thigh with bloody thorns, but he ran. He didn't duck a thick batch of leaves in time and it hit him in the mouth, but he ran. He ran and his gun was in his hand. He didn't hear the words, he only heard the voice, and his own panting, gasping urgency.

He broke free of the woods. The voice still intoned from behind the cardboard wall three steps away. Devlin brought his gun to bear in front of him, a two-handed grip for absolute accuracy, tight shooting with selective targets grouped dangerously close. One long left step. One short right step. One long left step, his right foot swinging up hard, hitting the cardboard crashing it even as he screamed wordlessly at the top of his lungs, bursting through the space between the rear wall and the front post, the cardboard crashing down in front of him, bursting through with gun levelled ready to send its six slugs into human flesh, bursting through and seeing the little boy with brown hair and a T-shirt and blue jeans scurry backwards from the picnic bench, his blue eyes wide with fright as a real monster crashed into his newly discovered, private hiding place, bursting through with a roar seconds before the child himself screamed, "Mommy! Mommy! Mommy!" at the top of his young and powerful lungs, bursting through moments before the mother cried out her answer as she ran up the hill in time to see a brutality-crazed cop with his snubnose .38 levelled square at her little darling. Who stood alone under the rain shelter.

But before the mother and the young uniformed cop and the two other patrolman charged up that hill where sunrise service is held each Easter (weather permitting), before that, Devlin realized the target he'd zeroed, realized as he whirled, looking for danger, looking for the demonic voice. His gunsights followed the rain-washed planks of the picnic table, followed them up to the small black box, the tiny Japanese transistor radio the little boy had carried for weeks, ever since Grandma sent it to him. The box didn't make cartoons or funny pictures like TV, but it was wondrous just the same. The boy's only trouble was understanding how to work the station dial to find something he liked. That morning, he'd found only one thing that wasn't loud music: The man who lived in his little box that morning sounded like the guy in the black robes at Sunday school.

fifty-one

"You better sit down for this part, Sergeant," cautioned the young policeman as Devlin paced back and forth in front of three cruisers idling at the park entrance.

"Why? What's worse? What could go wrong after me drawing down on a six-year-old I'm supposed to be saving? After calling out the riot squad for nothing? After scaring a mother and child to death?"

"We found the strange acting man the other kids reported. He was hiding in the bushes at the opposite end of the park."

"Who is he? Where have we got him? Take . . ."

"That's the part you're not going to like."

"What do you mean?"

"The guy is Liam McKinnon."

"Who?"

"The Duck, Sir. Sgt. McKinnon."

"Oh my God."

"No, Sir. The Duck."

"What the fuck is he doing here?!"

"He says he's working on special assignment for you."

"Oh my God."

"He was in plain clothes when we found him. The guys were a bit excited and didn't listen to him. Not many of them have ever seen the Duck out of uniform. They didn't recognize him, and went nuts when they found that cannon he carries. Then they found his badge."

"Oh . . . *shit!*"

"Sergeant? What should we do with the Duck?"

"Shoot him."

"What?"

"Shoot the son of a bitch! It should have been done a long time ago. Mercy killing. Hell, justifiable homicide! He's a walking fucking crime. Shoot him!"

"Sergeant . . ."

"I'll shoot the scum bag myself!"

"Sergeant! He's a police officer!"

Devlin stopped, his rage spent. He kicked a beer can standing not far from a full trash barrel. He'd assumed someone else had made a bad shot with an empty can. He was wrong. A beer-rainwater mixture sloshed out the tab opening to soak his running shoe.

"Tell the Duck to get the hell out of here."

"Yes, Sergeant!"

fifty-two

Jeff Stern's call came as Devlin shuffled back into the Homicide squad room after spending two hours fudging the truth as he explained to the Deputy Commissioner and the Lieutenant how one police officer almost shot a lost child while another police officer was arrested as a suspicious character. Devlin picked up his ringing phone without thinking. Stern's sputtering curses roared over the line before the detective could even say hello. The angry denuciation ended with Stern hanging up before Devlin could think of anything to say:

"I heard all about your escapade today, Sergeant Rourke. I just sent two hysterical parents home with their traumatized child. You're one hell of a tough cop. From gunning down an ignorant woman who wanted to surrender to almost blowing away a six-year-old kid for playing his radio in the park. You'll stamp out crime if it kills all of us, won't you, you asshole? Well you won't get away with this one. I'll drag you before every board of review, every court I can find. I'll run you out of the Department once and for all! You're rabid! I might even see you behind bars or in a padded cell. This is one time justice won't be fucked over by your shit-covered badge!"

fifty-three

Devlin went home that night sure that he'd done nothing to save an innocent child from death or his own ass from any one of a dozen deadly fates. Although the D.C., his Captain, and all his fellow officers understood the whys of his blunder, the error gave them all pause, second thoughts about his abilities, his soundness. The Lieutenant had said nothing, absolutely nothing, and his silence was more effective a condemnation than any speech he could have made. Tomorrow morning's *Star* would feature the story somewhere inside its thick Sunday edition. Devlin worked with the public-affairs officer to handle the newspaper reporters—including Devlin's friend Gary Ebbenhouse—and the television stations that had been called by Stern (who wanted to be sure Devlin's actions received "complete coverage"). The policemen managed to convey a Department embarrassed at a routine surveillance operation that had been compounded and confused by a routine lost child report. Drugs were implied, but no further comment on the nature of the surveillance was made. The reporters didn't know the truth, that an extraordinary event for extraordinary reasons had taken place in a quiet Baltimore park. Devlin didn't want them to know, for if the story got the wrong kind of play, the Reaper might realize he was in danger. Devlin was sure they'd fooled the reporters, or at least stymied them. But he saw Gary Ebbenhouse staring at him in disgusted disbelief when the question and answer session was over.

The story ran just before the sports report on the 7 o'clock TV news. Devlin saw himself stammering before the camera. He looked, sounded and acted like a fool caught with his pants down: "I guess I overreacted." What a hell of a line, he thought.

He shuffled through the stack of envelopes he pulled from

his mailbox. He glanced at the envelopes from the gas and telephone company, tossed them unopened to the pile on his desk. A letter from New York which looked like an offer to buy life insurance followed their flight path. The company's timing was good, but he had no one in mind as a beneficiary. A solicitation envelope from The Little Sister of Charity of the Desert sailed unopened towards the garbage can, slapped instead to the floor beside the desk. The last envelope puzzled him until he saw the return address: Dockside Laundry. He carefully opened the green paper envelope and took out the bill stamped "DUE." The dollar amount was blank.

"Oh, that's real cute," he said to no one because no one was in his apartment.

He tried to shower the day away, but all that happened was his body emerged cleaner than before. He dried off, knowing the dirty humidity in Baltimore's industrial air would turn his flesh clammy and greasy within too few minutes. He dressed, walked to his stash, then thought better of it: never do drugs or booze when you're down, to bring you up. That's how alcoholics and junkies are made. He put his stash away.

The long cord let him take his old black dial phone to the couch. Barbara answered a minute later.

"Hello?"

"Did you ever watch your ship sink?"

"I'm glad to hear you still survive."

"I'm glad one of us is sure."

"Why don't you come over to my hotel? I'll have room service bring us up dinner. Spend a little of that Texas money. We'll probably be in no shape to go out anyway."

"I'll probably be lousy. Company, I mean."

"We can talk about that."

"I might be too tired to talk."

"There are other things."

"I suppose I might as well."

"Your enthusiasm frightens me."

"I'm sorry."

"I'm not. How soon can you get here?"

"Half an hour, bit more."

"I'll be ready."

"Great," he said flatly after she hung up.

He sat quietly on the couch for five minutes, forcing himself to listen only to the hum of the air conditioner. He called the dispatcher with Barbara's number, and in effect told the entire police department he was going to a hotel room to get laid. He straightened his shirt, made sure his gun was securely clipped to his belt, and picked up a light sportcoat to cover that token of his profession. He turned off his air conditioner. Barbara's room was bound to be cooler, more bearable than his apartment. He fetched his shaving razor and toothbrush from the bathroom, put them in a paper sack with the index cards and other police paraphernalia he carried with him. One never knew when one might get an invitation to spend the night. He glanced around the apartment to be sure he'd forgotten nothing, then left.

And then came back again. He went to his stash, cut out a couple grams of cocaine and shook them into a plastic baggie. The idea of seeing Barbara lifted the rock crushing down on him just enough to let a glimmer of sunshine cut into his darkness.

And it was such good coke.

fifty-four

The Reaper ad burned out to Devlin from Page B-7 of the morning *Star*. The ad seemed more real in print than it had on paper. The ads surrounding it sold cars, summer suits and sundry toilet products, and still made no sense to Devlin or the men he met with that afternoon.

"I'm afraid that for now, the only answers are in Heaven," apologized Rabbi Cohn. The priest, the Methodist bishop, and the professor from John Hopkins University nodded their concurrence with their colleague as they sat in the thick, musty study of the Jesuit priest. The priest had a Sunday afternoon Mass scheduled in a few hours. He'd worn his sacred vestments to this meeting to be sure he wouldn't lose time dressing when secular matters were concluded—and maybe because he hoped such reverent trappings might invoke the powers of God where the strength of men had failed.

"The verse references come from throughout the Bible, with a heavy emphasis on Revelations," said the priest. "They imply he considers himself a chosen man of destiny. But also that this destiny keeps shifting. Perhaps he sees himself as several divine beings at once. He is a chosen messenger, a quasi-divine prophet, perhaps the Triad—Father, Son and Holy Ghost rolled into one. But we can find no clue to predict his pattern of behavior, other than to guess it will, God help us, be consistent with his past."

"I agree," said Dr. Weis who'd flown to Baltimore as soon as Devlin called him about the second ad. "I also agree with your alert to the playgrounds, nurseries, pre-schools and day-care centers, the amusement parks. And I agree with your attempts to keep the whole thing quiet. Aside from the obvious perils of a panic situation, we don't want to frighten him into either extreme caution or some rash act, say a multiplicity of murders to go out in a flourish as the "Forces of Evil"—you and other policemen, anyone who is chasing him—close in."

"One thought that occurred to me," ventured the Methodist minister, "is perhaps having us compose a similar Biblical ad directed at the Reaper, challenging him on that level, perhaps drawing him out somehow."

"I'd considered that too, Father. . . . Oops, I'm sorry, Reverend," apologized Devlin. "The collars get me confused. Eventually I rejected the notion. If we challenge him, he might explode, feel forced to prove himself in a spectacularly bloody way. We might scare him off or merely tip him to the fact that somebody undivine is onto his game. Then there's always the possibility that we'll have no effect at all. Maybe he won't even see the fake ad. He's gathered all the news he needs from the *Star*.

"Dr. Weis," said Devlin, "there's something I'd like you to try. The Reaper moves around a great deal, but he must have a base, some city he calls home. Maybe a city in which he's also killed. To me, Chicago sounds probable, because that's where he first killed. True, he might have gotten the urge while under the strain of unfamiliar environment, but this guy seems too much in control to let a thing like a strange city throw him. If he's got a base, a home, we might get lucky. Maybe he didn't always accept his madness, maybe at some point he sought professional help. I know there's a doctor-patient relationship, but I think we've got to try to push it, bend it a bit. I want you to work with the Department psychologist. Start in Chicago, and then work forward through the other eight cities chronologically, hitting all the psychiatrists, psychologists. Try and get the doctors in those towns to help you. You can tell them everything, as long as they keep it quiet. If they know a child's life is on the line, maybe they'll open up, at least to another professional. You know what we're looking for: a male with religious mania and a potential for violence."

"That sounds like one of the Crusaders," said the academician. The two Christian clerics were not amused.

"Stress that our guy would be mobile, too," added Devlin. "That's the big thing that's always bothered me about this: How is the Reaper so mobile?"

"And I can't come up with any answers," Devlin told Barbara as they lay in the darkness of his bedroom that night. "He could be a truck driver, I suppose, something like that. But then how does he find and stalk his victims? The whores are easy, but what about the kids? Where does a truck driver meet kids?"

Barbara had no answer, so she pressed her cheek harder against his chest to reassure him that she cared. She was half asleep, half listening, half smiling.

Devlin slept only half that night.

fifty-five

"We're having trouble," Bequai admitted the next morning when Devlin answered his cryptically-worded, through-Cowan-routed message to call. "We have to approach the houses we've identified as potential sites on a covert basis. Since we're using agents from outside the Baltimore area, and using them without the knowledge or cooperation of the local field office, we've got some hellacious logistical problems. We're bringing most of the guys up from D.C. Trusted guys. Clones, if you will, but good clones. They'll do a careful job, but it's not easy to see the inside of a rich man's home without an invitation, and black-bag jobs are hard since everybody these days worries about burglars. We'll need more time."

"That doesn't bother me right now. Oh, by the way, there's a friend of mine: Jack Mitchell. Works in the Department's special section on white-collar and organized crime. You owe him a couple big favors. Let him know and keep him under your wing. He may need you someday."

"Can I ask either of you how I incurred this debt?"

"Honorably, but neither of us will explain."

"Look, Rourke, this is getting old: One minute you've got me frantically sifting through the Baltimore area bar association looking for lawyers who own a home that fits an extremely vague description: library, French windows, circular driveway, country-sounding, church bells nearby and dogs. The next minute you tell me you're not bothered by a lack of results in this. I'm beginning to wonder where your heart lies."

"In my chest behind my badge, still beating, which is how I want to keep it."

"If you won't tell me what we're doing, could you at least give me a little something more to go on?"

Devlin gave the FBI agent the license numbers of all the vehicles he'd seen used by Matella's men. The city cop believed the information useless, but he didn't tell the Bureau man that, and giving him the chore of running down the numbers got him off Devlin's back.

That night Devlin left Police Headquarters at 8. None of the double-checking of reports, none of the patrols, none of the calls the psychiatric teams were making had panned out. He felt that the only thing he was closer to was defeat. And death.

fifty-six

"Not sleeping doesn't help," Barbara noted after she woke at 4 A.M., listened for a moment in the air conditioner-humming darkness, then rolled over and by the light shining in from 29th Street saw the man beside her staring at the ceiling. "In fact, it hurts. When you're tired, you have less ability to handle the problem. You can't sleep because the problem keeps you awake. If you don't sleep, it will be harder to solve the problem. If you don't solve the problem, you won't be able to sleep. Shitty circle. I've gone round it before."

"I don't mean to sound cruel, but I wish it were you there now instead of me."

"Me too."

"This just isn't me," he said, too tired to protect himself from the consequences of honest emotion. "My life is upside down. Normally this . . ." He waved his hand in the dimly lit bedroom. ". . . this is what I don't have going for me."

"What do you mean?"

"Everybody's got somewhere where they're in synch, where they're the best they can be and damn good at it. A . . . a talent, if you will.

"Me, I'm a great homicide cop. It's like God created murder just so I could chase killers. When I'm on a case, when I'm in the street . . . it all clicks for me, it all happens. Even on the hard ones . . . I bust through like I was born for it.

"But this . . . I've never been good at it, never done well."

"Done well at what?" she asked.

"You. Women. People. Hell, if it's got to do with a case, I can walk into a room of beauties and beasts, cool and clever, do my thing and shine like a star. But if it's just for *me*, if it's just me and not my badge . . . I burn out like a meteor, crash, roll into the room like a dull hunk of dead rock."

"Don't be so sure," she said. "Even the great Detective Devlin can be wrong."

"Not about this."

"Why not?"

He couldn't respond, which to him proved his point.

"You think you're a flop 'relating to people'?"

"No," he said, "just not much better at it than I was in high school."

"Especially with women," she finished for him. Then smiled. "So why am I here?"

"That's what's so funny, so upside down. I should be finding my luck in the street instead of in here."

"Want to trade?"

"I refuse to answer that question on all grounds."

"Maybe your luck is changing."

He felt Matella's green eyes touch him through the darkness, shuddered. "I hope not."

"Hey!" she called.

"Oh no," he said, "nothing personal, I . . . There, see what I mean?"

She laughed, shook her head. Kissed his cheek. "Maybe your luck isn't lost or backwards. Maybe it's just realigning itself. Maybe it's just now coming into its own."

"I hope so. I wish I knew."

"Then it wouldn't be any fun, would it?"

He shook his head, and she didn't understand why that idea seemed surreal.

"Maybe when this is all over you can go away somewhere," she said. "Take some time off to sort it all out. Maybe it will even be okay and 'unthreatening' for both of us if I go too. God knows I could use one, a real vacation instead of just shuffling my body from place to place. The last vacation I had was when Jimmy, his father, and I flew to the Bahamas the February before . . . before vacations became impossible. . . . Would you like to go on a trip with me, Sergeant Rourke? Hmm? If you know it's a no strings package?"

"Yeah. Maybe. If I can."

"That's what I like about you. Always a firm answer."

"Sometimes you can't give a firm answer."

"Mmm. Well, I'll settle for what I can get. But one thing: if we go on vacation, you can't bring that new briefcase I bought

you today. That's strictly for work. Strictly! Did you like it? I
know you said you did, but did you really, *really* like it?"

"I . . ." Devlin paused, leary about applying the word
even to something as grand and yet as still safe as the hand-
tooled, military dispatch style leather briefcase she'd surprised
him with at dinner. "I . . . loved it."

"Really?"

"Really."

"You don't know how glad that makes me. I know you feel
awkward about accepting a gift from me, and I know you are
appalled because you think it was expensive. It was. Fright-
fully expensive. But you needed something, a gift to perk your
spirits. I know you're not a briefcase person, but you need
something better than your pockets to carry all those index
cards and envelopes and reports and the radio gizmo and other
stuff. That'll hold a ton and besides, it's *so* classy! Just like you.
I almost had them engrave your initials on the outside like a
fancy lawyer. . . ."

"Ech."

"I know. 'D.R.' Sounds like a lightweight corporate vice
president in charge of B.S. So I settled for your name etched
in gold under the flap. But that's okay, isn't it? And I didn't
even sign it 'from Barbara' so any other woman can see it
without you feeling awkward. Aren't I thoughtful?"

"You are," answered Devlin in absolute sincerity, "without a
doubt one of the most thoughtful, kind, considerate, terrific
people I've ever known."

"I try."

"Why don't you try to get some sleep now."

"I'm awake."

"So am I. But there's no reason for you to lose sleep too."

"I can keep you company."

"Mmmmn. If I talk, it'll be even harder to fall asleep."

"I could take your mind off your problems quietly."

Devlin stared at her in the dim light.

"Well, sort of quietly."

His gaze was noiseless.

"I could tire you out a bit more to make you sleepier."

"You're inexhaustible."

"I'm alive." She slowly drew her thigh up over his leg, over
his stirring groin, raising herself up on one elbow to look down
at him. "And I've got lots of lost time to make up for." She

nuzzled in his neck, then lightly nibbled his ear. "And you make me want you very . . ." she said as her lips kissed his left cheek. "Very . . ." she repeated as her lips kissed his right cheek then trailed back towards his mouth, tingling his flesh as he cupped her breasts, her nipples stiff in his suddenly alert hands. "Very much. . . ." she said, then she covered his mouth with hers as she straddled him.

fifty-seven

Something new bothered him as he drove to work the next morning, something that nagged at his consciousness just out of reach. The closer he came to work, the more the something nagged, the more he felt in his guts that whatever was lurking where he couldn't see it meant more to him than he dared hope. He glanced to the briefcase on the seat beside him. Such beautiful leather. He'd stuffed the index cards inside that fine leather, plus a comparison data file created for him by Jackson Bricker's computer, plus some pens and a notebook, and odds and ends. Giving him a briefcase as sumptuous as this one was just the kind of thoughtful thing Barbara would do. She was an amazing woman. A fine woman. He remembered more of her wonders, and smiled. The traffic slowed on St. Paul, stopping him at a red light behind a long line of cars. It would be another hot day, according to the *Star*. The paper also told how the federal government had filed suit against Philadelphia, charging the City of Brotherly Love with extreme, regular police brutality. The paper also told how three smugglers threw 18 men, women and children off their boat and into the hungry Atlantic when authorities closed in on the vessel. Five children and one woman who'd left Haiti for a new life as illegal aliens in the land of Hope and Promise drowned with their dreams in the seas off Florida. Devlin looked down St. Paul Street, over the line of anxious commuters, down through the canyon of buildings to the polluted horizon. At the end of the man-made corridor he saw a passenger jet rising up, up and away like an old song he remembered. Maybe someday he would go away to some place cool, with a clean ocean and no debris in the Bay, where there wasn't such depression in the eyes of the people around him and life wasn't lived so close to its end. Maybe he'd go with Barbara. The classic late night orgy on a deserted moonlit beach. He smiled. Then the traffic light changed.

And then it happened.

Be calm, he told himself seconds later as the shock of suddenly realizing what had been nagging him wore off. *It's a dumb, dumb idea, not even good enough to be a long shot.*

But his hands trembled with excitement as he locked his car. He jogged instead of walking to the Headquarters' doors.

Breakfast hadn't been cooked at the Lopez house in Los Angeles when Devlin called. Little Matty Lopez's father groggily answered the phone.

"Mr. Lopez," asked Devlin after a fast introduction, "the first time we talked you mentioned Matty loved flying."

"I did?"

"Is something wrong? Did I misunderstand you?"

"No, it's just that . . . Oh, I know what you mean. Yes, Matty loved flying. He'd only done it twice though."

"By any chance did he go to the Bahamas?"

"The Bahamas? We don't make that kind of money, Detective Rourke. We had to scrimp and save as it was to all fly down to Mexico City for the wedding anniversary of Matty's grandparents, my mother and father. That was so long ago. Nearly . . . three years. We went six months before Matty died."

"Oh." Another idea gripped Rourke. "By any chance, do you remember the airlines you took?"

"The big one. Universal Airways. The others, they take illegals and deportees back. I didn't want to get mixed up in that."

"When would that have been?"

"It's so long ago. . . . I couldn't tell you the exact date. All our records were thrown out when we moved after Matty's funeral. But we probably flew down a couple days before January 16—that's their anniversary. January something, 1976. Is it important?"

"I don't know," answered Devlin as he scribbled the

information on Matty's index card and in his notebook. "I don't know."

Stay calm, he repeated to himself. *Do it right and it'll be the fastest way.* He quickly spread all the children's index cards on his desk. If the link was with them, he wouldn't need to bother with the whores. He paused for a second. To hell with any phone taps. She'll want to help if she can. He dialed his home number.

"Barbara?"

"Hi there, Handsome. Why don't you drop by and see me sometime?"

"Sit down: I'm totally serious."

As if he could see, he knew she'd lowered her shirt-clad body to his couch and was staring straight ahead.

"I'm sitting down. I'm listening."

"Last night you mentioned that you and Jimmy and your husband flew down to the Bahamas."

"Yes, the end of February, 1977. About 5 months before the Reaper . . . Does this have to do with . . ."

"I don't know," he insisted, cutting her off. The time lag between the flight and the death was different, but the computer would sort out such variations—and they might not be important. "Do you remember what airlines you took?"

"No."

Devlin swore to himself.

"But my husband, my ex, he'd know. He drove me nuts with his compulsiveness. He keeps a log he takes with him wherever he goes. He even writes down where and what he eats. I can call him; he can look it up."

"Would you? Call him right now?"

"Of course. I'll call you back right away."

'Right away' meant ten minutes. Ten long, agonizing, painful minutes while Devlin tried to steel his mind for what he would do if. If. If. Only if!

"Devlin? He had everything. Universal Airways, Flight 303 out of Denver, February 27, 1977, 9:15 A.M., arrived in Naussau . . ."

"Same airlines back?" interrupted Devlin.

"Yes. Flight 624, March 6, 8:10 straight through to Denver. Arrived . . ."

"For now that'll do. Stay there until you hear from me." He didn't bother to say good-bye. He'd already figured that with

the time differences, he could catch Mr. Stoner before that
man left for work in Kansas City.

"Flight?" said the murdered boy's father. "Yeah, we took an
airplane flight. The four of us, a couple of months before Andy
was killed. Went to Minneapolis to spend some time with the
wife's sister and her family."

"Do you remember the flight you took? Or the airline?"

"Christ, I can't tell you the flight. But I know what airline.
My wife has a cousin who works for them, so the three times
any of us have flown, we've gone Universal Airways."

"Thank you, sir! Could you please stay at home today, call in
sick? And look for anything more about that flight that you can
find?"

"You got him, don't you? You got him!"

"No sir, but I think we're getting close!"

"I'll tear the whole fucking house apart, but I'll find my
cancelled check and anything else we've got. I'll call that
number you gave me just as soon as I get them!" He hung up
before Devlin could thank him again.

Calm, thought Devlin, *calm*. The adrenaline pumped
through him. He'd been exhausted when he was driving to
work. Now he was charged, alive and alert. And maybe, just
maybe, about to nail the big one. He glanced around the
Homicide squad room. Detectives McKee and Perry were
teasing each other about something, preparing to go to court in
a week on a routine strangulation. Stony-faced Captain
Goldstein sat caged inside his glass cubicle of authority. Devlin
dumped all pretense of control and screamed, "Captain!"

His superior was at his desk in seconds. McKee and Perry
also gathered around him, and a uniformed officer who'd been
passing by in the hall stepped inside the room to be sure
everything was all right. Captain Goldstein glanced at Devlin's
desk, then at the face of the man he'd nurtured and observed
for three years.

"Whatever you want, son, you've got. You've got it now."

"I may need manpower, a lot of manpower, but not right
now. Right now, I need a little. If all of us, if you guys
. . . Each one of these cards is a victim. The kids are the
crucial ones. I've done these three, but they'll be checking
back. Call the next of kin on the rest of them. Find out if any of
the victims had at any time flown commercially. If so, what
airlines, flight number if possible. Call the local investigating

officer for help if you need it. I'm betting you'll hit Universal Airways every time. After the kids, try the whores, but . . . Son of a bitch! The first girl, the one with the big tits, Stephanie What's-her-name: she was a stewardess. If the next of kin don't have the info on any flights, call the airline in that city, see what you can get from them. I'll check out Stephanie's past."

"What do you think, son?" asked the Captain as he picked up the index card marked "Victim/Child—#1—Elizabeth Jackson."

"Remember how we couldn't figure the Reaper's mobility? I think he's an airline employee. A Universal Airlines employee."

Devlin and his fellow officers went to work on the telephone, the instrument which has replaced shoe leather as being essential to detectives. While the other officers called distant cities, Devlin assembled his forces and tried to track down Stephanie Phillips's employment record. If she were an ex-stew, then when someone who worked for an airlines went looking for a prostitute, he stood a good chance of cutting her path. Devlin located the Jesuit priest and had him assemble the God Squad. He found psychiatrist Dr. Weis at his hotel and dispatched him to the Jesuit's rectory. He called Jackson Bricker at the computer center, catching the man as he walked through the doors. The computer boss would check the city profiles to be sure Universal Airways flew to all eight cities. Devlin also asked him to print out all airlines serving those cities. Perhaps the Reaper had changed employers during his years of carnage.

Devlin collected all his index cards from his fellow officers as he checked their progress. The cards had served him well; he wouldn't abandon them now. Besides, the other policemen had made their own notes. He stuffed the cards in his briefcase as he explained what remained to be done to Detective Perry.

"Where are you going?" asked the Captain.

"To check out the wide skies of Universal Airlines."

fifty-eight

"Even if I wanted to help you—which, of course I do—I couldn't. We at Universal pride ourselves on being the most cooperative airline. All of us employees have *strict* instructions to be as helpful to our customers and friends as possible. But I'm afraid this is out of the question. I mean, not only can't I help you because it would break company rules I would not break without a court order or specific instructions from our New York headquarters, I physically cannot help you. Yes, we have the information you want, but no, we don't have it here. We've moved all such systems ability to Baltimore-Washington International Airport. And even if you're there, even if you can use the computer system, you'd need to reprogram it. You could do that from there. We are plugged into the central computer. But the data isn't stored in those sequences you need."

"But it's at BWI. Or I can plug into your computer out there to get it."

"Yes. That is, assuming we let you do so."

"Give me your phone."

The harried desk clerk hesitated, then reached over the counter to hand Devlin the receiver with the touch tone button built into the handle. The clerk was miffed and a little frightened by this wild-eyed policeman who'd come barging into the small ticketing office in the heart of downtown Baltimore, a squawking radio in one hand, a blue-and-silver badge mounted in a leather case in the other, rudely shouting questions before he'd even been properly greeted with the company salutation. The clerk watched and listened while this madman made three phone calls:

First call: "Jackson? . . . Can you jimmy stuff out of somebody else's computer? . . . I think so, they say it's got everything. . . . Bring one of those telephone hook-ups with

188

you and make sure you've got somebody on your end ready to receive in your machine. There'll be a squad car in your driveway pronto. Identify yourself to the driver, and he'll take you to BWI. Universal Airlines. Wait for me there. . . . I'll tell you when we've got more time."

Second call: "Tell the Deputy Commissioner it's Sergeant Rourke. . . . Yes, Sir, if Goldstein told you, that'll save time. . . . I appreciate it. Right now I need access to all records Universal Airlines has. They're reachable through a computer in their BWI office, which is where I'm headed. A court order would take too long. If you can find some way to explode their bureaucracy. . . . New York City . . . Good. Two more things: Send a cruiser to pick up Jackson Bricker in front of the Computer Services building at Johns Hopkins. It's just off the main entrance. Ferry him out to BWI Code 3. And send an escort cruiser to do the same for me. I didn't take the time to get an official car. I'm in a blue Camaro, parked out front of Universal's offices at Sheridan and East Baltimore. Oh, I may also need some big manpower. . . . Thank you, Sir. And you better inform the state police that I'll be at BWI. If we're lucky, we'll need them to make an arrest out there, but I wouldn't count on it."

Third call: "Find me Kibler." The airlines clerk heard the wail of a siren growing closer, closer, closer until a police cruiser screeched to a halt behind the wild-eyed detective's old blue car. The radio squawked, and the madman holding the telephone with one hand radioed to the police car that he'd be out shortly. The cruiser didn't even have the decency and discretion to turn off its spinning blue light. "Kibler? This is Rourke. I'm calling from the downtown offices of Universal Airlines. I need help, and I need it now. I need access to Universal's computer files at BWI and their regulations say no. Their home office is in New York. The Department should be banging on their door by now, but I want to be sure. That's a big, interlocked, bureaucratic company, and I thought maybe somebody we know might know somebody big there, some-body who could put his foot down on this right now. . . . I don't have time to fuck around calling you back for a progress report, just do it!"

The clerk's beady eyes squinted behind his thick metal-rimmed glasses as this insane petty official punched his thumb down on the phone's cut-off button, thus uncivilly ending the conversation with the poor man at whom he'd yelled. The policeman then had the audacity to snarl at *him*, toss—not hand, mind you, but *toss*—the phone back to him (he barely caught it) and run from the office without so much as a thank you.

Such a terribly rude individual!

fifty-nine

"Mister," announced the agreeable shirt-sleeved manager for Universal Airlines who, with Jackson Bricker, his city policeman escort, and two state police officers met Devlin at the airport door, "I don't know who you are or what you want, but you got it. I got a phone call three minutes ago from the president of the company himself. A vice president and a corporate attorney are on their way here in a company Lear-jet, just in case you need them. As of this minute, you are running Universal Airlines. You can do anything, up to and including grounding all our flights anywhere in the world."

"First I want all you know," said Devlin as he hurried through the automatic opening glass doors ahead of his entourage.

Normally it's a minimun 20-minute drive from downtown Baltimore to BWI. Devlin made it in a siren-screaming 12 minutes. BWI's main building is 1200 feet long, a low, layered "C" of black smoked glass and concrete supported by house-thick red-tiled columns. Inside, the open ceiling is a criss-cross web of thick tubes, space age girders supported by mirrored columns that distort the bodies hustling through the terminal. The Universal executive led Devlin and his group to a conference room on the back wall of the second floor. A square ring of tables filled the large room. In one far corner, two technicians were busy attaching a desk-sized computer terminal on wheels to a phone box. Bricker raced over to help them. The other far corner was blocked out by a private office within the conference room, a glass cubicle like Captain Goldstein's, but one in which privacy could be attained by closing the floor-to-ceiling curtains. The curtains were closed then. The entire far wall was a glass window overlooking the runways from which 720 planes took off every 24 hours.

"I figured this would be best. The computer terminal will hook up here, you got privacy, everything you need. What can I do? What else do you want?"

Devlin explained what he wanted to both the Universal executive and Bricker. "Can you do it?"

"Well . . . I think so," said Bricker. "I'll need to pick up their programming system by playing with the machine, but that shouldn't take more than four minutes. Give me a couple more minutes to think, a couple minutes to reprogram the computer, a minute or two for it to digest it, another two minutes for checks to be sure because if we miss, we might not know it. Then we should be ready to start. Say . . . half an hour at the outside."

"Hit it."

sixty

"So far you've got six kids, right? All on Universal. And the one date and flight number we're sure of is Jimmy Austin. First let's see if we can't pop out the other five from the computer archive's passenger lists."

Jackson's fingers danced over the typewriter console. Two minutes passed. Then the green TV screen lit up and a beam of light burned five rows of letters behind the glass—name, date, flight number. A printer at the rear of the machine chattered as the same information clacked its way onto an unfolding roll of paper providing a permanent print-out.

"Bingo! Now let's do two things. First, I'll push this data over to the University, start that machine checking on general correlation matrices. Maybe The Reaper hits victims in a progressive series of days after they fly together.

"Now let's do the biggie. Any correlations of people on those planes, passengers . . . and crew."

"Holy shit," said Jackson three minutes later when the light burned four names across the screen:

CAPTAIN JOHN ANDERSON
STEWARDESS CHERYL LIND
FLIGHT OFFICER JEROME KARRIS
NAVIGATOR MICHAEL GREELY

"I know all of them," commented the man from Universal. "They've all been with us five or more years."

"First let's shuffle those names off to Johns Hopkins for analysis," said Jackson, pushing a button. "Then let's see . . . We want to avoid as many runs as possible, so let's . . . Let's run assignments by each of those four people to the eight cities where our boy has been. If they don't have assignments to those cities, maybe we'll rule them out. This will take a few minutes."

Two to be exact. During which time Devlin asked, "Is it common for that many people to serve together that often?"

"It's really not all that often," explained the airline official. "We're talking about several years. Besides, we've been trying new things with our personnel, both grouping for assignment and rotating them, as well as voluntary assignment whenever possible. We think it makes sense to keep a crew together— they get accustomed to each other, work better as a team. Of course, there's a curve on that that shows an eventual downside: They get too used to each other, they get . . . well, I don't know what the shrinks call it, but I call it sloppy."

The burning green light on the screen cut short the company man's discourse. Three of the four names showed assignments in all eight of the Reaper's cities since he'd first murdered:

CAPTAIN JOHN ANDERSON
STEWARDESS CHERYL LIND
NAVIGATOR MICHAEL GREELY

"Okay," said Jackson, "now let's see . . . We know that these three have all been on planes with five of the kid victims. Let's see what we come up with when we feed the other three kids' names, their home cities as points of origin or arrival on passenger lists, and these three Universal people through the sorter. The machine will reach way back, since the Reaper could have hit on one of those kids one, two years before he killed them. That'll take more time. We'll come back with flight numbers, dates, but hopefully just a single correlation with the employees. The odds must be getting pretty long by now."

Analysts at Universal Airlines later established the computer sorted through over 1,950,000 names and places, then correlated those names and places with three different constants. The process took 26 minutes. During that time Devlin had the Universal executive track down the three employees' present whereabouts.

Navigator Michael Greely was guiding a plane to Los Angeles. Devlin arranged to have Greely met by L.A. police detectives, just in case.

Stewardess Cheryl Lind was due in any minute on a flight from New York. She'd replaced another stewardess on a commuter shuffle between Baltimore and The Big Apple. Devlin dispatched another Universal employee and two armed officers to meet her when she got off the plane.

Captain John Anderson, a seasoned pilot, had the day off. He'd flown into BWI frequently for the last two months. The company dispatcher listed him as staying "in the area, not on call." He had a flight scheduled to San Juan in two days.

The light burned the name on the screen, the one Universal employee who had flown with all the dead children:

CAPTAIN JOHN ANDERSON

"Can we get his picture? His personnel file?" asked Devlin.

"I don't believe it! I . . . yes, of course. Excuse me, but I've known John for . . . eight years, ever since I was a dispatcher out of O'Hare. He's . . . he's one of our best pilots!"

"His records?" repeated Devlin.

"I'm sorry, but the main flies are kept in Kansas City at our training facility. But you can punch up abstracts from the computer. Right here."

"A picture, we need a picture!"

"Well . . . yes, it'll give you that. Like a newspaper wire. The quality isn't terrific, somewhat above a Xerox machine but below a regular photograph. I know how to punch in the codes, so if . . ."

Devlin gestured towards the machine. The company man hit the keys, and a minute later the machine burned the demanded data across the television screen.

JOHN WILLIAM ANDERSON

AGE: 46

SINGLE/N.M.

CAUC.

HT: 6¼

WT: 194

B.A., UNIVERSITY OF OHIO, ANTHROPOL-OGY/AFROTC

AIR FORCE SERVICE FOUR (4) YEARS

ATTACHED TO FIGHTER INTERCEPTOR SQUADRON, NO COMBAT EXP.

HONORABLE DISCHARGE, 1959, SEV. AF COMMENDATIONS

AIR FORCE RESERVE, TRAINED IN CARGO TRANSPORT PILOT PROGRAM

ONE YEAR POST-GRAD, UNIVERSITY OF CHICAGO, NO DEGREE

ACCEPTED, UNIVERSAL FLIGHT PROGRAM, 1962

FLIGHT ENGINEER 1962–1964

NAVIGATOR 1965–1967

CO-PILOT 1968–1970

PILOT 1971–PRESENT

OUTSTANDING SERVICE AWARD, 1973

SPECIAL BONUS AWARD, 1974

RUNNER-UP, PILOT OF THE YEAR, 1975

PILOT OF THE YEAR, 1977

QUALIFIED ON ALL UNIVERSAL PLANES,
   DOMESTIC & OVERSEAS
17,952 hrs/air (all w/UNIVERSAL & exclusive AF
   time)
HOME BASE: CHICAGO

"Also butchers little children and helpless whores," added
Devlin, when he'd finished reading the data.

Jackson handed him the computer-created picture. Fuzzy,
black and white, but still a quality likeness of a somewhat
average-looking middle-aged man. A lean but square face, a
few wrinkles, a tight smile on thin lips, evenly spaced eyes
(BRWN., according to the computer). And short light hair.

"He's had white hair ever since I've known him," said the
company manager. "Not snow white, more a pale blond. He
once said he'd looked that way since he was 18."

"Have this machine print up three dozen more of these,"
Devlin ordered Bricker. While the computer man went to
work, the Baltimore detective summoned one of the two
uniformed patrolmen. He handed him Anderson's photo. "As
soon as the machine spits out three more of these, you blast
them back to Headquarters. They'll be set up and waiting for
you."

Devlin turned to the state police officer, who'd been joined
by the head of airport security. "Most of these copies coming
out of the machine are for you. You know how to do it on your
turf. I want all the exits and entrances covered. Let him come
in. Let's take him inside the building. He's not scheduled to
report for another 19 hours, but he may drop by, he may be
early. As soon as he gets in, put a plain-clothes team on his tail
until we work him someplace where we can nail him. If you
need more manpower, I can supply it."

"We'll be fine."

"Now," said Devlin, "where does this guy stay when he's in
Baltimore?"

"I don't know," answered the company manager. "He's not
on call, so he could be anywhere in the area. We don't make
them tell us. They'd feel like they're on a rein. Our company
psychologists dissuaded us from that old tight tab system.
Now, if they're on call, they carry a beeper. We don't know
where they are otherwise. They have privacy.

"Most of the guys stay fairly close. It's easier. But John and a few of the others like to go into the city. Get away from airports. I know where some stay, but John is real private."

"Would he have told anybody?"

"I doubt it. I'm his . . . He knows me best here in Baltimore. He didn't tell me."

The patrolman headed for the door, the still-warm printout pages in his hand. Devlin called the Deputy Commissioner. After telling him what he knew, Devlin said, "I want every cop you can get. Have the lab duplicate the pictures as quickly as they can. Send teams out to check all the hotels in the area, all the suburbs. Call the rent-a-car places. He probably uses his real name, but maybe not. Get the pictures out to the radio cars on patrol too, they might spot him. And the state police. I don't want to go to television yet. If we tip him off, he might go berserk on us or run or both. Have our Vice guys take it to that hooker Jade and the people at the Flame. Have a judge set up with a search warrant for Anderson's person, his property, any car he might be driving, room he might be renting, you name it. If you need it, I'll call in the deposition part as soon as I can. If anybody spots him and they can't guarantee a solid, clean arrest, tag him and call in me and back-up. I don't want anybody going up against him alone. The guy would probably kill a cop with the same type of divine approval he gets to slice up kids.

"Now," Devlin said, turning back to the man who was the maniac's friend. "What can you tell me about him?"

"Well, only that . . . I'm shocked! He doesn't seem . . . crazy. Oh God! It's just sinking in! Think about it: Not just the kid or the women you say he's . . . But think about what he *does*! All day long he's up there, a couple hundred lives in his hands at twenty thousand feet. And he's crazy! Absolutely crazy! Do you know what this will do to the passengers, to the airlines, to the company when it gets out!"

"I'm worried about what he's got left to do in Baltimore. Now tell me about him."

"He's extremely private. I'm probably his only friend here. I knew him at Chicago O'Hare, LAX too. He flies almost more than we like our pilots to. He loves it. Up there in the air, in charge of the airplane. He once told me that was . . . his mission in life. To fly people where they had to go. He volunteers for static assignment—that means we hop him where we need him. A few pilots like that make it easier on guys with families to work out of their home base."

"Any girl friends, ex-lovers?"

"None that I'm aware of. Everybody assumes pilots are getting a lot of the stews. It's not necessarily so, but . . . you know."

"So there's nobody he's close too and he's a shy, quiet man."

"Well . . . Not like it sounds. He's terrific with passengers. We get more letters praising him than any other pilot. He especially . . . Oh God."

"What's the matter?"

"He's especially good with children. He takes them up to the cockpit lots of times, shows them around the plane. He always . . . loved doing that."

Jackson looked at Devlin, but the detective didn't change expression. "Does the company have psychological profiles on pilots?"

"Of course. They're in the computer too. But the access is guarded. It might take a couple calls to get the right code."

"Sgt. Rourke?" interrupted a state trooper. "We've got the stewardess."

Devlin told the company manager to "make those calls" while he interviewed the stewardess.

Cheryl Lind was a pretty brunette whose huge brown eyes were wide with fear. Cops are dangerous. Widespread distrust is an occupational disease of law enforcement. Devlin stared at the petite woman before him as he reassured her that she was in no trouble, that she had nothing to fear. Her nerves calmed, but not enough. She should have been nervous being questioned by police, but not that nervous. Devlin wondered if Cheryl supplemented her stewardess income or lifestyle by smuggling contraband in her usually uninspected luggage. He reached toward her. She shrank back as if his touch meant death. But his hands were fast: They went not to her purse or luggage to search, not to her body to poke and pry and grab like a hundred male creeps on as many flights, but to her uniform, a simple navy blue blazer and skirt, one which could pass for an ordinary store-bought outfit. He fingered the simple fake brass buttons on her cuff.

"Do the men's jackets have these too?" he asked.

She nodded and the manager said, "It's a new style we're trying. We'll probably discontinue it though, because we found people like to see the gold braids and stripes on the pilot's sleeve. We thought dressing them in standard-looking clothing, men's blazers that are suitable for street wear, simple-cut stew outfits, that they'd feel less like they were passengers on an airplane, more like they were flying with friends. It's cheaper too. We use common material, standard design."

"But the men's blazers look . . ."

"Just like the one you've got on. Only dark blue, our company color. Cut functional, but not too distinctive. You can wear them to parties and no one knows what you do. The same as hers."

"Right down to the buttons," said Devlin.

Cheryl Lind knew little. She'd crewed many flights with Captain Anderson. He was her first pilot out of stew school four years earlier. She respected him greatly. He always maintained a proper, commanderial role with the crew, with her. His flights were efficient, even happy when he charmed the passengers, the children. But he never loosened up with the crew, on-duty or off-duty. She knew nothing about his personal life, what he did, where he stayed, where he liked to go.

They'd been flying out of BWI together this round of assignments. No, he hadn't talked about Baltimore much. Oh . . . There was one thing: When she saw him day before yesterday, the day they'd both subbed for a short hop to Chicago and back, he'd mentioned something about having some unfinished business in Baltimore. But that was all.

"How can you protect yourself, your kids?" Jackson whispered to Devlin when he joined him at the computer terminal after questioning the anxious stewardess. "You guard against all the obvious dangers, against the straight burglars and creeps. But how can you keep them and yourself safe from contact with a nut like the Reaper? Somebody who for some reason decides you're it after you meet him?"

"You can't," said Devlin. "When you get those psychological file codes, plug them through. Let's see if anyone else thinks Anderson is nuts. And while we do that, see if there's any mathematical pattern to when the kids flew and what happened to them. Maybe we can narrow it down to what flight with a Baltimore kid on it he's picked this time."

But the psychological file told Devlin little he didn't already know. The rudimentary interview examination was designed to measure how Anderson withstood stress and whether he exhibited such outward signs of instability as excessive drinking. The company psychologist believed Anderson's assertion that he seldom drank anything but wine with a meal. All the tests showed Anderson performed exceptionally well under stress. "He has a fine sense of command, of authority," noted the report. "If he has a flaw, it is his tendency to assume too much responsibility."

"No shit," said Devlin. He turned back to the company manager. "Can't you tell me anything more about this man? He blends into a crowd like a flu bug. Doesn't he have any peculiar traits, quirks, mannerisms, habits? Anything?"

"Well," said the manager after a moment. "He's methodical as hell. And a neatness freak. Once I brought him a bum set of flight instructions on the runway. The tower radioed him that I had incorrect papers. Normally a pilot would chuck his copy away, but he took the time to tear them in two a few times first, just to be sure they wouldn't be confused with the correct ones. Then since a trash container wasn't handy, he put the pieces in his pocket. I remember teasing him about that. The only other thing I can think of . . . It's probably not important, nothing you'd notice on the street, but he shaves with a straight razor, the old-fashioned kind barbers use."

sixty-one

"You're not going to like this," Jackson told Devlin. The policeman had instructed him to program the computer for all children under 12 who'd flown on any of Captain Anderson's recent flights. After age 12, the airline didn't request the passenger's age. They targeted from that general list all children from the Baltimore area. The printer clicked and the green light burned line after line onto the TV screen.

"A bunch of that is a special flight," explained the manager. "About a month ago. Some kind of school tour. The kids sold candy, washed cars so they could go to New York City. We gave them a special rate."

"Captain Anderson is great with children, great with that group," said the stewardess who was not totally aware of what was happening.

"And there's two, three dozen names coming out now off other flights he'd taken in the last month. If we go back further, we'll hit even more. Some of the Reaper's victims flew with him as long as eight months before he killed them."

The long snake of paper jerking out of the machine mesmerized Devlin. The technology ticked out the names like a carpenter hammering nails in a coffin:

Steve McNamer
Frank Hodgson
Whitney Kilburn
Kenneth Applegate
Richard Bechtel
Judith Isander
Stuart Johnson
Robin Gratsy
Lindsay Baker . . .

Devlin's plan had been to find all the potential Reaper victims, call their parents, dispatching cars to look for them when the telephone failed. Put a circle around all those in danger and snare Anderson if and when he showed up.

"How many kids so far?"

Bricker glanced at a number on the screen. "One-nine-eight, and counting."

"Oh shit," said Devlin. "Oh shit."

sixty-two

He had to beat the clock. The only way to do that was to beat the mad mind racing against him. Devlin sat in the conference room's curtained-off private office, staring out at the runway. Jets landing, jets taking off. Somewhere out in the streets was a pilot who could command such mechanical monsters, a man who'd held the lives of thousands of people in his hands, a man who'd finally decided he had a right to claim life as well as ferry it from point to point. That man was the Reaper. Of that there was little doubt. Beyond all the assumptions, beyond all the statistical certainty, there was evidence:

A button that could have come from his uniform, which the lab might be able to establish when they located the uniform.

Papers torn in the methodical way he tore papers.

A memory from a dead woman who'd called him cloud-head. Perhaps because of his whitish hair? His talk of flying, of being up there in the kingdom of clouds with so much power and glory?

Not much, not enough for a conviction. But more than enough for an arrest. And with the arrest, Devlin was sure he could find more evidence, evidence to end the Reaper's reign.

But right now, convicting Anderson wasn't foremost in Devlin's mind. He wanted to stop him from reaping another innocent victim.

But how? Devlin felt like he'd moved back to square one. He knew who the Reaper was. But he didn't know where he was or how to get him. He didn't know when he would strike (but believed it would be soon), or where, or quite how. But most important, he didn't know why.

Which Devlin felt sure was the key. It was not enough that the man was simply mad. There was a pattern to his killings, a *why*—of that Devlin was sure. A pattern that he simply couldn't see! Anderson was too methodical a man, even in his madness, to act with irrational fury. If Devlin knew the pattern, he could find the next victim, perhaps in time to save that child.

The routine of standard police procedure was in full swing. The D.C. dispersed 131 officers in the Reaper hunt. Most of them were hitting bars, hotels, motels, boarding houses, a grid search looking for the Reaper's lair. The rest were contacting parents and the administrators of the major tour. The computer eventually coughed up 396 names. This was summer. Vacation time. Children being flown with parents, without parents. A splurge they wouldn't forget in later tight-money times. A sacrifice of parental love. A fatal gift for one of them, if Devlin didn't beat the Reaper.

He had to gamble on himself. The routine would work—in time to save the child or not, but it would work. Routine wasn't good enough for Devlin, not good enough by half. That child, that last child, was his to doom or save. There was a pattern: he could sense it, he could feel it, he could smell it, he just couldn't *see* it!

The private office was cool and quiet. The computers needed an average 70° temperature for optimal performance. No sweat waited on Devlin's brow as he forced the wrinkles in his skin to relax, forced his mind to relax. He'd gone over and over every aspect of the case in his mind, flipping through his notes, flipping through the index cards, shuffling and reshuffling and finally stacking them near his open briefcase on the table. Now he was trying to relax, to let the tension leave his mind so it would work, so it would flow. He was alert and exhausted at the same time. He needed that flow, for with it he might crack the pattern he couldn't find with naked logic.

His elbows rested on the table as he leaned forward to cup his face in his hands, close his eyes. The neatly stacked index cards, computer printouts, his briefcase, pads and pens waited on the table—tools that weren't working, tools that weren't helping. He tried to think, to find a fresh viewpoint for all that knowledge at his fingertips. But his brain hurt. He felt a terrible dread of inevitability: this could be it. Until the Reaper killed again, until he caught him—two eventualities that were inevitable unless Devlin pulled off some miracle play—this could be it. He'd worked himself as far as he could, and he'd ended up impotent in an air-conditioned office while his opponent stalked the streets. Devlin would get him, but not soon enough, and not on his terms. He was so close, he could feel that, but he couldn't find a way to jump the gap.

And wouldn't you know it: when he raised his face from his hands, leaned back in his chair, he knocked over the styrofoam cup of coffee. The milk-tanned liquid raced out in a flood across the table. Devlin quickly pushed the stack of index cards out of its path, threw the computer printout further down the table. He dropped his arm in the puddle, soaking most of it up to save the records, felt the tepid, sticky liquid soak through his shirt and glom on to his flesh.

Nice, he thought, *real nice*.

He found a box of tissues in a secretary's desk, mopped what was left of the spill on the table, sponged his arm as dry as possible. He reshuffled the chaos he'd made on the table (*as if that made any difference*, he thought glumly), bent down to pick up the stack of Reaper index cards he'd swept to the floor.

They'd been stacked in chronological order, a nice, neat array of the box score: Reaper: 8 kids, 9 whores, 3 leads tagged on base. So far the home team had zero. While the prospects had improved for a dazzling and victorious final inning, the odds now showed the opposition racking up one more bloody score before the game was over. His jaded eyes roamed over the recipe cards.

Here was little Matty Lopez's card. He was number 3.

Then came Pete Jenkins from San Francisco, he was number 7 in the lineup.

And Jimmy Austin, Barbara's boy. What had he been like? What would her child have been like? He came in at sixth place. Poor little Jimmy. The pictures showed him with her smile. Poor little Jimmy. Or rather, James.

Then came Mary North, in second place on the chronological list, fourth in his disarrayed order. Had the Reaper killed them in the order he wanted, or in the order he found them? wondered Devlin. Matty, Pete, Jimmy, Mary and the others. Or rather, Matthew, Peter, James, and . . .

And then it hit him. Hit him like an outfielder slamming into a brick wall when he had his eye on the fly. The memory popped out of the catechism lessons of his youth, the schooling he'd eventually been kicked out of before confirmation. Maybe, just maybe . . .

He dialed the number as fast as he could punch the buttons.

The Rabbi answered. Devlin hesitated, then asked for the Jesuit. His memory was Catholic.

"Father, the name Matthew is from the Bible, isn't it?"

"Yes," said the Priest, not quite sure of the question's intent, "Matthew is the first book of the New Testament. He was one of Jesus's disciples."

"How about James?"

"There was also a disciple named James."

"Peter?"

"There were several Peters, including another disciple of . . . Oh dear Lord!" Devlin heard him yell: "The Bible! He's killing discip . . . No!" yelled the Father back into the phone. "It can't be disciples: What about . . . Mary, the Mother of Christ! Good God!"

In the phone's background Devlin heard the Methodist minister yell, "And Andrew! Another disciple!"

"What about Elizabeth?" cried the Priest to Devlin and his fellow Biblical scholars.

"Mary's cousin! Mary had a cousin named Elizabeth. The angels told Mary about her to convince her she could bear a child!" The academician's voice.

"I've got the list here!" yelled the Rabbi. Devlin envisioned them excitedly rushing around the somber, book-lined rectory, yelling to each other.

"What about Thad Gardner?" shouted Devlin. "His name wasn't shortened, no nickname. Just Thad."

"One of the 12 disciples had the surname of Thaddaeus!" answered the academician. "The Reaper just extrapolated a bit with Thad!"

"But that leaves us with Maggie O'Donovan," said Devlin. "I don't remem . . ."

"Another extrapolation!" shouted the Priest, emphatically ecstatic, happy with his understanding of the blasphemy he unravelled out of Hell. "He already had one Mary, he needed another, but a different one: Mary Magdalene. He figured Maggie was close enough! Remember, Maggie was number 8. Maybe he's getting less fussy."

"Let me talk to Dr. Weis," said Devlin. "Doctor, does this make sense to you? That he'd be killing Biblical characters associated with Christ?"

"Yes, yes, the coincidences blended with the religious mania in the ads is compelling logic, buy why . . ."

"Oh Jesus, Doctor!" shouted Devlin. "Don't you see? Of course! He's a pilot. He *takes* people places where they need to go. He's the Reaper, he's taking, no, he's *gathering* the Holy cast together in Heaven. He's the instrument of the Lord preparing for Armageddon!"

"That's crazy!"

"Yeah, Doc, that's crazy. But it also might give us the edge we need. We know the names he's worked with, we've got the list of potential victims. We can match the list with Bible names. Especially Christ-related names."

"Everybody's name is in the Bible," said Rabbi Cohn in the background.

"We don't know what text he's using for his list either," said the Priest. "Perhaps several. And how he'll handle repeats of names. For example, St. Luke lists two disciples named Simon, both of whom are also called by different names." The Jesuit quickly read Devlin the disciple list from Luke.

"But we can narrow our field, guard against his attack better. You guys better pull out the reference books. I'm dispatching a list of 396 names for you to work on. I'm going to headquarters, but I'll be in radio contact and I'll call you as soon as I land."

Devlin hung up, ran for the door, dashed back to the desk, shoved the index cards and his copy of the computerized list of children into his briefcase, then jerked open the door yelling orders.

First he sent the remaining Baltimore policeman racing to the rectory with the passenger lists for the God Squad.

Then he made sure that none of the people assembled outside would leave: he didn't know when or how he might need them, and he wanted them where they could be found.

He called Captain Goldstein with the latest news.

He made the stewardess look over the list of names with him, but there were *so* many and Captain Anderson had been *so* good with children, talking to them, taking boys and girls into the cockpit where he presumably talked with them at greater length, always asking where they were from and where they were going, who their folks were, that kind of thing. Not all the children got such treatment, of course. Especially not when there was a planeful, like that tour. But enough did, so many she couldn't even begin to count or name them. The list of children was merely so many words to her.

Devlin checked the security arrangements at the airport. If the Reaper returned to BWI as Captain John Anderson, the only way he would exit would be in custody or in a coffin.

As Devlin was about to leave, Jackson Bricker handed him a torn square of manila paper. Devlin glanced at him, and the computer man said, "I had a hunch. There's a parking lot here that passes these out."

Devlin smiled. "You're supposed to process data, Jack, not find it."

"We're all trying new things these days."

sixty-three

Suddenly he knew it all.

He was backing his straining old Camaro down from 75 to a speed safe enough to maneuver through the traffic on the edge of the city when he remembered a name on the list, when he suddenly knew. It was as if the Reaper sat on the seat beside him, dark blue suit, white shirt, snow-cloud hair and pale, pale skin, perfect teeth flashing in a smile as one long finger pointed to the briefcase and in it to a name.

A commercial strip lay not far off the highway. Devlin quickly glanced in the car mirrors, looked around him, then jammed on the brakes and wove across three crowded lanes of honking traffic to an exit ramp. Once again he cursed himself for not being in a cruiser with its blue light and siren. He shot through a red light, missing a collision with a Chrysler and a Coca-Cola truck by inches. He didn't glance at the drivers as he roared past them, whipping off the access road to a serve-yourself gas station with a lone phone booth. He skimmed his copy of the Reaper's last ad. It had to make sense! He leaped from the car and jogged towards the phone booth.

But seconds and steps ahead of him was a ruggedly handsome salesman on his way to the phone booth to answer the message relayed to him over his car radio. Perhaps he'd sell another bulldozer today. The salesman was anxious for the business, but generous and easygoing. Devlin wouldn't have needed to use his badge to wave the salesman away from his right to first use of the phone. But Devlin didn't have the time to find out, so he pulled his leather folder and flashed the shield.

The airline executive answered the phone: Somehow Devlin knew he wouldn't do. "Give me Jack," he said. Devlin pulled the computer list from his briefcase. "Hang on!" he ordered the computer man. Devlin crammed the phone receiver into the fold of his neck, and ran his finger down the list. One name accidentally seen, accidentally remembered. The phone receiver started to slip, but the waiting salesman grabbed it with one strong hand and held it to Devlin's ear. Devlin found the name. The address burned into his mind as if the computer light were tracing knowledge on the green TV screen. He knew the salesman read that crucial line too, didn't care. He shouted the name to Bricker: "Call that home number and keep calling until you get someone! I'm not far from there, I think. I'll get there as fast as I can. Don't call it in to the Captain, I don't want it over the radio yet."

"Why?" asked Bricker, astonished at this last instruction.

"Never mind!" snapped Devlin. "Just keep calling that number until you get somebody to guard the kid!"

Devlin nodded to the salesman, who hung up the telephone. The detective stuffed the list back in his briefcase. He glanced at the big man in front of him. The salesman pointed and said, "Three traffic lights up that way, take a left, about half a mile, six blocks down on the right. I've got a lot of renovations being done in that area. Whole blocks are torn up."

"Thanks!" yelled Devlin as he raced towards his car.

"Don't mention it," said the salesman, although he knew the cop couldn't hear him over the squeal of old tires tearing across cracked pavement.

Hell of a day! thought the salesman. He had a hell of a story for the customer he was about to call.

Devlin cut through the traffic on the main artery as fast as the other drivers allowed. He was in the Dawson section of

Baltimore, once a poor neighborhood where unrehabilitated townhouses bordered on disintegrating slums. Many of the blocks of sagging buildings, deserted homes and businesses had been razed; heavy equipment churned brown earth to his left, diesel smoke belching out to dirty the already heavily fouled, hot industrial air. Downtown Baltimore, Police Headquarters, the Block, they waited a mile or so up the road. A grey stone, castle-style gothic tower loomed on the skyline. The 357-foot building had once properly been called Emerson Tower, but was popularly known as the Bromo Seltzer Building after the most popular product of the drug firm it housed. At one time, a 17-ton revolving replica of a Bromo Seltzer bottle slowly turned atop the tower. The replica was 10 million times bigger than the 10 cent bottle it represented. While inflation has not increased the drug's price that dramatically, the 10 cent bottle is a thing of the past. So is its replica, which was sent to the scrap heap in 1935. The building is now called the Arts Tower Building, housing municipal offices and smaller private concerns. The only prominent remnants of the tower's past are the world's largest four-dial gravity clock, capping the building above the 14th floor. The hours on each of the four clock-faces are designated not by numbers, but by the letters in the words "Bromo Seltzer." The tower looked down on the Dawson section, watching it also change with the times. Someday, if the recession didn't suck away all the renovation money, Dawson would become a showpiece neighborhood of middle-class life. Already some homes showed a break with the area's dreary past. Devlin turned left on Angelos Drive, the street of the angels. Another Biblical link. More than ever he was convinced he was right. More than ever he felt the urgency of his mission.

He didn't dare use the radio—not because of the Reaper, but because of Matella. The emerald-eyed monster was as dangerous a factor as any in this game. Devlin believed beyond doubt that by now Matella had been alerted to the progress of the hunt. By now his minions were monitoring the police radio frequencies. By now they might be mounting a plan which Devlin had no way of knowing. He instinctively knew Matella's plan would violate anything Devlin would want. He had to get to the Reaper-Anderson first, he had to control him if he were to survive the game. The *entire* game.

So the radio was out. Besides, most of the Baltimore police force was already engaged. He was as likely to be as close to the house as any officer, as likely to be in the right place as anyone. Devlin didn't worry that Matella was on his trail. Perhaps they had followed him to the airport, perhaps they'd put a tail on him when he'd been there. Perhaps they'd been behind him on the road. But as crazily as he'd charged through the traffic, no watcher could have stayed with him without showing up in the mirror for Devlin to notice. And he saw no one behind him now as he headed towards 5317 Angelos Drive.

Judith Isander. Shown on the airline records as female, age 7. Another poetic permuation: Judith to Judas. Isander to Iscariot. Judas Iscariot, the disciple who betrayed Jesus. Who lived on the Street of Angels. Who flew on the airplane with the Reaper. Who lived in the city where the Reaper's ad preceding his murder of a child included the phrase, "he that thrusts his sickle to clean and harvest the earth shall not rest until his work is worked, yea, even till all the false prophets and the betrayers have been taken before the heavenly throne." Judas. The disciple and betrayer. Judith. The innocent and doomed.

He slowed as he reached the 5000 block, checked for rental plates on cars parked along the townhouse-lined street. He found none. He pulled into a space in front of 5317. No pedestrians shuffled down the street, no men with white hair. Or green eyes. Devlin slowly strode up the sidewalk leading to 5317, a squat, newly renovated townhouse of pale brick with maroon wooden shutters, a heavy black door, and even here, even in the "new" Baltimore, the obligatory white marble stoop. He heard the insistent peal of a telephone through the open windows. His fire-tight impulses told him to kick down the door. But he knew he had to play it straight, play it careful. Perhaps he was more than in time. Perhaps. He turned his left side to the door, slipped his right hand inside his coat to rest it on his gun butt. He didn't need another madcap scene like the park. Then loudly, firmly, he beat on the wood with his left fist.

For over thirty seconds he hammered. When he'd almost decided to kick the door in now and worry about the consequences later, he heard the lock slide back. The round knob slowly, slowly turned.

sixty-four

"Who the hell are you?" Devlin demanded of the scrawny, pimply-faced teenage girl with long stringy hair, a tube top and dirty brown cords. She looked at him in exasperation and disbelief.

"Oh wow man! First the fucking air conditioner breaks down! Then the goddamned phone won't quit ringing! Then you practically break the fucking door down, you know what I mean? I mean, it's just too fucking much man, too fucking much!" She stared past Devlin, her eyes rolling listlessly from side to side as if searching the street for yet another excess.

"Who are you?" demanded Devlin again. He guided the girl back into the house as easily as a man commands his shadow. "Who are you?!" he said again as he glanced around the living room. The TV was on, but almost inaudible. The phone kept ringing. And on the coffee table, on top of *Better Homes and Gardens* magazine, he saw a square of tinfoil the girl hadn't even bothered to hide. A faint aroma of burned hemp rope teased his sensitive nostrils.

"What is it?" he demanded, hoping to crack through her emptiness. "What the hell is it you're on?!"

"Oh wow man, this Angel Dust is too fucking much! I mean like my head is going a million jillion miles an hour and all this fucking noise keeps happening!"

"What are you doing here?" he asked, trying to keep harshness out of his voice, trying not to frighten this stoned-out child. She was on a killer drug: Angel Dust. PCP. She was lucky to be still alive, no matter how many or how few times she'd mixed the soft white dust with khaki marijuana, the favorite way for the million some teenage users of that deadly dreammaker. Modern medical science developed PCP as a surgical anesthetic, but now, because of its unusual and

unpleasant side affects—including disorientation, muscle
rigidity, paranoia, speech impediment, and euphoria—PCP
has been legally restricted to animal use. The *least* it does is
scramble the nervous system. Devlin wanted to scream at her
about responsible drug use. Such a peculiar concept. But now
was not the time, she was not who mattered.

"You were banging on the door," she announced calmly.

"Where's the little girl?"

"Who?"

"You're here, you must be a baby sitter, so there's got to be a
little girl."

"Oh yeah, her. She's playing outside. I mean it's so fucking
hot in here without the air conditioner and anyway, she's too
little to blow some stuff. I mean . . ."

"Where outside?" Devlin grabbed her arm.

"Don't pick on me! Out front or out back or out I don't know
where. What difference does it make? She can take care of
herself."

He raced through the house to the back door, leaving the
scrawny girl stammering to herself. Judith hadn't been out
front. "Out back" was a small lawn surrounded by a 7-foot
redwood plank fence with a gate. He was almost to the exit
when he heard it.

"Meewrown! . . ."

". . . Yow!"

Devlin jerked open the gate, his hand reaching for his gun.
A scruffy calico cat fled down the alley to his left. A peculiar
singed hair odor seemed to linger in the cat's panicked wake,
then it vanished in the summer smells of a humid, garbage-
strewn alley. Houses interspersed with vacant lots and pas-
sageways stood before Devlin. To his left, the direction the cat
fled, the alley ran empty to the street. To his right, leaning
against a fence, was a chubby boy of about thirteen smoking a
cancer-causing cigarette and picking at three red, just-beading
lines scratched down the inside of his left forearm.

At least he isn't stoned, thought Devlin.

He was worse than stoned. He was spoiled, sadistic, an
arrogant meanness of a child pampered on television and
envied macho. Devlin flashed his badge. The boy's poise
cracked for a moment, and his eyes darted to where the cat
had run. The animal was out of sight. That fact buoyed the

chubby, T-shirted lad's confidence, and his sneer returned as Devlin asked, "Son, I need to know . . ."

"I don't need to tell you nothing, cop!" The boy spat the words from his pubescent mouth, his tone squeaking with the changes of his physical maturity. "I know my rights." The boy tried to flick ashes from his cigarette, but the coal was too fresh.

"*What?*" Devlin didn't believe what he heard.

"I don't need to talk to you, cop. Get a fuckin' warrant."

"Look, I don't care about anything but what you might have seen. If you've been here long enough . . ."

"I've been here long enough," answered the punk. He wished the kids who laughed at him were here to see how cool he really was. But they'd know someday. Just like that fucking cat.

"The little girl who lives in that house, Judith. Have you seen her? She might have been with a tall man who has whitish hair."

"So?"

"Kid, this is important! Did you see them?"

"I told you already, I don't gotta tell you noth . . ."

Devlin's backhanded slap knocked the cigarette from the punk's face. Before the boy could register his surprise, Devlin pushed him against the wooden fence. The kid's hands flew to his face, but couldn't stop a steel vice from gripping his throat.

"You're going to talk the truth to me straight and now, punk, or I'm going to rip your fucking face apart!" Devlin tightened his stranglehold. "One time, one time only: Did you see the girl with or without a guy like that, when and where?"

The punk frantically nodded, his face pale with fear. His parents had barely ever scolded him.

"A couple minutes ago," he gasped as the grip around his neck eased to let the words out. "The dopey little girl in one of those frilly dresses and some guy like you said, blond hair and taller than you. They went through there, through the passageway!"

"What's out there?!" Devlin demanded as he backed away, already moving towards the gap between two houses.

"Honest mister, just a vacant lots they're working on and a ways away an old factory. I didn't mean nothing," he whined, starting to cry. "I didn't mean . . ." But he was crying to an empty alley.

The passageway ended in a torn-up street. Beyond the street the land resembled a bombed-out city—vacant, scarred, rubble-filled lots cut with a drainage ditch and high embankments.

They walked silhouetted against the backdrop of a deserted factory with rows of broken windows, two figures hand in hand. A little girl in a frilly play dress she'd promised Mommy not to get *too* dirty, and a tall man in a dark suit, his light hair blowing free in the hot summer wind. Judith Isander, age 7, of 5317 Angelos Drive, Baltimore, Maryland. And the nice pilot who'd shown her all around the airplane and talked with her while Mommy and Daddy beamed from their seats. Nice Pilot John, who Mommy and Daddy liked, who they wouldn't mind her going for a walk with, who she could trust. John. As in John Anderson. As in John the Baptist, who brought salvation to the flocks. Who saved souls. Whose head was severed. Who shaved with a straight razor.

Devlin tried to run silently, to get as close as possible before they noticed him. He drew his gun, but kept his right hand turned back, hiding it as best he could while he ran.

Now he could see them clearly, the red-and-green-checkered pattern of Judith's dress, her white anklets, her brown shoes skipping over the darker brown earth. His heart pounded against his sweat soaked shirt, and his lungs heaved foul air. He could see the gold buttons of the man's blazer, he could hear them laughing. They bore to their left: a gorge cut by the bulldozer so heavy rains might drain off the reworked land blocked their way to the dark, empty factory but a hundred yards distant. They turned to climb the embankment, beyond which might lie a path to that special place he'd promised Judith, promised her even though he said she'd been bad before. She was sorry she'd done something wrong, and anxious to please this nice man. They turned when Devlin was but 25 feet away—too far to make a safe, quick charge, too far to risk a shot with the girl standing on a rise between him and his target. The man in the dark suit smiled at his young charge—and then saw what must be the devil running up behind him.

Suddenly the nice man's grip tightened on Judith's arm and he drew her close. The pain scared her, but he was a grown-up. There must be a reason for it. The man running toward them must be bad, and the nice plane driver must be trying to protect her. She saw the sun flash on something her friend pulled from his pocket, but then he held it high above her head. Caught in his tight hug she couldn't look up to see what that bright thing was. She clung tightly to the protective arm encircling her. She wanted to close her eyes, but she was too scared.

"Don't Reaper!" cried Devlin, stumbling to a halt as he saw the sun glint and the long, suit-clad arm point to the sky.

There it was, that shiny, 3-inch steel edge glistening high in the air above the pale-haired man with the outraged, determined look, high above the wide-eyed little girl with her head pressed back against his body, the pounding pulse of her pure white throat seemingly visible to Devlin.

"Don't Reaper!" pleaded Devlin in a softer voice. He ventured another step closer, stopped when the razor trembled in the sun. The policeman kept his gun-heavy hand behind his back. He held his left palm forward in supplication. "Don't Reaper! It . . . it would be wrong!"

"Who are you?" demanded the bass voice. "Who dares to interfere with Divine will? Who challenges this Holy mission?"

It had to be good. It had to buy him time, buy him a few steps closer.

"I'm . . . Don't you recognize me?!" snapped Devlin. Go for it, try it! "Don't you remember me from Heaven?!"

"I . . . I . . ." The Reaper's brow furrowed.

"I'm the Message Angel," insisted Devlin, wishing he could come up with a Biblical name. "I'm the Message Angel sent here to help you, to guide you in your work."

"I have never seen you before! Your voice has never come to me in the heavens or in the night!"

"That's because you never needed me before," explained Devlin. He shrugged his shoulders to cover a step forward. Perhaps 22 feet. He could make the shot. Soon he might be able to risk a charge. Perhaps he'd be fast enough. The little girl might get bruised, but she'd live if Devlin hit the Reaper in time. "You never needed me until now."

"But all is well!" insisted the prophet. "I have satisfied my vessel of flesh! I blessed the wicked harlot, healed her with my touch, cleansed her with my purpose, baptized her with her blood, sent her soul to Satan so that I might be purified and the balance maintained, so that Hell will have its soul and a child of the Lord may ascend to Heaven, so that I might fly the saint there on the wings of innocence and strength by shedding the Lamb's blood!"

"But this is not the time for *this* baptismal!" Devlin remembered the list the Jesuit had read him. "Is it not written that Judas the betrayer was the last?" Fake it, go! "You're out of order on the most important of all your missions, Reaper!"

Devlin saw the man's lips tremble. The razor-tipped arm lowered—not to strike, but in hesitation. Behind him Devlin heard a car bouncing over the vacant lot, the motor racing toward them. *Bricker must have called the Captain*, thought Devlin. He heard gravel crunch, the sounds of a car skidding sideways to a stop. Dust torn from the ground reached him seconds before he heard two doors fly open. He dared not let anyone charge towards the delicate balance of death on the embankment, yet he feared breaking eye contact with John Anderson. And if he spoke as other than the Angel Messenger . . . But Devlin heard running feet. The Reaper broke their gaze first, his eyes darting beyond Devlin, so Devlin knew he must turn too.

But no police car waited in the settling dust. No representative of law and order sent that tan Mercedes. Kibler was stepping out of the passenger door, ducking low, away from the field of fire of the chauffeur who was leaning on the hood of the car, drawing a bead with a long barrelled .22 target pistol. And behind a highly polished rear window Devlin saw the twin green flames of Matella's eyes, the pure snow crest of his head.

"No!" he cried as he realized the shooter's target. To them, the girl was expendable, although Devlin sensed that with his special marksman's pistol and that classic, confident pose the driver would have no trouble hitting his target.

Then, not because he didn't want the pilot to die, not because he knew that somehow he'd been used again, not because of the danger to the girl or himself from .22 bullets or a hastily swung razor or even because of the law or his own pride did Devlin fire those three quick shots. He saw a merciless, mercenary killer targeting another killer who was insane with his own divinity. Devlin fired because justice disintegrated if such play decided the game.

Devlin's first shot winged high over the Mercedes. His second bullet screeched across the waxed hood of the car. The mob marksman had been told to ignore the cop, not to worry about him. Now two shots from a police revolver had barely missed him. He swung the long, skinny barrel of his .22 towards a new target just as Devlin's third bullet slammed into his chest. The marksman's concentration oozed away. He crumpled to the ground on the far side of the Mercedes.

Devlin whirled to scream at the Reaper, to reassure him of his safety, to convince him that he was the true messenger who had just saved him from agents of Satan, to forestall his errant sacrifice. As he whirled, Devlin thought he heard the sounds of another car motor, thought he saw white metal moving up behind the Reaper on the far side of the drainage ditch. But the detective's eyes were locked on that shiny steel razor still held high above a little girl's throat. Again he yelled, "No!"

Then his body exploded forward, the air rushing from his lungs, his hands flying wide and his gun dropping to the torn soil, ground glass and dead weed dirt. Devlin sprawled flat, all the air driven from his lungs, his back smashed by Randy's crackback block. By Randy, 6'6", 285 pounds of barbell-built muscle. By Randy, who swung wide, out of the marksman's way, then looped back as hard and as fast as his steel piston legs could propel him, a double team effort against the primary target with a secondary responsibility of one lone cop.

Judith screamed.

Kibler shouted, "Don't kill Rourke!"

Devlin's badly shocked body curled inward, his rump raising in the air, his gasping mouth filling with dirt as he tried to suck oxygen back into his lungs. He raised his head, forcing his eyes open and up, up to where he could see the bottom of a skirt and a brown shoe racing down from an embankment of death, up to the sight he'd replay in his nightmares until he died: Randy's right hand, that huge baseball glove of satin-skinned steel buried in the red flesh of John Anderson's neck. Randy's fingers closed on cartilage and tubes and muscles and bones. He lifted the pilot off his toes with that one strong right arm, lifted him high until Anderson's feet danced madly in the air. Anderson's eyes bulged to the edge of their sockets, his left hand clawed frantically at the unshakeable girder which held him up to the heavens. Anderson's right arm flopped lifelessly.

Devlin had been face down in the dirt when Randy's charge smashed into the Reaper and his victim. The detective didn't see the little girl knocked free from the man she trusted. The detective didn't see Randy stop the downward slash of Anderson's razor, catching the madman's right arm in his monster left fist, halting all that insane energy with a calm, detached professionalism. The detective didn't see the two-second squeeze and flip which broke Anderson's wrist and flicked the carefully cleaned razor unbloodied to the dirt. The detective didn't see Randy's carefully calculated jerk which pulled the pilot's arm from his socket, or the lightning grab that locked Randy's other hand in the death grip around a man whose claim to immortality was about to be tested. That grip choked off any screams as Anderson's dying body slowly rose above the earth.

Devlin saw the end of the Reaper. And as he watched, his own will came back to him. He couldn't stand yet; he certainly couldn't walk. But he could crawl. Only a few feet, only a few sliding feet. His left hand was but inches from the barrel of his snubnose .38 when he heard the sound he never forgot: the *snap!* of a spine, and the death gurgle as Randy opened his hand to litter the ground with the scrap of what had once been John Anderson, an ordinary man who'd wanted only to be the best, the most important helper in the universe. Devlin touched metal, the .38's small circle bore which was still warm from three fired bullets. His fingers crept over the cylinder where three more bullets waited, towards the checkered combat butt, around it.

When Randy's huge, shiny, custom-made shoe covered the back of Devlin's hand and pressed down.

And then a cannon exploded.

Poor Duck. He'd been trying so hard with his special mission from Detective Rourke. But he'd goofed in the park. For the first time in his professional career, he'd felt shame. He had heard snickers from his fellow officers as he'd walked away from that debacle. He'd wanted to cry. Since then, he'd tried even harder. Today he'd driven to the outskirts of town, parked his cruiser behind a burned-out factory. Rourke couldn't *conceivably* show up there!

And then came the radio call. A disturbance reported by some workmen in a vacant lot just around the corner from where he carried out his lonely watch. A low priority call routinely radioed over the air. The dispatchers knew most of the force was searching the city for a crazed airline pilot or protecting a seemingly endless list of children. They assumed some unit in the area would routinely respond.

But not the Duck. The dispatchers automatically ignored him when they sent officers out on the great manhunt. When he heard that call, that low priority public disturbance routine call he'd heard thousands of times before, he thought *maybe*. Just *maybe*. Maybe he could combine his duty to Sergeant Rourke with some routine police work. Maybe that extra bit of initiative would wipe some of the stigma of the park from his otherwise untarnished badge. This was his chance! It was obviously something easy. Probably two weak old drunks rolling around in red wine-soaked mud. Maybe even a false alarm.

The Duck swallowed his nervousness. He grabbed the mike, and in classic tough guy fashion radioed, "I got that public disturbance." He garbled some numbers so the dispatcher wouldn't realize who was responding (in case they wanted to avoid overloading him). The dispatcher didn't bother calling back to get a clarification on the cruiser I.D. There was too much going on to worry about coordinating a public disturbance response.

Behind that burned-out factory, the Duck slipped his idling air-conditioned cruiser into gear, turned on his blue light, and surged the heavy machine around the corner, down one curb and over the other, the excitment building in him as he rumbled over the junk-filled field toward some figures scrambling on the other side of a ditch. Just like in the movies. He swung his cruiser parallel with the gorge. His tightly rolled windows, the growl of his engine, plus the squawks from the radio mixed over three quick sounds he might otherwise have recognized as shots. The Duck carefully adjusted his hat and sunglasses in the rearview mirror, pulled his billy club from its built-in door sling, sighed for the loss of air conditioning, and stepped outside his vehicle to do his duty. He swaggered the ten steps to the edge of the ditch, peered across to the figures on the other side—and suddenly realized that he was in the middle of major police action.

He saw a man even huger than his own considerable bulk

shaking another man like a gorilla shakes a rag doll, shaking him and then letting him crumple to the ground.

He saw a little girl "fleeing the scene."

He saw an expensive car with a man looking out of the rolled-up back window and another man standing by its trunk.

He saw all this clearly, as his side of the embankment was slightly higher than the other, where he now saw the gorilla-sized man quickly step across to a figure on the ground.

He saw all this but he wasn't seen; rather, he wasn't noticed. The concentration of the men on the other side of the ditch was riveted elsewhere. And Duck's emergence, for all his huffy officialdom, had been smoother than their play. Duck realized they didn't know he was but 50 feet from them, cut off by a wide, deep ditch. He also realized that the man on the ground was Detective Devlin Rourke, and that the giant gorilla in the three-piece suit was about to do something very unpleasant to his fellow officer.

For the first time in his life, the Duck drew his huge .44 Magnum revolver in a street situation. Whenever he'd drawn that cannon in target practice all the other shooters left the range.

The Duck's first shot roared past the man attacking Sgt. Rourke. The booming explosion of his first shell sent Randy diving to the ground. Kibler scrambled for cover beneath the expensive German automobile.

Duck's second shot ripped over the crawling form of the ape who'd attacked Sgt. Rourke. The ape pressed himself flat and immobile against the earth.

Duck's third shot flew harmlessly over the Mercedes, eventually falling in the seventh hole water trap of a suburban golf course.

So did the Duck's fourth shot.

Four rapid rounds threw the Duck off balance. He tried to pull his bucking arm down, to aim where he wanted the bullets to go. But he overcompensated. The fifth round slammed into the dirt at Duck's feet, kicking blinding dust into the air. His eyes instinctively squeezed shut, and he threw his arms up, including the arm attached to the hand holding the three-pound pistol.

The next shot was purely accidental, his nervous finger twitching too much, too soon. The gun boomed one last time, sending final round six racing behind the Duck. The bullet shattered the only pane of glass on the top floor of the deserted factory which vandals had been unable to reach before that hollow lead slug splattered against a rusty girder. The mighty kick of the .44 Magnum twisted the gun from his hand, breaking the Duck's trigger finger and thumb in the process. He grabbed his injured hand, screamed, doubled over, threw up, staggered backwards, and collapsed in a dead faint against the side of his cruiser.

Rourke's left hand throbbed. Randy hadn't had time to crush it before the Duck's blast drove him to seek shelter, but the pressure had neared the breaking point. Rourke rolled closer to his gun, his right hand cupping it just as Randy (who'd wisely counted the shots) realized the cop on the other side of the ditch needed to reload. Randy glanced across the abyss. He didn't understand why the blue uniform slumped against the cruiser, but he sensed that that cop was no longer a threat. He leapt to his feet, prepared to neutralize Rourke.

Devlin raised his body as high off the ground as he could. He took his best aim, and shot Randy through the Italian loafer-clad foot. The muscleman screamed, and stumbled to the ground, his huge hands reaching for his pain. Devlin scrabled towards him over the dirt. The policeman slammed his gun butt down on Randy's carefully cut hair. The giant slumped still.

The energy flowed back. It didn't mask Devlin's pain, but it gave him the strength to tolerate it, to stand, to quickly see that somehow he'd been rescued by a somehow now unconscious Duck, to see the broken form of the Reaper sprawled on the downward slope of the ditch, to see Randy, unconscious and helpless. And then he whirled.

Kibler was crawling from underneath the car. Devlin staggered towards his "buddy."

"Hey! Hey! Hey! It's okay, I won't hurt you! I don't carry a gun!"

The cop eyes never left this man's face. He thrust his gun barrel deep in Kibler's stomach, then pulled back the hammer so that if the man even sneezed hard, the motion would trigger the bullet to kill him. Devlin's throbbing left hand discovered that Kibler hadn't lied. Feeble moans came from behind the Mercedes as the wounded chauffeur slipped in and out of consciousness.

"How?" hissed Devlin.

"We had another trace bug hidden behind your badge all this time," he blurted. "With all the action, all the radio calls, we just hung tight, out of sight. But we had you on the screen all the time. We pieced it together, turned the corner on you. There it is."

Rourke glanced to the rear of the Mercedes.

What he saw there killed any further comments.

From where they stood, the car looked deserted. The front passenger door gaped open and that compartment was empty. No one could be seen in the rear passenger compartment.

The rear window closest to them fit snugly in its slot, tightly rolled up to keep the air-conditioned air inside and the dust outside, away from the lungs of a healthy but older and thus more sensitive human being. The middle of this glass was dotted by a hole slightly smaller than a golf ball, the size hole a .44 Magnum hollow point slug makes when it punches through solid glass. The side rear window directly opposite this hole was snugly rolled up too. That once clear safety glass was now a pink crimson cobweb of lines leading from a hole the size a hard-pitched baseball could make.

"Oh boy," whispered Kibler.

The two men slowly walked closer to the rear door. They peered—briefly—into the back seat.

"Oh boy," Kibler whispered again.

Devlin leaned away from the tan car. He didn't bother to keep his gun on his prisoner. He glanced across the ditch to where the Duck was struggling to his feet. He saw Randy slowly stirring to life in the dust not far from the ditch where a dead madman lay. The badly wounded chauffeur moaned loudly and called for his mother in a gurgling, lung wound gasp.

"Yeah, Kibler, there it is. There it is. How's this one going to play out? Huh, old buddy? How's this one going to play out?"

sixty-five

"I don't believe it," Captain Goldstein told Devlin Thursday evening some 40 jumbled hours later.

"I mean, the part about you catching the Reaper, tracking him down, that I buy. Good police work, maybe even brilliant police work. I expect that from you. But not this other crap.

"Stand in my shoes. Roll all this out in your head. You chase the Reaper down. To this vacant lot, right?

"Which turns out to be extremely busy for a regular-type summer afternoon. Not only do we have an attempted murder by a madman in progress, we have an eccentric rich old barber from Brooklyn and his accountant, who have caught on to a scam two of the barber's employees are pulling on them, a scam that turns sour right there—though we never get an explanation of *why* they're right there. So this scam turns sour right then, right there. The embezzlers turn stick-up men. They see all this action around them. They hear you yelling police. They figure you and the madman are cops coming in to bust them. God knows how they figure the little girl in it. . . ."

"She's so confused she doesn't know what happened out there, Captain."

". . . So this chauffeur character pulls out his target pistol and this pretty muscle boy goes to work with his hands. The Duck shows up shooting that cannon of his. Blim! Blam! Bloom! All the bad guys are down! You take out the chauffeur and the muscleboy, but not before the muscleboy takes out the Reaper who's flipped and is attacking everybody with the razor, everybody *except* the little girl he's trying to kill. She gets away. The Reaper doesn't get to take out anybody for once. The only believable part of the whole thing is the Duck fucking up and accidentally blowing up that old guy's head while trying to make like the Seventh Cavalry."

"That's how it finally played out, Captain."

"What that is, is a crock of bullshit."

"You got a signed statement to that effect from Kibler. You've got my report—which is based largely on Kibler's statement, I will admit. You got the Duck's report—which is based largely on me helping him, I will admit. You've got confessions to that effect from the chauffeur and the muscleman. I bet they'll plead as soon as they get from the hospital to the court. I bet they'll take their sentences without a whimper. They've got the best criminal lawyer in town, who, as you may know, is a political hotshot in Annapolis and even in D.C."

"Funny about that, isn't it?" said the Captain. "Them coming up with a high-powered attorney out of the blue? And these days nobody flat out confesses, but all of a sudden we got two big city goons begging for the chance, no plea bargaining demanded."

"I spent four hours sometime around dawn with the Chief Prosecutor," said Devlin. "He doesn't think any of this is funny. Who will he give the case to?"

"Not your friend Biz. Old Charlie Adams, been with the prosecutor's office for years. He's already got a hearing date before Judge Wilson."

"Judge Wilson? Judge Emmett Wilson?"

"Know him?"

"No, I've never been in his court. Maybe I read his name on a list somewhere."

"You think he'll buy this bullshit story?"

"Want to bet?"

Captain Goldstein shook his head. No one could hear them in his private glass cubicle. He looked at the exhausted, unshaven, sniffling man across from him.

"Couldn't you have come up with something better? Something I could tell the Commissioner and my wife with a straight face?"

"There wasn't a whole lot of time."

"I'll bet. Will you ever tell me the truth?"

Devlin smiled.

"Listen: one thing we need to know for absolute sure true: That pilot Anderson who's stretched out in the morgue. Was he the Reaper?"

"No question. We found enough evidence to back up my eyewitness account and convict his corpse a dozen times over."

"How the hell am I supposed to relax and travel again, knowing there could be some nut running the cockpit?"

"Try prayer."

"Nearer my God to Thee, huh? Like the pilot?

"At least we look great," continued the Captain. "Baltimore's police department captures madman where eight other departments fail. Ain't it amazing how that reporter Ebbenhouse dug out all that behind-the-scenes stuff way before anybody else? For once, even his stories make us look good. If we believed all of it, you'd ride that kind of press to a lieutenancy. Hell, to my job!"

"I like it where I am."

"That's good, because not everybody thinks you're a boy wonder. You'll have to settle for a medal and a citation. And some vacation time."

"And no more questions?"

It took his boss 30 seconds to smile. "And no more questions."

sixty-six

The envelope which appeared on his desk that morning contained a statement from Dockside Laundry and Dry Cleaning: no amount shown, but stamped, "PAID IN FULL." Devlin shook his head, then dropped the bill in his briefcase. He stuffed his rancid collection of dirty laundry in there too. They'd allowed Barbara to bring him fresh clothes during the 40 hours he'd spent never leaving Headquarters as he wrapped up the Reaper case. The Deputy Commissioner offered to send a fellow officer on whatever such errands he needed, but Devlin declined that offer, saying (truthfully) that he wanted the excuse to see her. An unspoken truth was his reluctance to have any representative of the law other than himself poking around his apartment where something entirely unexpected might be discovered in a drawer.

He fastened the straps on the briefcase and shuffled to the hall.

There stood the Duck. Sergeant McKinnon had been waiting for almost an hour, trying to build up his courage to face the man he'd let down again. They hadn't talked since Sgt. Rourke crossed that ditch to explain the situation to him, to make sure he was not seriously injured, and to use his radio to call for the meat wagon and back-up units. The Duck swallowed. He shyly waved his bandaged hand.

"Sgt. Rourke? Could I . . . I have to ask you . . . Sergeant, are you mad at me?"

Devlin yawned. He'd catnapped for maybe 5 hours off-and-on during the last 40.

"Mad? Why should I be mad?"

"Well . . . I didn't do like you said and stay away from you. A couple times I goofed up, in the park, at the . . . the building thing."

"Factory."

"Yeah, the factory. And you know what else?" The Duck paused until Devlin shook his head. "That little black capsule you gave me? I lost it somewhere a few days ago. I'm sorry."

"I'm not: you charged down in the nick of time, saved my ass, helped me break the biggest case of my career."

"Yeah. I did. Didn't I?"

Devlin nodded.

" 'Course, there is that thing with that poor sweet old guy."

"There is that."

"I never meant to hurt him! Honest! Even the shooting team knows that. They called it 'an unfortunate incident'." Duck enunciated those saving words slowly, with memorized precision. "He probably wasn't a bad fellow. I bet he was a good barber. I bet he always gave kids a lollipop after their haircuts."

"I'm sure you're right."

"Shame he had to get mixed up with those crooks. Old guy like that, couldn't take care of himself like as not. Trusting, never hurt a fly, never thought anyone would hurt him either."

"A shame."

"Yeah." But then the Duck's mood brightened and guilt slipped from his conscience like water off the ass of his namesake. " 'Course, he was getting old. And it's probably better he went this way: quick, sudden-like rather than ending up toothless and drooly in some nursing home. You might— *you just might*—say I kind of did him a favor! Bet he's in heaven now, still kind of dazed about it. But maybe just a bit tickled 'bout him getting . . . a peaceful surprise."

"Sergeant, you're one hell of a guy."

Worry creased the Duck's face once more. "Uh, Devlin, uh, out there, when I got through firing, uh, it kind of might have looked like instead of being knocked unconcsious by flying bullets like we said, maybe it looked like . . . that maybe I . . ."

"Fainted?" volunteered Rourke helpfully.

"Yeah."

"Never crossed my mind."

"It didn't?"

"No. Why, Sergeant, you're amazing! You were overwhelmed by total incompetence and through amazing luck survived to prosper! Few men can made that claim! I bet they'll even have to give you a mcdal for all this!"

"Really?"

"Really." Devlin walked to the elevator. The doors slid open as the Duck excitedly waddled after him. Devlin got on the elevator alone.

"Hey!" said the bandaged officer as Devlin turned to face the front of the machine in full compliance with Maryland state laws and Baltimore city ordinances governing the use of elevators. "Maybe we can do this again!"

Detective Sergeant Devlin Rourke silently stared straight ahead as the elevator doors closed.

sixty-seven

Devlin got as far as the front desk.

"Hey Fleetfoot!" called the desk sergeant with the scars from his throne, "they piped a call down here for you." He handed Devlin the receiver.

"Sgt. Rourke."

"This time I've got you!" Stern hissed into his ear. "All that heroics in the newspapers can't hide everything. I'll show you up for the crazy cop you really are!"

"Always nice to hear your voice, Counselor, but what the hell are you talking about?"

"Talking about? Talking about? I'm talking about the way you brutalized poor Steven Bensley!"

"Who's Steven Bensley?"

"You don't remember?! My God, you don't even remember! If I had you here in my office right now with Mrs. Bensley and this poor, precious young man you punched and slammed around. . . . Why, I'd commit assault myself!"

"Punched and slammed ar . . . *Him*? Stern, watch yourself! Don't show him your back! He almost let the little girl die! He's a spoiled, snot-nosed monster with no respect for anything!"

"I'll teach you about respect! Sure you saved that little girl. And caught that madman. As much as you disgust me, I'm grateful as any citizen for that. But you can't play God with one hand, Satan with the other, and expect to get away with it! Not while I'm around. I'll demand a full review of this. I'll take this to the City Council, to court if I have to. I'll get your badge, I'll . . ."

"Counselor, I just left a man who's so stupid he blunders into brilliance and now I'm talking to you who are so brilliant you blunder into stupidity. It's all too cosmic for this poor cop."

Devlin handed the phone back to the smiling desk sergeant, who gently but firmly settled it back in its cradle as Counselor Stern screamed.

sixty-eight

"What should I believe with this whole thing?" asked Bequai from behind his borrowed desk in the Federal Building. The FBI agent wrinkled his nose and glanced at Devlin's briefcase. He leaned forward and through the loosely-closed flap saw a muddy sock. "Do you always carry your dirty laundry around with you?"

"Doesn't everybody?"

"That's your problem, Rourke: you never remember the way the game is played. I ask the questions, you answer."

Devlin smiled.

"But that doesn't mean much to you, does it? You sold some crap story to your people, and figure that I can't make enough waves to wash the truth out of you."

"No, I figure you can make it pretty rough. But you won't. Matella is dead, not like either you or I wanted or planned it, but he's dead. It wasn't murder, if that's what you're thinking. I didn't set him up to be hit. Amazingly enough, he died legally, probably the only thing in his life he did within the law. You and I ended up with a bigger play that we could have imagined. I know it bothers you. You don't know whether you won, whether you should be happy or not, whether you should feel cheated or tricked. But there's some times when you just need to be content with good fortune, and let the questions slide."

Bequai showed the strain of the last few days. But Devlin saw a freshness in him, a freshness Bequai probably couldn't recognize. Yet. The G-man finally said, "And all you want is for us to backstop your buddies in the Department without asking why?"

"And be there if I need a big favor or two. And leak a little something on all that local O.C. stuff I told you about Cardozo and Baltimore in such a fashion that a reporter named Ebbenhouse at the *Star* gets one hell of a scoop. He's kind of expecting it, so he might hawk our friend Danny Cowan. Who, by the way, is expecting the go-ahead from you to slip him some stuff out the door."

Devlin waited, but Bequai didn't reply for a full minute. And then he smiled. Devlin lifted his briefcase off the desk and walked to the door. He turned back. Perhaps a friend watched him.

"By the way," said Devlin. "Randy and Matella's other guy, they got a hell of a lawyer."

"Gee. I wonder how. I wonder where they got the money. I wonder why he took their case."

"They go before Judge Wilson."

"Never heard of him."

"It's an old Maryland family name. WASP money and credentials from way back. Big house in a ritzy neighborhood. Raises Dobermans as a hobby."

Bequai cocked his head.

Devlin shrugged. "Maybe another little bonus for you. But for now, go home. This is finished."

"I don't have a home. I have an office."

"Maybe that's another game that's over."

And he shut the Fed's door.

- - -

sixty-nine

The black limousine with mirror windows and the telephone antenna on the trunk slowly followed him for three blocks as he walked down busy East Baltimore Street toward the parking lot where he'd left his Camaro. Better here on the street, the decided, than in an alley somewhere. He stopped, turned to face the car. The long black machine purred forward, stopping effortlessly when the back door was opposite him. The electric mirror glass window hummed down, and a smiling Kibler leaned out.

"Hey Buddy! How you doing?"

"Moving up in the world, Joe? From the front seat to the back?" The only other person in the car Rourke could see was the driver, who kept his eyes locked on the ornament at the end of the long black hood.

"This? Oh, this is a little something some friends loaned me to help take care of some errands, clean up a few things. Come on in. We'll give you a ride to your car."

"Why am I reluctant to accept?"

Kibler laughed. "Hey pal, if they wanted to make trouble for you, they wouldn't need to be half so tricky as sending a limo. Besides, that's not my line. Come on, we need to talk."

"So how did you find me this time?" asked Rourke as he settled into the crushed-velvet cushioned seat. A bar was built into the back of the front seat, and a small color television flashed baseball action live from the stadium where the Orioles battled yet another opponent on their way to the Pennant. The score at the bottom of the screen read: *0-0, Top of the Fourth*. "A tracer bug in my ear? I thought I pulled the last one of those from behind my badge."

The Oriole batter drove the baserunner home with a line drive to left field.

"You did. But we know a few people in that Federal Building. They call a certain number whenever they see something interesting, somebody fascinating who goes in or out of a couple places there."

"I suppose for that they get a Christmas card from the firm."

"Chanukah too. We don't discriminate."

The Oriole batter struck out, retiring the side.

"So if Cardozo told Matella that I tried to co-opt him too, why didn't you drop that on me too during the second snatch?"

"Oh, that. Mr. Matella figured you thinking you were in a different jam with Cardozo would keep you from being too much more creative. He had a hell of a mind, that Mr. Matella."

"Until the Duck blew it all over the inside of that Mercedes."

"Accidents happen. Nobody bears a grudge against anybody for that. I want you to be sure that's true."

"I got a letter."

Kibler laughed. "Yeah, I heard. Those were Mr. Cardozo's personal touches. Funny, huh? He's really a very funny guy."

"Barrel of laughs."

"Yeah. Listen, I want you to know I appreciate the way you played our little factory scene. That could have been sloppy for everybody. We all appreciate it, even Randy and the man you put down."

"It worked out."

"Yeah. Don't worry. We'll be sure it stays worked out."

"What are you going to do now, Kibler. Fade away now that your master is dead? Or are you a company man? You going to shuffle off to serve somebody else?"

"Oh, I'll do a little of this, a little of that. Maybe even help you now and then, if you need it. Not to worry about that either. Or about you or your friend in the police lab. All that's about to be dead and buried."

"I don't care for that phrase."

"Just a figure of speech. And remember, I can be reached if you think otherwise, or need a little favor."

"Let's hope we don't have to do that."

"You never know."

The Oriole catcher fired the ball down to the second baseman in time to stop the stealing baserunner and end the inning.

"Listen, Mr. Matella planned to give you a little something if you did your job right," said Kibler. "He knew you wouldn't take cash or like it if we helped you jump your way up in the Department, so . . ." Kibler pulled a football-sized package wrapped in plain brown paper from a compartment in the limousine door. "So he arranged for you to get this."

"What is it?"

"Two pounds of cocaine, the same batch minus about two ounces—the stuff what we already gave you. Matella joked that it could be a lifetime supply for you."

Pause.

Devlin slowly adjusted.

Pause.

"You expect me to take it?" cried the detective.

"Why not? You know we don't need to frame you or set you up. You already have my word such notions are forgotten, dead and buried. Mr. Matella already had this planned. If you don't take it, I'll need to channel it back through the market. Or throw it away. Any of that will disrupt things and generally piss everybody off."

"That's almost $100,000 worth of coke!"

"Oh we'd turn over much more than that with it. This is uncut."

"Why? Why give it to me with Matella dead. Why would he give it to me at all?"

"To tell you the truth, I want to get rid of it and it's only fitting you get it. See, nobody ever questioned what Matella did, but if I suddenly say, 'Hey, I got 100 G's worth of coke!', somebody might not understand. That could be awkward. And if they find out I had the coke and didn't do like Mr. M. said, even if I dump it in the trash, well, that could be worse. *That* nobody would understand. So I'm stuck with it.

"As for why Due Smeraldi wanted you should have it if you did right, well, there was him thinking that if he paid you this way, not only would he be clear of the debt—remember, he was big on not owing anybody, always paying off one way or the other, that kind of a great guy! If he paid you off with this stuff, you'd be more likely not to do something foolish and fuck around with him for having come to you with his friendship. Giving you a present like this saves killing you, which he considered a vast waste of talent, plus a minor inconvenience. And personally somewhat boring."

The Orioles were in the field again, with one man out, a runner on first, and the designated hitter standing at the plate. The big batter blasted a line drive toward left field, but the Oriole third baseman jumped high and diagonally, snagging the ball with what would have been an impossible catch if he hadn't made it, stopping what would have been at least a safe single base hit by the batter. The third baseman compounded his stunning play by whipping the ball across to the waiting first baseman who tagged the frantically returning baserunner (who'd tried to steal on the wrong pitch) for the double play. The crowd roared to their feet.

"And part of it was his sense of humor. These are a very funny bunch of guys. He loved life, all its challenges and mysteries. He told me when we got this stuff that it would be fascinating to see if you had the mark of a true genius, a man who can handle all the dangers and temptations of his weaknesses without destroying himself.

"He said that challenge was partially why you indulged in coke, why you were a cop too. He said you like cutting life close, walking over the abyss on a cold steel razor's edge. He said someday your feet won't be tough enough and you'll slice yourself clean through, or you'll lose your balance, something will knock you off. Any way you cut it, the fall is down and bloody. He figured the heavy-power illusion dust would hone your razor. You'll love doing it even as you know the next snort may be the zing that cuts you down.

"Me, I say take it as a favor. And enjoy."

Kibler carefully packed the brown paper package inside the briefcase, wrapping Devlin's dirty laundry around it.

"See? Fits like it belongs. We're at your car."

Devlin climbed out. The limo door slammed behind him. But the glass slid down again before the detective moved away. "Oh, by the way, there's a little momento from me in the package. My own idea, but I think Mr. Matella would have loved it. We had a hell of a game, didn't we, buddy?"

The mirror slid back up, and the limousine glided away.

"Hell of a game," said Devlin.

seventy

Barbara stood by one of Baltimore's hard-to-find taxis in front of Devlin's apartment building. *As if she were paying off the cabby, getting out,* he thought, his tired heart beating faster in memory and anticipation he knew he'd need to delay until after he'd slept. He'd found a parking place only a block from his building. As he walked toward his home he pretended there was no reason to be nervous. He clung to the heavy briefcase Barbara had given him as if it held his life.

Today she looked especially sharp. Her suit was new, classily tailored, her hair artfully combed, her makeup perfect. She saw him, hesitated, then gave the cabby a bill from her purse. But instead of pulling away, the cabby's brake lights went off and the vehicle stayed where it was. He's waiting, probably slipped into PARK. She paid him to be sure he'd stick without complaining. Which meant she isn't coming. She's leaving. She walked far enough away from the cab so the driver couldn't hear them over his blaring radio's broadcast of the Orioles game. The voice without a body floated from the cab, announcing it was 5 to 3, Orioles, top of the ninth.

"I'm going," she said.

"So I see," he replied.

"I thought you'd be at work."

"I've had a hard couple weeks. I took the afternoon off."

"Oh."

"Where you headed."

"Home."

"Denver?" he asked with some surprise.

"Home is where you don't get hung up or feel like you've got to run."

"Which is it here?"

"A bit of both. Besides, I'm not the only one who's getting anxious to back away."

Devlin stared blankly for a few seconds. He nervously twitched, supressed a smile. His shoulders shrugged, then he broke into a wide grin. They both laughed.

"Well hell," he said, "all that Texas money made me nervous."

"Sure it did. Just like I couldn't stand the worry of you going through life walking down dark alleys with a gun on your hip betting yours was the best brain and the strongest karma in the darkness and that that would be enough to let you come out the other side. We're both alive, really, really alife. Me for the first time in too long a while. I've been resurrected from the merely not dead. You, well, you got a pleasant eye-opening detour to spice up your time and show you there might be more to life than you thought you could have. And a briefcase. What are you carrying in it now that you don't need the Reaper cards?"

"Just stuff. My dirty clothes. Some crime things. Good

dreams and nice memories. The kind of ordinary, everyday items everybody packs with them. Only in a more interesting and expensive bag."

"Oh Devlin! You're so precious! Only you would sincerely treasure a $300 briefcase and at the same time use it for a dirty laundry bag! You're . . . wonderfully unique!"

"Really?"

"Really."

"You aren't so bad yourself. But I never . . . I never had time to get you anything. Not even daisies."

"You gave me a great deal more than daisies. Besides, as a parting present to myself, I took four *extremely* long lines from your stash. I left some bucks for you in your cookie jar to replace them—and don't try to interrupt! I know you wouldn't want money for it, but I also know how expensive it is and difficult for you to get. Paying you lets me do the vice my way. I put your keys in the same envelope as a note that couldn't say it all so it says almost nothing. Shoved the envelope under the door.

"And that stuff, that wonderful white stuff. You've got to promise me you'll be careful with it. You're so special, so alive, with or without it. So be careful. Don't go wild with it when you get a little. It's dangerous. Insidious. It's too good to be true."

"I promise. I may give up my old motto."

"What was that?"

"Push The Limits."

"Sure you'll give that up. For what?"

"I haven't decided yet. Maybe 'Moderation In Moderation.' Where will I ever find a woman like you?"

"Mmmnn!" She moved close to him. Right there, in broad daylight with randy hard hats and unsatisfied housewives and laughing schoolchildren passing all around them, she embraced him. The weight of his briefcase kept his left arm pointed straight down to the ground. She took his right hand and pressed it against her left breast. He felt her nipple stiffen through her clothes as her right arm looped around his neck. The last words before she kissed him deep and long and wet and burning were, "And where will I find another man who knows how to appreciate me so very, very well?" As she crushed her mouth against his, she boldly reached between his thighs with her left hand and caressed him until his passion surged. Maybe 20 seconds, maybe 20 lifetimes later, she drew back. They were both panting. And then laughing as she broke the embrace.

"I'm not worried about you!" she said. "Or me either."

They walked hand in hand to the cab, no regrets. She kissed him lightly, then gracefully slid into the back seat. Barbara smiled out the window. Just before the cabby jerked his chariot into gear and away forever, she said, "You'll find somebody. You're the detective."

seventy-one

The note read, "Terrific! Thanks! Good-bye. Barbara."

Which was a lot more than nothing. He switched on the stereo system. The selector was on radio. Seconds after he flipped the switch, the announcer said, ". . . will be going home disappointed. That does it today for our Pennant-hopeful Orioles. Final score: 6 to 5, in favor of our mighty Birds!" Devlin hated post-game wrap-ups, so he flipped the switch to activate the record player. He sat the heavy briefcase on the coffee table, then slid Charlie Byrd's "Encores at the Maryland Inn" out of its tan protective sleeve and put the record on the spinning turntable. The briefcase waited on the coffee table.

Tired as he was, sleep seemed wrong. He left the briefcase on the coffee table, and walked back to the kitchen. The tea kettle was still hot: Barbara. He'd been drinking coffee all morning, and his kidneys would soon need relief, but so what? Within seconds he had the kettle hissing and made himself another cup. She'd even left him fresh cream. Real cream, not milk. He walked back to the living room as the guitar-bass-drum trio played the Beatles' "Michelle." Devlin put Barbara's letter in a desk drawer he seldom used.

And looked at the briefcase on the table. He sighed, crossed the room and undid the straps to flip back the lid. His dirty laundry went on to the heap in the bedroom. The brown-paper package sat on his coffee table while he took off his foul jacket, his tie and his gun. The package waited. Charlie Byrd somehow didn't seem right any longer, so he crossed the room and switched the record for Keith Jarrett.

"Well, shit," he finally said. The plain brown-paper package didn't reply.

He unwrapped it slowly. Two squat plastic bags, one of which had previously been opened, each about the size of a small loaf of bread, both filled with shimmering white crystalline powder. Taped to the top of one of the plastic packages was a small brown jewelry box, the kind designed for expensive watches. The present from Kibler.

And inside the jewelry box, an ebony-handled, cold-steel straight razor, brand new and shiny, unsoiled by any kind of cutting.

There was neither card nor need of one.

Rourke carefully reopened the one plastic bag. The over-powering odor of alkaline drifted up to him. He assumed it wasn't poisoned. Why go to all that trouble? Even those *very funny guys* didn't have that peculiar a sense of humor. He abstractly noted that he would need to break the bulk down into more manageable parcels to avoid clumsy disasters. If he kept the coke. He'd also need to find a good stash, a large, safe, dry place. If he kept it.

"Hell," he said. "The coffee is still hot."

He moved the steaming cup off the coffee table. No accidents allowed. He took a black book from the shelf for a cutting board. His safety razor blade was in his old stash across the room in the rolltop desk and he'd absentmindedly put his clasp knife on his dresser when he'd taken his laundry back to the bedroom.

Damn! he swore, momentarily irritated that such small, insignificant details would interrupt the flow.

And then he picked up the new straight razor. The hard, harsh blade flipped open. Why not? It could do double duty.

He dipped the long blade into the soft, snowy pile of the open bag. He balanced a mound as big as a thimble on the edge of his shiny new blade, then shook three-fourths of it back into the sack. Moderation. Next he carefully tapped the remaining mound on to the book, chopped it finely with the razor, then drew out four thick lines. He rolled one of the five $20 bills Barbara had left him, bent over.

"*Mmnffphtt!*" First the right nostril sucked up one line.

"*Mmnffphtt!*" Then the left nostril sucked up another.

Fight the sneeze back, fight the fire. After all he'd used lately, he'd need to abstain for a while or risk burning out his sinuses, straining his heart. After today. The unsubtle swell of euphoria roared through him.

Too good to be true.

He stood, paced around his room, looked out his bay window. His kidneys demanded attention.

And he felt Matella's green eyes on him. He felt them . . . laughing. Devlin's mind flew a million miles an hour. Due Smeraldi loved this joke. Devlin's kidney's increased their urgent request. He absentmindedly picked up Kibler's black-handled razor, the pound bag of cocaine he'd resealed. He jostled it in his hand as he drifted back to the bathroom, set it beside the razor on the back of the toilet while he urinated.

Even in the grave that brilliant mind behind those green eyes was having its way with him. Matella had pushed him out further along the razor's edge. If he kept the cocaine, Matella owned a piece of him, no matter how Devlin justified it. Matella even had the sport of wondering if the cocaine would ultimately take charge of Devlin, seduce and destroy him. The green-eyed monster gave him a weapon for his own destruction, and could watch him use it. Throwing the cocaine away presented a not much more liberating choice for Devlin, because he'd already succumbed to the temptation. He might deny it, but even after the cocaine was gone, he'd be tortured by the *if only's*. Devlin remembered the priests' lectures about how wanting to commit a sin was almost as damning as following through and committing it. He felt those emerald eyes laughing at him. Matella had been the ultimate rational mind, and he'd created an ultimately rational trap for Devlin that even if it didn't destroy his body would snare his soul. *There's no way out of this one*, thought Devlin as he readjusted his clothing, reached towards the flush handle. No way to beat Matella at this game.

And stopped. No *rational* way.

He jostled the pound coke bag in his hand. One of two, equal with the other for all intents and purposes. Rationally it was the same, rationally they were a package deal. He tossed the bag in the air, caught it above the basin of his waste and water destined for the Chesapeake bay.

In one smooth, sweet motion Devlin grabbed Kibler's razor off the back of the toilet, flipped it open, tossed the heavy bag in the air, caught it and held it down out over the toilet much like Randy had dangled the Reaper above the earth.

Then Devlin slashed the razor through the plastic bag, spilling a powdery avalanche out and down into the toilet basin, the water splashing and hissing as the bulk hit it, an alkaline blizzard filling the bathroom as Devlin shook the plastic bag, then dropped it in the toilet—to hell with what it might do to the plumbing.

The fishes will have fun tonight, he thought. As he wondered where he'd keep the remaining bag he felt those eyes realize what he'd done—one slashed and one thrown away: that made no sense! That wasn't rational!

And that closed those laughing emerald eyes out of Devlin's life forever.

seventy-two

"This is a police emergency!"

"Then why do I hear some scratchy old record playing in the background?" insisted the whiney female voice.

"How old are you?!" demanded Devlin suddenly.

"Wha . . . what?!"

"You heard me! This is an official police emergency that you're not cooperating with and I demand to know how old you are!"

"I don't see what . . ."

"How old are you?" screamed Devlin.

"I'm 19, as if it's any of your business!" snapped the girl on the other end of the phone. Maybe that would satisfy this creep.

"Nineteen? Nineteen? They let you out in the world at that age *alone*? For your information, that scratchy old record is the Beatles singing 'A Hard Day's Night,' which is what you're going to have if you don't get her on the phone right now! This is a fucking police emergency! I ought to know, I'm a fucking policeman, and I know a fucking emergency when I fucking well see one and this is a fucking emergency!"

"Don't you talk that way to me! This is no police emergency and you can't scare me! I know who this is. She told me all about you. You're that crazy Sgt. Rourke. I'm sorry I told you her home phone number that night! She gave me strict instructions never, and she meant *never* to put you through to her again! Especially when she's busy preparing her opening statement for court tomorrow, which is what she is doing now."

Be cool, he thought to himself. *Stay calm. You're tired, dead tired, running on hope and the confident desperation that lies beyond exhausted courage. Plus you're stoned, coked to the gills.* He glanced to the coffee table. The remaining victory bag (as he now thought of it) of coke was stashed in his rolltop desk. Only a cleanly wiped, black-jacketed book waited there. One minute before two totally unnecessary white lines had followed their immediate past four predecessors god-knew-where. Try a new tack. Professional failed. Friendly failed. Hyped professional failed. Raving professional failed. Pitiful sweet groveling might work.

"Listen, Mildred—It is Mildred, isn't it? It usually is. Can't you please help me? I desperately need to talk to her. You're the only one who can help me. I called because she once told me how understanding and good you were. I know you know how these things are. Won't you please, *please* . . ."

"I'm sorry, I'm not going back on Ms. Grey's orders, and she told me . . ."

"Mildred," whispered Devlin in a cold voice so quiet the secretary on the other end of the phone strained to hear it, "you get in there and you get her on the phone right now— N-O-W—now, or I'm going to do the most disgusting thing in the world to you!"

Hope, thought Devlin, just hope he'd sliced through

Mildred's stubborn loyalty to some deep fear he couldn't have named if his life depended on it.

Maybe it was the whisper instead of the shout, maybe he just finally wore her down, maybe he actually did touch that one dark nerve all of us try to protect, that fear we dread above all: A hairy tarantula slowly stalking up our naked belly. A man with bamboo slivers for our fingernails. Quicksand slowly rising above our ankles, our calves. Heavy breathing in utter darkness which draws closer, closer. The phone suddenly hummed in the peculiar way he recognized as "on hold." Whatever, he knew he'd won. That victory might cost him a great deal later, but for now, he'd won.

"Rourke, damn you!" shouted the voice he realized he'd longed to hear. "I told you never to call me again and now you pull this kind of shit! Just because you're a big hero now doesn't give you the right to bully my secretary and threaten her and abuse her with your foul mouth and filthy mind! I'm long past hassling with this shit you and Cowan use me for! I'm not going to be your patsy anymore! I ought to file charges against you, criminal charges! Abuse of the telephone system! Harassment and half a dozen others! I wouldn't even need to make any up! Obstruction of justice, for Christ's sakes! I'm preparing an important prosecution and you're interfering with my concentration! I . . . They . . . You . . . You should be locked up!!"

She sputtered out of breath.

Then, in what anyone would recognize as honest, gentle innocence, he asked, "Do you *really* think I'm cute?"

ABOUT THE AUTHOR

Born in Shelby, Montana, JAMES GRADY describes the town as "a cross between *American Graffiti* and *The Last Picture Show.*" He began writing at the age of four, dictating stories to his mother. His other early love was politics, and at the University of Montana, he was involved with antiwar politics of the era. During college breaks, he studied with a Chicago Black community action group as well as worked as a journalism intern on the staff of U.S. Senator Lee Metcalf of Montana.

After graduation in 1971, Grady did a stint as a research analyst for Montana's state Constitutional Convention. Then, after a burst of traveling, returned to Montana where he held a myriad of jobs from fire hydrant inspector to juvenile delinquency prevention worker. These odd jobs allowed him the time to finish his first novel, *Six Days of the Condor.*

After several rejection slips, he received that phone call from a publisher saying, "We like your book, kid." Within a few short weeks the book's publication plans were formulated and—amazingly—the property was sold to Hollywood.

On the political front, he won a fellowship as a legislative aide to Senator Metcalf. During this time the film starring Robert Redford, Faye Dunaway, and Cliff Robertson, but now called *Three Days of the Condor*, went into production and Grady was polishing up two further books, one a sequel to *Condor.*

In 1975 he joined the staff of syndicated columnist Jack Anderson, working there as an investigative reporter till mid-1979, when he left to devote full time to writing fiction. The next year *Catch the Wind* was published and subsequently his work has appeared in many papers and magazines, including *The Washington Post, Newsday,* and *Washingtonian* magazine.

In writing *Razor Game*, an original for paperback, Grady has drawn on a number of experiences and some specific

research. His Jack Anderson days spent investigating organized crime helped, as did weeks of riding around with D.C.
homicide and prostitution squads, and talking with Baltimore
police and newspaper reporters.

A prolific writer, he lives in Washington where he is
working on a number of projects, among them another book in
a series which features private eye John Rankin, who first
surfaced in *Runner in the Street*.

Coming soon in paperback . . .

THE
AQUITAINE
PROGRESSION

by
ROBERT
LUDLUM

The modern master of the superthriller returns—with his most gripping adventure yet. THE AQUITAINE PROGRESSION is the story of Joel Converse, a man who stumbles onto a shocking international conspiracy involving the world's most renowned military leaders, a conspiracy bent on creating Aquitaine— Charlemagne's dream of an Empire engulfing all of Europe, and the lands across the Atlantic as well. Isolated, running for his life, Converse is the only man alive who can prove that Aquitaine exists . . . that the day of the generals is at hand.

Don't miss Robert Ludlum's THE AQUITAINE PROGRESSION, coming in March 1985, from Bantam Books.

SPECIAL MONEY SAVING OFFER

Now you can have an up-to-date listing of Bantam's hundreds of titles plus take advantage of our unique and exciting bonus book offer. A special offer which gives you the opportunity to purchase a Bantam book for only 50¢. Here's how!

By ordering any five books at the regular price per order, you can also choose any other single book listed (up to a $4.95 value) for just 50¢. Some restrictions do apply, but for further details why not send for Bantam's listing of titles today!

Just send us your name and address plus 50¢ to defray the postage and handling costs.

DON'T MISS
THESE CURRENT
Bantam Bestsellers